"YOU DID ~~~~ NK TO WAKE ME ~~~~ A KISS?"

She took a quick breath.

"You thought about it."

"No." Her mouth was a firm, tight line of denial, but her eyes betrayed her.

"Think about it now."

Her glance, wary and fascinated, flickered over him once. "There's no need now. You are awake."

"There is more need now." His heart beat madly. "You could find out what more there is to want," he whispered.

A moment passed. Rosalind leaned forward. His hand came up and slid into her hair, binding her to him, ensuring the union of their mouths.

WINTERBURN'S ROSE

KATE MOORE

AVON BOOKS ◆ NEW YORK

WINTERBURN'S ROSE is an original publication of Avon Books. This work has never before appeared in book form. This work is a novel. Any similarity to actual persons or events is purely coincidental.

AVON BOOKS
A division of
The Hearst Corporation
1350 Avenue of the Americas
New York, New York 10019

Copyright © 1996 by Kate Moore
Inside cover author photo by MGM Photography
Published by arrangement with the author
Library of Congress Catalog Card Number: 96-96181
ISBN: 0-380-78457-2

First Avon Books Printing: October 1996

AVON TRADEMARK REG. U.S. PAT. OFF. AND IN OTHER COUNTRIES, MARCA REGISTRADA, HECHO EN U.S.A.

Printed in the U.S.A.

RA   10 9 8 7 6 5 4 3 2 1

For Loren

Chapter 1

"Burn it."

"My lord?" George Ralston glanced at his new employer. Winterburn stood at the window where a March gale blew heavy rain against the glass. George felt the distance between them as a thing of rank rather than the width of the narrow room. With a crackling fire in the grate behind him, he could not have heard Winterburn properly. He wiggled his pinky discreetly in his right ear. Clearing his throat and straightening the pile of papers before him, he ventured to speak again.

"I meant, what do you want to do with the hall, my lord?"

Winterburn looked over his shoulder, a dark glance of careless certainty. "Burn it."

George blinked. For the better part of the morning, he had been leading the new earl step by step through a prudent course for the recovery of the Nash fortunes. Now he sensed that Winterburn had reached this point ahead of him and had been waiting all along for George to arrive. He

1

felt a warm flush suffuse his face. The columns of figures in front of him blurred.

"The waste of it!"

"I suppose."

"Winterburn Hall is not some trifle you can throw away. The marble alone. The facing stones for the east side, the . . ." George was beginning to babble. The hours of calculation, the pages of notes.

"A fitting pyre for Marcus."

"Better a profit than a pyre, my lord." The impudent words slipped out, and George held his breath.

Again the dark glance. "Your frugal soul is offended, Ralston?"

George loosened his hold on the sheaf of papers, laying them flat, smoothing the curled edges, recovering his professional air. "Naturally, as your man of business, my concern is your best interest. The late earl would not have wanted you to be dependent on your mother's goodwill."

Winterburn cocked one black brow. "How am I to find a measure of independence in all this?" A barely perceptible gesture indicated the papers on the table.

"It will take time to be sure. With the news of Bonaparte's escape, we'll not find buyers for your brother's goods just yet. The house is the only valuable thing left."

"Sell, then."

"As you wish." George bowed his head, concealing a grin that made him feel more foolish than the flush of a moment before. "Actually, my lord, your creditors will be patient if we merely advertise the property. With a prudent alliance and sound investments, you should be able to retain the hall."

"Investments, Ralston?"

"Ah, I was coming to that, my lord. Your brother did overlook a source of income we can use to your advantage."

George did not miss the flicker of interest in Winterburn's gray gaze. They said in London that he was the coolest of the Nash brothers, though they also said it was not entirely Nash blood that ran in his veins. He certainly had a better tailor than either his father or his oldest brother, but he hadn't their sleek, ruddy looks. The face was too lean, the hair too dark, black really. And the gray eyes had a capacity for mockery which made George feel he was back in school, mishandling his cricket bat and letting the side down.

"If you will excuse me just a few minutes, my lord, I will order some supper, and we'll continue."

Winterburn nodded, and George bowed himself out of the little room.

It was the only habitable room left in the hall, an anteroom off the long gallery. Winterburn—that's who he was now, not plain Leigh Nash as he preferred any longer—had ample time to contemplate the dreary view from the window. In the forecourt below, neat piles of stone rectangles stood like soldiers mustered for review. The stones apparently had been intended to cover the north face of the hall, now exposed to the elements.

For three days Leigh had been trying to reconcile the present state of the hall with his memories of it. It had never been home. His father had brought them here as boys for hunting and fishing. He and Richard and Marcus and Trevor had made it a sort of camp, nothing permanent about it, just a place to come when exhausted at the end of the day's hunt. Grander than any of his billets in Spain, but equally temporary, nothing to be attached to. His mother had never been here.

A gust of March wind splattered rain against the glass. The days of his careless youth were gone. He'd never thought the house would be his. What could he do with a house? Ralston seemed to relish the details of the debacle. He apparently had traced every penny of the fortune Marcus had squandered on his unfinished renovation project. Abandoned scaffolding blocked the larger rooms, while the smaller rooms were stocked like warehouses with assorted goods and furnishings. There was a room filled with gilt wall brackets, another with mirrors, a third with bolts of brocade, a fourth with Sèvres figurines, even one with shoes. Folly or madness? Leigh did not, and never would, know. Marcus was dead.

He pressed a hand to his side and stretched cautiously. The damp cold of the day had settled deep in the newly healed wounds in his shoulder and ribs. The fire in the hearth on the opposite wall had no power to warm him. Richard, too, was dead, buried in the Pyrenees, where they had fought their last battle together. Leigh was now the eighth Earl of Winterburn, and he was ruined.

Behind him the door to the little room opened and closed with a draft of cold air as Ralston returned. The Nash man of business reminded Leigh of the best sort of hunting dog, the kind that would not be deterred from his quarry, intense, a bit nervous, and not very flexible of mind.

"They've just delivered some provisions from the Bear. Mrs. Noakes will bring a tray up shortly." Ralston gripped the cloth-wrapped handle of a steaming pewter pitcher with one hand. In his other hand were two battered crockery cups. "A bit of punch to warm you, my lord?"

Leigh nodded. With a final glance at the dreary day, he crossed to the table that served as a makeshift desk. He cleared a spot so that Ralston could set the cups down. "Ralston, did you know what Marcus was doing?"

Ralston shook his head. He began to pour the steaming mixture of rum and citrus. "When his late lordship came to me about breaking the entail, it seemed a reasonable request. Your mother was treated very favorably by your father's will, and your brother had little cash for improvements. He proposed to sell off three of the outlying properties in order to restore the hall."

Now there was no cash. Marcus had spent madly. Leigh accepted the cup that was offered him and took a swallow of the warming punch. After a moment he remembered that his new rank required him to sit or keep his scrupulous man of business standing. He pulled out a chair and sank into it, motioning for Ralston to be seated.

Leigh set his cup in a space free of papers. "When did Marcus lose control?"

"I don't know, my lord. He was very cagey with his records. He allowed his tenants to buy him out, but I suspect he gave them the money to do it."

That, Leigh could imagine. Marcus had liked to give gifts. He had always seen to it that his brothers had extras at Eton. Once he had even contrived for a load of supplies to reach Richard's regiment in Portugal.

"My mother never suspected what he was doing?"

Ralston shook his head.

Leigh understood. As long as Marcus remained at the hall, their mother would not have cared what he did. Neither quick nor graceful, slow of speech, with a vacant, uncomprehending air, Marcus had never pleased her. She would be grateful that he had died so young and with so little inconvenience to his family, a weak heart overtaxed by exertion in the pursuit of a vain grandeur.

Now Leigh was expected to handle any tiresome details of assuming his new position and hurry back to London, where it would be his duty to marry well and quickly. There was the sticking point. Leigh propped an elbow on the table and rested his forehead in the palm of his hand.

"You were saying I could save the property," he said.

"The first step is a careful alliance."

Leigh raised his head, offering Ralston a level glance. "You mean if I do what titled paupers have ever done and sell myself on the marriage mart?"

He could see himself in a glittering ballroom, lifting a gloved hand to his lips, leaning to whisper in a delicate ear, his breath disturbing an artful curl. Around him, peering over the edges of fluttering fans, assessing eyes would be weighing his person against his lack of fortune.

Ralston studied the contents of his cup. "A man of your lordship's obvious attractions will easily find a lady of birth and breeding who will be pleased to join her wealth to your family name."

No doubt his mother had several prospects lined up. Why did the idea stir such distaste in him? He knew the folly of rebellion. Richard had made his rebellion in the army; Marcus had made his here. Both dead.

"And the investments?" He could not imagine what Marcus had overlooked in his rush to financial ruin.

Ralston had a smug, satisfied air. He was enjoying the moment. "You've six benefices in your gift, my lord."

"Benefices?"

"Church livings. You may sell them. The least is worth some fourteen hundred pounds, and the rest upward of that. I daresay we could get ten thousand for the lot of them. If we put that amount in the funds . . ."

Leigh let Ralston carry on, the man's voice

rising and falling, muffled to Leigh's ears like noises in a swoon. An odd, unsettling flash of Portugal, a vision that had troubled him there, overcame him again. A dusty road bathed in white light led him to the hub of an old cartwheel entwined with the delicate blooms of a climbing rose. At the convent where he had recovered from his wounds Sister Luzia had insisted that the disturbing image was his calling.

He came back to the present. "Does one sell them? I thought it was customary to appoint a vicar to a living when a vacancy occurred."

"It is, but with so many young men in want of a situation, a careful father will purchase a living for a son, against the day that the incumbent . . . leaves office."

"Dies?"

"Well, yes." Ralston put aside his punch cup and leafed through a pile of documents in the upper corner of the table. "Here we are. Upworth, Appleford, Menthe, Haythorne, Blithedale, and Rowdene. In truth, Rowdene is vacant. The vicar died not two months past."

"You mean I could appoint someone to the living at Rowdene."

"No. No profit in that." Ralston lined up three pens by their tips. "I mean that, although it's a small parish, its value is high at the moment because it's available immediately."

The clutter on the small table faded. Leigh saw his path with that clarity that inevitably came in the smoke and din of battle, when he could say to his men, "This way." He'd been caged, and suddenly the door had opened. "Where is it, Ralston?"

Ralston studied the sheets of notes he'd compiled, running his forefinger down the page. "In Wiltshire, near Malmesbury."

Wiltshire. Stretches of rolling, green hills, no close ballrooms. Leigh did not have to become his mother's dependent. He did not have to sell himself to the first woman of fortune who would have him. He could appoint himself the Vicar of Rowdene. There would be a parsonage, an income, freedom.

"Ralston, are there any restrictions on whom I may appoint?"

"None that I know of, my lord."

Again his Portugese vision flashed before his mind's eye, the wheel and the rose bathed in the peculiar white light. He hesitated, then shook it off. The vision meant nothing here in England. "Then I appoint myself."

"You?" Ralston opened and closed his mouth. His fingers twitched, knocking the pens out of line. "You are not ordained."

"I could be. Uncle Ned's a bishop. Ordination isn't much. A fellow I knew at Balliol spent a few weeks reading Paley, had a meeting with his bishop, and it was done."

"Of course, it may be done," said Ralston slowly, "but you've no vocation, have you, my lord?"

"A true calling you mean? Some sort of vision, blinded on the road to Damascus?" He shook his head. He would not mention his vision, an aberration wrought by pain and the strange fevered atmosphere of Portugal. His brothers' deaths and his inheritance of an encumbered estate had nothing to do with the experience of white light he'd had on a road in Portugal. Providence had not troubled itself to bring the Nashes down to make a worldly fellow like himself into a vicar. He was simply making a practical choice which freed him from his family and from a distasteful state of dependence.

"My lord," said Ralston. "Have you considered the . . . simplicity of such a life?"

"The lack of income, you mean?"

Ralston nodded, disapproval plain in his pinched expression. Ralston had no doubt heard something of Leigh's reputation.

"What is the income, roughly, do you think?"

Ralston consulted his notes. "Four hundred a year at most."

"A soldier manages on less."

"You could never maintain the hall on such an income."

"We're back to that." Leigh stood. "Burn it."

"You are frivolous, my lord. I am not a religious man, but the charge of souls requires a certain . . ."

"Piety?"

"Indeed. You would not put your financial affairs in the hands of a man with no head for figures."

"You think the Church of England requires saints to read sermons and collect tithes, Ralston?"

"No, my lord."

"Remember Becket, a man of the world in every sense." Leigh moved to the door. "Perhaps this is God's jest, Ralston, making a vicar of me."

Lady Winterburn's London drawing room combined the informality of a men's club with the elegance of a private palace. There, on a raw afternoon in late March, a small crowd of gentlemen gathered around the countess. Bonaparte's return to the Continent had all of London worried. Leigh recognized two cabinet ministers and several diplomats, among them his younger brother, Trevor.

Trevor, three years Leigh's junior, had their mother's look, at once shrewd and indifferent, calculating and unconcerned. But his features were rounder than hers. He had the broad forehead and straight brows, but a smoother line of cheek and jaw and fair, florid coloring. He was his father's son as well, inclined to yield, to turn away from an open fight. He came immediately to Leigh's side.

"You took your time, brother." Trevor raised an eyebrow. "A fortnight in town and not a word to mother?" He signaled a footman to offer Leigh a glass of wine.

"How are you, Trev? Still on Castlereagh's staff?"

Leigh glanced about his mother's elegant drawing room and experienced a mild shock that it was all so familiar. It was a place where a man felt his empty pockets keenly. Though it was but a short way from his lodgings to the countess's house in St. James's Square, he had not called on her until his plans were certain.

Trevor shot him a penetrating glance. "Did you think mother wouldn't hear what you've planned?"

"I was sure she would."

"Advertising the hall?" Trevor's voice was sharp with irritation. "You might have warned us. Every tradesman in Mayfair has been dunning us."

Leigh smiled at the thought of a tradesman attempting to intimidate their mother. He accepted a glass of burgundy from the attentive footman. He was cold again, or still, as he had been since his return to England. By late afternoon his wounds ached. Glancing around the room, he saw that other gentleman noticed him. He returned nods and greetings. Their easy acceptance of his presence caused him a second shock. They saw no change in him. They expected him to resume his old life as if he'd never been to war.

His mother gave him a mocking, heavy-lidded look. In her fifties, she yet retained the habits of her youth. She still met men in dishabille, her black hair loose about her strong face, her perfume subtle but unmistakable. A painting on the wall behind her depicted a satin-clad courtier sighing for the favor of his lady's hand, just the supplicating position his mother liked a man to adopt. And there was a new man in that position, leaning toward the countess where she sat on a sea-blue brocade sofa. The crowd around her shifted, and she lifted her face to smile at the gentleman bending down to her. It was a gesture as unmistakable as a siren's call and probably as fatal. "Who's mother's latest beau?"

Trevor's gaze followed Leigh's. "Barton, a would-be baronet from Dorset. Lent her a few guineas, and now he fancies himself her next lover. Gets close enough to smell the dew on the blossom."

Lover. A careless word, but it stirred the old question. Which of their mother's lovers had fathered him? Leigh studied the new suitor, a tall, thin fellow, pale and sharp-featured, with a hungry look that the countess would not miss. She had instructed her sons too often in the ways of the world for Leigh to doubt her opinion of Barton. A man had power, she would say, or he became the tool of those who did. Leigh was about to ask what use the countess planned to make of Barton when Lord Eldon, the chancellor, joined the brothers.

"Glad to see you here, Winterburn." Eldon looked him over, extending a hand for Leigh to shake. "Recovered from your wounds, I see."

Leigh kept his countenance impassive as the chancellor urged him to take his place in the House of Lords. There was no need to mention that he was turning his back on the life he was expected to lead. Eldon turned his gaze to the countess.

"Your mother's held us steady on our course through all this disturbance over the Corn Bill."

Leigh nodded. The bill would raise the price of bread, and rioters had torn the iron railings from the chancellor's house the week before.

"Elizabeth should be in the cabinet," Eldon suggested. "She would never give in to the rabble."

It was true. Elizabeth Nash rarely yielded to anyone.

"Ah, Leigh," she greeted him an hour later when her guests had gone. "You must be chilled to the bone. Do sit by the fire." She indicated a tapestried chair apart from the couch she shared with Trevor.

She extended a silk-clad arm to offer Leigh a cup of tea. The little silence was broken only by the tinkle of a silver spoon against fine china. Without looking at him, his mother asked, "You've received Lady Candover's card?"

"Unfortunately I won't be able to attend her dinner."

A look of concern crossed his mother's face, so real he might have been taken in by it. "Then you've not . . . fully recovered?"

"I have other plans, Mother, as you've no doubt heard."

"Inappropriate plans." She shrugged her shoulders. "You, a clergyman? You've had a woman in your bed since you were . . . sixteen?"

Fifteen. She waited for him to correct her, and when he did not, she cast a glance at Trevor.

"What are these plans of yours, Brother?" Trevor asked.

"I've taken the living at Rowdene and will be ordained within the year."

"Fancy a bishop's miter, then, do you?" Trevor offered a smile which was patently false.

"The collar will suit me."

"Rector of Rowdene?"

Leigh took a swallow of tea. "Perpetual curate."

"My dear brother, a mere curacy? You won't be able to pay your tailor."

"Then I must dispense with his services."

A look of annoyance passed across Trevor's smooth features. "What *did* happen to you in Portugal?"

"I doubt I could explain it."

He couldn't. Not here, in this room, where he had only to reach out a hand to pick up a snuffbox from the regent, or raise his eyes to the jewels at his mother's throat to see a sign of Lord Maitland's favor. Twice he had been pressed to marry, not so much a woman as a position, the place in the world his mother intended him to take. Once he had chosen the army; now he was choosing an obscure village and freedom.

His choice had nothing to do with the vision, however. Portugal was like no other place he had been. He had seen for himself a chapel made of human bones and heard often enough the story of Prince Pedro, grieving for his Ines and eating the hearts of her murderers. His vision was but a mild form of the passions that ruled the place.

His mother rose with apparent composure and crossed to her desk with a whisper of her silk gown. She took up a letter and returned, dropping the missive into his lap. "You may be grateful to the little flock of nuns who nursed you back to health, but to throw your life away in this manner . . . is excessive, and I will not allow it."

He looked at the writing. "Uncle Ned has confessed all."

"He was very wrong to encourage this folly, but I gather you threatened to join the Methodists or, worse, the papists."

"The church has always been an acceptable occupation for a younger son."

"Not my son." It was as close as she ever came to acknowledging that his father had no part in him. He belonged wholly to her. "Persons of rank marry to extend the influence and credit of their families," she concluded.

Leigh put his cup down. "Arrange a marriage for Trevor. It will advance his career."

"Spare me the rebellious poses. The stage is not for you any more than the church. You are nothing if you are not a Nash, and you have a duty to this family, which I expect you to perform."

It was true. He was nothing without the Nash name, but she would not cast him off, could not now that he had inherited the title. She merely would seek to bend him to her will. "I am, of course, sorry to disappoint you, Mother," he said, rising, bringing the interview to a close.

"How soon do you expect to take up your duties in Rowdene?" Trevor asked.

"Within the week."

"Ah, but you can't properly act as curate until you've been ordained, can you?"

It was the weak point in his plan, he knew. It made him vulnerable to his mother's will and his own selfish nature. "No. There's another fellow who will preach and manage the services for me for a while."

"What's the delay?" Trevor was probing, and Leigh had to be grateful that Uncle Ned's letter made no mention of any of his reservations about Leigh's rakish past.

"I want to do a bit of studying first." Uncle Ned had given him six months to win over the villagers and prove himself capable of managing the affairs of the small church there. His uncle had been very direct about how Leigh was to conduct himself in Rowdene. "Carnality in a clergyman," Uncle Ned had said, "is an evil which cannot be permitted." No scandals that would give the Evangelicals an advantage. Leigh was to remain chaste and avoid his former companions.

He bowed and took his leave. His mother did not offer her hand.

"He won't last a month," said Trevor after his brother had gone.

"He musn't last a fortnight," his mother answered. "I must have him back in London for the season. The Candover girl will not wait forever." She crossed the room to look out the window, down into the street.

Trevor could see that the encounter with Leigh
had upset her. Leigh was the one she couldn't
manage. From his days in short coats, Trevor had
understood that his mother ruled the family.
When their father died, there had been no question of her removal to dowager apartments. Their
oldest brother, Marcus, had simply retreated to
the country. Richard had fled to the army years
before. Only Leigh had ever braved her wrath.
Only Trevor didn't mind her interference. He had
learned that he generally could get anything he
wanted by offering his mother some concession in
exchange.

Trevor could see the beauty in their mother's
plans. The match was an excellent one. His mother was brilliant to see it. The Candover chit had
been rejecting suitors for three years while Leigh
was away. The return of the wounded soldier with
his new title would be just the thing to pique Miss
Candover's jaded interest.

And Leigh could win her. Their mother would
see that he had every opportunity to court her.
His looks and manner would do the rest. There
was no girl Leigh couldn't get when he put his
mind to it. He had scandalized all London with
his open pursuit of the courtesan Lucetta King.

And Trevor didn't mind really. Their mother
would find someone for him when the time was
right. Now was the time, with Bonaparte loose, to
advance his career.

"Patience, Mother. I'll wager all Leigh will have
with this curacy is small tithes. Three hundred,
four hundred pounds and a glebe farm. Dirt. His

coats will be threadbare, the company dull, and the celibacy wearing. He'll be back."

Lady Winterburn turned to her son. "Do you suppose he prays?"

"Leigh on his knees? I can think of only one reason for him to assume such a posture, and it's not to address the diety."

"Then what has happened? What accounts for this foolishness?"

Trevor cast a sly glance at her. She was asking where she had failed in the raising of her favorite son, for there was no denying that Leigh was her favorite, the son of some lover she had taken perhaps to please herself. Trevor had always had to work for her notice. While she approved of his ambition, his cunning, and the flexibility of his scruples, his successes had never brought her the satisfaction that one of Leigh's exploits had. "Perhaps he's impotent."

She shot him a sharp glance.

Trevor went on. "We don't know the extent of his injuries or their effect. He was in that damned convent for nearly a year, six months before we knew where he was."

"And I'm sure there's a little sister or two who has broken her vows over him. He's whole. I know when a man's lost his carnal appetite."

"Then perhaps he's developed a taste for village maidens and means to seduce his share in Wiltshire."

Lady Winterburn smiled, a smile of genuine approval, and Trevor sighed. She was going to ask a favor of him. He came to his feet.

"We must see that he does. We must supply him with a willing maiden. You can arrange that, can't you, my dear?"

"Mother, I should return to Vienna directly if I'm to advance at all from my work at the congress."

"Yes, you should, dear, so just do this one thing for me, and I will take care of the rest." His mother touched her cheek to his and turned away, and Trevor knew he would do as she asked.

Chapter 2

Rosalind Merrifield found her neighbor Mrs. Fowler seated in a wooden armchair in a patch of wan March sunlight from the east windows of the parsonage drawing room. For three days they had been packing Jane's things. The room was cold, stripped of its family detail, but the old carpet remained, muting the sound of Rosalind's steps.

"Jane?" she said softly. At her touch the crisp bombazine of Jane's mourning gown crackled like a thin frost.

Jane lifted sad blue eyes. Her hands closed tightly on the iron ring of keys in her lap. "I can't leave."

Rosalind dropped to her knees at her friend's side and pressed Jane's cold, thin hands in hers. "I know."

The hands in hers shook, and Rosalind gave them a slight squeeze.

Jane's gaze wandered over the handsome room, seeming not to see its present emptiness. "For a moment, sitting here, I thought he was just in the

21

next room." Her voice broke, and she bowed her head, staring at their joined hands. Rosalind struggled to subdue the ache in her throat.

"The Earl of Winterburn is a beast to turn you out like this."

Jane shook her bent head. "This house was never truly mine or Theo's, though I let myself think so."

"It's more yours than anyone's. Winterburn's haste is indecent. He should have given you a month's notice at least. Then you would have had time to reach John." Rosalind rubbed Jane's cold hands in hers.

Jane shook her head. "My dear, Lord Winterburn could not know my circumstances nor my son's."

"He could have inquired. He should have consulted the warden and the vestry. After all I'm sure Mr. Vernon's duties at St. Andrew's are not very great. He could have continued to look after the congregation in Rowdene until you were properly settled."

"But so many young men need situations, my dear. Lord Winterburn must have had this Mr. Nash in mind even before . . . before Theo died." Jane sighed and looked up. With a bit of her old spirit, she pulled her hands free and straightened her black lace cap.

Rosalind met her friend's brave gaze. "Well, I promise to dislike him heartily—for your sake."

"Oh no, you musn't. You know how these young men are, with their threadbare coats and their zeal."

"Yes, tiresome." Rosalind ventured a smile. The pompous Mr. Vernon was just the sort of young clergyman she most disliked, and she feared the new curate would be cut from the same priggish cloth. "Winterburn should have appointed a married man in any case, for what can a single man want with such a grand parsonage? And who will care for your garden?"

"I was going to ask you, dear. If Mr. Nash has no interest in roses, could you come from time to time?"

"Every day. Now I've put some tea out, and you must warm up a bit before Mr. Turnbull arrives with the gig." Rosalind stood, drawing Jane up with her.

At the drawing room door Jane halted as if she'd just remembered something. "Rosalind, dear, I've not done very well by you."

"Nonsense." She tucked Jane's arm in hers and patted her hand.

"Before Theo died, I always thought someday I would take you to Bath. You should have suitors, dear, and balls and outings."

"How could I leave Merrifield?"

"But you must. It's your brother's house, and . . . he's not all that a brother should be to you."

"It's my home."

Jane sighed. "It should be," she said fiercely. "Women should have title."

Rosalind laughed. "That would be a revolution."

"A wise one. What do men know of housekeeping? They inhabit places but hardly make them habitable."

"You see, Jane, you agree with me after all. Winterburn should never have given the living at Rowdene to a bachelor."

"But he has, and you, Rosalind, must give him my keys." Jane slipped her arm from Rosalind's and pressed the heavy iron ring into her hands.

"I shall, and I shall take him over every inch of this house. I promise you he shall feel his good fortune."

The view of Merrifield Hall from the top of the park lifted Rosalind's spirits, as it always did. Not so grand as the houses that appeared in the guidebooks perhaps, but more happily situated. It sat midway down a long incline, a sweep of trees and lawn that drew the eye to warm brick and stone, arched windows, and the lovely curve of the center roof over the barrel-vaulted library, her father's treasure. Beyond the house the ground fell away in a vista of trees and hills stretching to the distant horizon. *Home.*

The sharp edges of the keys in her pocket jabbed her hip. Jane's present circumstances rankled. By the system of church livings, a parsonage belonged to the vicar, of course, but such a system did not do justice to the woman who made a parsonage a home. Now Jane was forced to accept a spare room in her brother's parsonage in Clyro. She must go from mistress of her own home to poor relation. Worse, Jane would be separated from all that reminded her of a dear husband while her grief was still new. Rosalind had offered Jane a room at Merrifield, but she was not surprised when Jane refused. It would be too hard for Jane to see a new man in Theo's place.

The bishop's letter had not helped. It made no mention of Theo's years of service, only of the new man, Nash, and his immediate need of the parsonage. Rosalind knew where to lay the blame for such evils. Winterburn. She tried to picture the distant earl, at ease in some grand apartment with soaring ceilings and marble columns, dictating Jane's fate to his secretary. "Deprive the good widow of her home so that the ambitious young man may rise in the world." No wonder gentle Jane thought revolutionary thoughts.

Rosalind's situation was better. Though her brother, Gerrie, had inherited the hall when their parents died, he had no interest in living in it. She was saddened by Gerrie's defection, but glad in some selfish corner of her heart into which she tried not to look very often. Until he married, as she supposed he must some day, Rosalind was mistress of Merrifield Hall.

That cheering thought died as she caught sight of a drayer's cart drawn up before the side entrance to the house. Two men in carters' smocks were lifting a chair into the cart. Her spirits sank. Quarter day was coming. How could she have forgotten? Gerrie was home and out of funds again. She broke into a run.

At the house she caught her breath enough to ask a footman where Gerrie was.

"In the dining room, miss."

Not the dining room. How much did she have on hand to give him? She heard his voice raised in protest as she reached the door.

"That's a damned paltry offer, Hinkson." She stepped into the room, and Gerrie glanced her way. He looked distracted, his chestnut hair standing up where he had run a hand through it, his waistcoat gaping, the buttons misaligned with the holes. He set down the tankard in his hand.

"Hello, Roz. Just in time. Would you tell this fellow here about this plate?" He swept a hand across an array of dishes on the table. "It's Viennese, ain't it? Worth a pretty penny."

Rosalind nodded to the other man. "Gerrie, we must talk."

"Not now, Roz. Hinkson, you can do better than that."

"Gerrie, you can't sell mother's dessert set."

"Dessert set, is it?" Gerald grinned. "Serve a good deal of dessert, do you, Roz?" He turned to Mr. Hinkson. "You see, Hinkson, you can't make some kitchen-cupboard offer for this stuff. Priceless stuff."

"Twenty, that's my final offer."

"Be damned to you then."

"Gerrie." Rosalind kept her voice even in spite of her anger. "We must talk."

Gerald looked at her, seeming to see her for the first time. He glanced back at Hinkson. "Going to palaver with my sister a bit, Hinkson. Think again about this set." He turned and stalked through the open doors to the drawing room.

Rosalind strode after him. She caught back the exclamation that sprang to her lips at the sight of the room. The drapery had been removed from the windows, and all the lighter chairs were missing. Gerrie must be hard-pressed.

She took a deep breath. "Gerrie, how much do you need?"

He lifted the tankard and took a deep draft. "Beastly week. Davies had all the luck. Won five thousand at hazard, the bastard."

Rosalind clasped her hands tightly. He couldn't have lost five thousand pounds, could he? He couldn't imagine that she had so much lying about or that the house could yield so much. She tried not to think of what might be on the cart already. "Gerrie, how long are you staying?"

"Not staying, Roz." He lowered the tankard and looked about, as if just realizing the furnishings were gone. He staggered to the long sofa and dropped down on it, putting the tankard on the floor and lowering his head into his hands.

Rosalind crossed to his side and seated herself next to him. He smelled of sweat and ale and foulness. He'd clearly slept in his coat and dined in his soiled linen. She remembered him fine and teasing, when he'd come to Miss Hester's school to take her and her friends for Sunday drives. She'd been the envy of those friends for such a handsome brother. Joan Talbot had declared there was not a finer pair of hazel eyes in England, and Sally Candover had said he must kiss one of them.

"Stay, Gerrie." She tried to be patient. "I'll have Mrs. Simms do up pancakes. You haven't had your Shrove pancakes, have you?"

Gerrie lifted his head. "Shrove pancakes? Roz, grow up. You sound like a schoolroom chit. We should be thinking of getting you married off." He gave her a thorough scrutiny. "The Rose of Rowdene, that's what Father called you, isn't it? On the shelf. Got to get you fired off while you've got your looks, while you're in bloom, so to speak."

Rosalind felt a little spurt of real panic. She wished he wouldn't look so serious. He doesn't have the resolve for it, she told herself. "Well, you don't have a husband in your pocket, do you? Not one who'd pick a dowerless country girl."

Gerrie swallowed another draft from his tankard. "You're a well-looking girl, Roz. There are fellows who'd take you." He gave her a long, sliding glance which made her squirm inside. "Too much color, too much hair. Get you one of those new crops, curls about the face."

Rosalind shook her head. "I'll keep my hair, thank you, Gerrie."

He was now examining her closely. "Brown eyes can't be helped, but some fellows like the red hair. A sign of spirit, they say."

"Well, they can admire spirit in someone else, I think."

"Don't set yourself so high up, Roz. There are fellows who've got their pockets lined with silver and want to set up their nurseries. I could look into it for you."

"Gerrie, I would never meet someone like that here."

"No, London's the place. We'd have to get you a season."

London. The idea gave her another scare, but she knew how to get Gerrie off it. "We don't have the money for it."

"Mother's sister . . ." He rubbed a hand over his face. "Aunt Elinor, she should do it, take you in, fire you off."

"Well, Gerrie, I haven't heard from Aunt Elinor in some time. I doubt I could impose on her. Besides, I'm fine here."

Gerrie rose and stretched, rolling his shoulders. He was already losing interest in the subject. "Suit yourself then, Roz."

Mr. Hinkson appeared in the open doorway. "The cart's near loaded, Mr. Merrifield."

"Have you come up with a decent offer for me, man?"

"Twenty-five pounds."

"Hinkson, you bandit, give me thirty."

"Done, sir."

"That's better, that's more like it." Gerald turned back to Rosalind. "Roz, I'll be off."

"Gerrie, stay. One night. It will do you good."

"Can't. Meeting a fellow at the White Hart, then we're off for Newmarket. Couldn't miss that."

Rosalind stepped up to him and touched a finger to his waistcoat where the buttons gaped. "Take care of yourself then."

He brushed her hand away and fumbled with

the tiny buttons, succeeding in fastening one of them. "Don't worry about me, Roz. My luck will turn."

"If it doesn't?"

"You're such a Friday face, Roz. I've got friends. Say, maybe what I need is a wife—a rich one."

Rosalind caught Mr. Hinkson at the foot of the drive and negotiated the return of her mother's Viennese plates. She hadn't enough funds on hand to buy back the hangings and chairs. Mr. Symonds, the bailiff, had urged some repairs this spring, and until harvest she must be frugal. So she turned her eyes from the slow progress of Mr. Hinkson's cart up the slope to the main road.

From the outside the hall gave no hint of the depredations Gerrie's gambling had made within. It looked solid, prosperous, welcoming, but the encounter with Hinkson shook Rosalind's confidence. Gerrie's visits revealed her secret shame. She wanted Merrifield for herself. She had discouraged Gerrie's interest in it from the beginning. She had stepped in and taken over, had never relied on him. Maybe it was her fault that the hall no longer mattered to him.

She stopped at the door, unwilling to enter and see the emptiness of the familiar rooms. She took the brick path to the garden, where Gerrie's gaming had not yet worked any harm.

She must do something. Gerrie could lose money faster than she could collect rents or harvest grain. This week it would be races, next week faro again, the week after that a boxing match. They would lose Merrifield if he went on as he was. The inevitability of it was plain, and she'd known it for some time. There her thoughts seemed to stick.

She needed advice, though she'd never been good at taking it. She would have turned to Jane, but Jane was on her way to Clyro. Her mother's friend Lady Ellenby could no doubt advise her, but Rosalind had no relish for her views. Lady Ellenby would tell Rosalind to find a husband and leave home.

Her school friends had done so. Letters from Elizabeth Seegrim and Joan Talbot told of lives filled with domestic concerns and babes. As closely as she read the letters, however, Rosalind could get no sense of their husbands. In her friends' letters husbands seemed no more than bank accounts, drawn on to provide gowns and hats, furnishings and carriages.

She tried to picture a rich husband. He would be a kindly, white-haired old gentleman, a bit like Theophilus Fowler. She would make sure he had uninterrupted hours for his books and a well-regulated household, and he would encourage her gardening and her work with the tenants. And every quarter day he would supply her with a generous draft on his bank that would keep Gerrie and Merrifield from ruin. The fantasy lasted but a moment until she thought of her third friend, Sally Candover.

Sally had been the boldest of them in school. She had experimented with kissing and reported all her shocking adventures to the others. An heiress, she remained unattached, finding her suitors more amusing than intriguing. Upon Elizabeth Seegrim's marriage, Sally had written, "Don't think of marriage, Roz. You have all the advantages of the institution already—a house and independence."

But Rosalind suspected there was more to marriage than she could see from the outside. There seemed to be a mystery in it that neither Elizabeth nor Joan with their contentment nor Sally with her boldness had discovered. Men and women were drawn together by a compulsion Rosalind could not fathom. It had nothing to do with bank accounts and comforts, and it made them wretched or joyful beyond anything. Though she had never felt the mysterious pull herself, she'd seen its effects. Like the way Jeremy Braithe, the bold shepherd, cast such burning looks upon widowed Mrs. Cole, the dairywoman. Surely, Rosalind thought, the woman's apron must catch fire.

Rosalind entered the greenhouse and took up an apron and gloves. She moved along the trays of seedlings, picking out those that were too crowded and repositioning them in trays she had prepared before her stay with Jane. The familiar task restored her sense of herself. Miss Merrifield of Merrifield Hall need not marry to find a situation.

She laughed. That was pride speaking and pride in circumstances that were hardly of her making. Jane had not been able to afford such pride. Neither could poor Mr. Nash, the new

curate. She supposed Jane was right not to blame
him for seeking a position.

She stripped off her gloves, pulled her apron
strings, and left the greenhouse. Hints of spring
were everywhere, in the buds above her head and
in the moss cups and green cinquefoil runners
beneath her feet. To her delight she found a patch
of violets.

As she walked, she noted the garden chores
neglected during her stay with Jane. She would
have to have the hedges clipped and . . . She cut
off the flow of thought. It was so easy to become
caught up in her daily tasks, forgetting the threat
to Merrifield that Gerrie's gaming posed. But
making cuttings and seeing the hedges trimmed
would not save the hall. There must be something
she could do so that Gerrie would not sell the roof
over her head.

She looked back at the late sun lighting the
windows to fiery brilliance, and an idea came
which made her steps falter, her eyes sting. She
could sell her father's books. At the thought a
flock of memories rose, winging into conscious-
ness. She spun away from the house, striding
determinedly.

It was dark when she swallowed the ache in her
throat and turned back. It must be considered
rationally. She could write to London, to her
father's man of business. Though Gerrie didn't
deal well with the man, Mr. Harwood would help
her find collectors who knew the value of Papa's
library. The books must be worth thousands of
pounds. She doubted she could sell them all at

once, but if she could realize a few hundred pounds at a time, she would be prepared for Gerrie's next visit.

She stopped and looked at the hall. It was enough that she must hand Jane's keys over to a stranger. She would not be driven from her own home.

Chapter 3

Frost covered the bare fields when Rosalind opened the parsonage door to a sharp knock. The polite greeting on her lips died. Her unprepared gaze swept over the stranger on the porch from his gleaming boots to the dark-blue coat that lay smooth across his broad shoulders. There was nothing clerical about him. His left hand tapped tan gloves and a gray top hat against his thigh. His weight, resting on his right leg, gave a tilt to his hips which drew her glance to the very flat plane of his fawn breeches where they met the edge of a white silk waistcoat.

Her stomach took an unfamiliar plunge. For a moment she thought Jeremy Braithe had played one of his tricks. Watching the stranger had the most peculiar effect on her, like the slow burn and quick shiver of an icicle sliding down her spine. No clergyman had hair that black, nor eyes so heated.

Leigh was not aware of breathing. He blinked as if he had stepped into the bright glare of a

Spanish noon. Some trick of the morning light set the girl's face glowing with all the warmth the day lacked. The early sun lighted her deep-red hair to fiery brilliance. Her cheeks had the tint of dawn, her eyes the brown of the deepest woods. Her breath made a bright vapor in the chill air.

The moment passed. He recovered himself. The girl was undoubtedly a servant, and the church would frown on curates who gaped at serving girls. He would get her to call her mistress and pretend their exchange of glances had not occurred. "Is Mrs. Fowler at home?"

She shook her head. A light shiver passed through her, jingling a ring of keys in her hand.

"Mr. Nash?"

He nodded.

She regarded his boots critically, as if puzzled by them, then drew in a breath and raised her eyes to his again. "There must be some mistake," she said, her tone assured, her accent well-bred.

He looked more closely at her pale gown and serviceable brown cloak. She was not a servant then. "Mistake, Miss . . .?"

"Merrifield." She tilted her chin up. "I ought to explain. Mrs. Fowler was obliged to leave Rowdene yesterday. She asked me to show the house to the new curate . . . a Mr. Nash."

Their glances caught and held. "May I come in, Miss Merrifield?"

She understood him then, but she did not open the door so much as a crack further. This time her pointed look settled on his coat.

"My coat offends you?"

"Your patron does not require you to adopt clerical dress?"

"My patron?"

"The Earl of Winterburn."

The name was evidently distasteful to her. He smiled at the irony of it. He hadn't even considered giving up his coats for a clergyman's black garb. With perfect honesty he informed her, "Winterburn has no strong opinions on the matter of clerical dress."

She hesitated a moment longer, then stepped back, allowing him to cross the threshold. He closed the door, and the narrow space contracted, filled with her presence. A fragrance of leaves and grasses snared his senses. His body, which had not responded to a woman in months, suddenly wakened. Forgotten messages hummed along his nerves, rousing his senses. He glanced about the cramped space for something on which to fix his attention and settled on a small half-moon table in the hall beyond. When he'd laid aside his hat and gloves, he found her staring again.

She had a plain, straight nose, thick brows, and a high, broad forehead with a widow's peak. She was undeniably beautiful, but, he told himself, her beauty should not unsettle him. In London, where thin, painted brows and pale cheeks marked the fashionable miss, the vividness of Miss Merrifield's person would be thought vulgar.

"Would you care for some refreshment, Mr. Nash?"

"No, thank you, Miss Merrifield."

"You will want to see the parsonage then," she said briskly.

"Lead on." What he wanted was space, a bit of distance from the girl.

She separated a key from the others, holding it up for his inspection. "This one opens the dining room," she said, turning and leading him into a room on the right. "Mrs. Fowler has left you her table and chairs." She stopped at the far end of a cherry-wood table, running her hand across the polished surface.

His eye followed the fond, appreciative gesture. He nodded and turned to the hearth.

"The stone is local," she told him with obvious pride.

He glanced at her over his shoulder, a mistake. "How does the chimney draw?"

Her too-revealing eyes said the practical question offended her.

"I never heard the Fowlers complain." She pushed open a pair of double doors and led him into a second room. "This is the drawing room, renovated just last year." With another key she opened one of the wall cases.

He strolled to the tall south windows, putting the width of the narrow room between them. There was a silence, then the rasp of a key in its lock.

After a time she said, "You can see the church and glebe farm from here, and to the west, the road and the village."

He did see the church, a block of gray stone, as dull as the lifeless winter landscape. Perhaps the world had been robbed of its color to make her hair such a deep red, her eyes so brown. It was an odd fancy for a man of his experience to have about a village girl, even a well-bred one.

"The study is next, Mr. Nash," she said, calling him away from the relative safety of the windows. He followed her into a small, sunny room with a large desk. She crossed to some bookshelves, brushing past him, her elbow grazing his, an ordinary, unremarkable event, but one that disturbed his pulse momentarily. The scent of her enveloped him, a fragrance that made him think of woods, of the sun on pine trees.

He caught her glance, the look of a patient tutor waiting for a slow student. "Go on," he said.

"This room has its own entrance, which Mr. Fowler found convenient for meeting visitors without disturbing Mrs. Fowler."

"Did Mr. Fowler have a great many visitors?"

A swift look pardoned his stupidity. "A vicar always does. Of course, he loved this room for its books." She indicated the floor-to-ceiling bookcases. In one was a handsome set of leather-bound volumes.

"Mr. Fowler's sermon collections," she said, unlocking the cabinet and slipping the iron ring of keys over her wrist.

"What a great many keys you have, Miss Merrifield," he said, unable to resist the promptings of his body that urged him closer. Their breaths mingled briefly, the top of her head just above his shoulder. With a slight lowering of his head he could kiss her.

Her eyes widened as if she guessed his thought, and she stepped back abruptly. "Have you brought many books with you, Mr. Nash?"

"Almost none, Miss Merrifield." He frowned. The girl muddled his brain. He might have no calling for the church, but he thought he could give a reasonable semblance of a curate, not a London rake. Only he had years of experience seducing women and but a few months' experience being chaste among them.

The faint line between her brows became a crease, her generous mouth contracted tightly. "You'll write your own sermons then."

"I plan to."

He scanned the titles on the shelf. "Which is your favorite?"

She pointed to a slender volume. "Sherlock." He picked it from the shelf and let it fall open in his hands. The words were a blur, but it was wise to occupy his hands with turning the pages.

"Did Mr. Fowler write his own sermons?"

"Very good ones."

He looked up from the page, caught by the sincere admiration in her tone. Lord, he was on the point of flirting with a girl who liked sermons. "What do you admire most in a sermon—feeling or delivery?"

He had blundered again. Her face told him the question was wrong. The Winterburn side of his nature took offense instantly. "Don't tell me, Miss Merrifield, that you have never lamented a Sunday spent listening to a dull sermon?"

A faint flush stained her cheeks. Her eyes

revealed a struggle with her temper. "A polished delivery can never make up for want of feeling."

"You want passion from the pulpit then?"

His scorn goaded her. No struggle this time. Her eyes flashed defiantly. "I don't judge a sermon chiefly on its presentation but on the effect it has on our lives."

"So, the poor preacher who wants your approval must deliver feeling with polish and provoke a reformation. You have exacting standards for the clergy, Miss Merrifield."

Her angry gaze dropped. She clasped the ring of keys in both hands and studied the floor for a moment. He suspected she was practicing forbearance.

"I have only Mr. Fowler to judge by," she said, raising her eyes again. "He was a kind and conscientious man. And I think that a clergyman like him achieves the greatest effect through his private character and general conduct."

The deep-brown eyes measured him. He knew that look; he'd seen it in Portugal in the face of sister Luzia, who wanted him to believe his vision from God. This girl would expect him to be better than he was. He closed the book in his hands and turned away.

He was clever enough to come up with sermons that would satisfy the villagers' demand for high-mindedness, but it was most unlikely that he could develop a new character. He was lucky his uncle had the power to ordain him, not this country miss with her impossible expectations. He'd had enough of others' expectations of him.

He stepped around his prickly guide and pushed open the study door. "What's next, Miss Merrifield?"

"On this floor? The kitchen and pantries."

He followed her into the kitchen, where she opened a series of doors with brisk efficiency, indicating a scullery, closet, and larder, plainly expecting him to be impressed. But she merely taxed his self-command. She slid her keys into so many locks, opened so many narrow doors, asked him to admire the charms and convenience of the house while he was conscious only of her bright hair and sweet, low voice. When she paused, he peered over her shoulder into the dark recesses of the larder.

"The most spacious larder in England, I take it," he said.

She spun his way, a flash of injured pride in her expressive eyes. "It should suffice for a single man, Mr. Nash." And then, relenting, she added, "Mrs. Cheek from the village helped the Fowlers in the kitchen and will be happy to offer you her services if you need some."

"Thank you, Miss Merrifield. I have a man who will do for me. Mr. Dowdeswell will be along shortly with a cart." He did not say that Dowdeswell was his watchdog really, appointed by Uncle Ned, charged with reporting to the bishop Leigh's fitness for ordination—or lack thereof.

She turned from him and relocked the closets. He noted again the authority in the way she handled the keys and wondered if she would surrender them to him at all. They passed back through the kitchen. On a work table lay a basket, a pair of gloves, and a pot of tea which must have grown cold as they'd toured the house. She had intended a kinder welcome than he'd allowed her to offer.

"Will you see the upstairs now?" she asked.

"If you insist."

Rosalind gripped the keys tightly. A few minutes more and she must surrender them to this proud stranger, making the parsonage his, not Jane's. So far she had failed to make him appreciate the least aspect of his good fortune. He had observed every feature of the lovely house with polite disinterest. The spacious rooms, the wide views, and all the convenience and charm had left him unimpressed. Apparently he was used to finer, grander things. His gray eyes hardly seemed to see his surroundings, except when he looked at her. Then his gaze was steady and consuming.

He moved with a wicked grace that drew her eyes to his form more often than was seemly. Other men of her acquaintance differed from women in their interests, their talk, their duties, but this man was fundamentally different. His height made the rooms seem smaller. His clothes did not so much conceal his person as reveal a hard sort of leanness. There was a moment when Rosalind had the startling impression he might kiss her. Rosalind stepped on the hem of her skirt and stumbled. His hand was instantly on her elbow, steadying her and sending a surprising jolt of warmth through her.

She attempted to give her thoughts a sensible

turn. It was common practice for clergymen to take more than one living. "Do you intend to fill the living, Mr. Nash, or will you hire a curate to discharge your duties?"

"Rowdene is my only benefice, Miss Merrifield."

She stopped at the top of the stairs. It was satisfying to look down on him. "The parsonage was intended for a family, of course. There are six bedrooms on this floor and two smaller attic rooms."

His gray gaze moved up her person. "And did the Fowlers have a large family?"

She swallowed. "They did at one time. Mrs. Fowler has just a son left now, in the navy."

He seemed to digest the information as she led him past the smaller rooms along the north side. She opened the cabinets and linen closets for his inspection.

"You were a good friend to Mrs. Fowler, I take it."

"Rather, she was to me and others. A clergyman's wife does a great deal for a neighborhood, you know."

"That's an ill-disguised reproach, Miss Merrifield." One of his black brows rose a fraction.

"I beg your pardon. I don't wish you to be without a situation, if you need one. But you can't deny the fitness of Rowdene for a family."

"Perhaps I mean to marry, and this living is my only means of supporting a . . . wife."

The word transformed their conversation into something intimate, something unlike any conversation Rosalind had ever had with a man. His gray eyes had darkened to slate. Rosalind struggled for an easy, indifferent tone. "We shall welcome your wife if you choose to marry."

"And every clergyman in easy circumstances ought to marry? That's your opinion, Miss Merrifield?"

They had reached the master bedroom, a large chamber with views to the south and west. She hesitated on the threshold, then entered and went directly to the windows.

"Mrs. Fowler's left me the bed, too?" he asked, his gaze fixed on the handsome four-poster.

Rosalind nodded, irked that the man made her conscious of things she ought to take no note of, like the bed.

He turned to her, caught her gaze, and held it trapped in his. She felt that look like the weight of a gray sky, pressing its heaviness on the land.

"You inspire most unclerical thoughts, Miss Merrifield."

She crossed her arms, hugging her elbows. "I don't mean to," she said firmly, praying he would not press the matter further.

From below came the sound of a vehicle. He moved to the window and waved to a man in the parsonage drive.

"That's Dowdeswell with my things, Miss Merrifield. Shall we go down?"

"You don't wish to see the garden?"

He laughed. "No, thank you. This tour's been enough for me. I have no desire to see the surrounding vegetation."

She stood her ground. "You can have no objection then if I stop by from time to time to tend to Mrs. Fowler's roses."

An odd look of surprise came into his eyes, as if she'd guessed some secret of his.

"Of course, tend the roses, Miss Merrifield." He bowed and indicated that she should precede him.

When they reached the hall, she stopped and handed him the keys. He passed around her and pulled open the door. A cart stood in the drive, and two men in smocks were bent under trunks. A third man, carrying a valise, seemed to be in charge. He was tall, with a heavy head too large for his narrow shoulders and long, thin body. His blunt features in a deeply creased face made her think of a solemn old hound. He stopped and frowned in obvious disapproval.

"Your lordship," he said.

"Dowdeswell."

Rosalind did not hear the rest of his reply. She spun toward Nash. "'Your lordship'?"

The carters passed between them. "In Rowdene I am Mr. Nash."

"But elsewhere Lord . . .?"

"Winterburn."

"You appointed yourself the living." She didn't need a reply; she could see the truth in his eyes. Jane displaced for a rich man to play at service. Rosalind wanted to snatch the keys back. "You are not ordained then?"

"I will be."

"I will see that the vestry protests to the bishop."

He stepped closer. "It's irregular but not illegal. Rank does not bar a man from God's service."

"But surely self-interest does, lack of character does. Deception does."

"There's no deception here." He looked at her as if he were enjoying her anger.

"To call yourself Mr. Nash is not a deception?"

"I am Mr. Nash, Curate of Rowdene."

"In that coat I think not. Good day, your lordship."

Chapter 4

The sun was setting when Leigh left the parsonage. Across the road at the foot of the hill stood the Church of St. Nicholas of Rowdene, a Norman structure with a squat, crenellated tower and a short nave of four bays whose rounded arches preceded the Gothic by centuries. The windows had a dull, leaden look. Patches of lichen and moss covered the rough, gray stones, as if the landscape meant to overtake the church. The iron gate in the churchyard wall hung open, beckoning Leigh past the tilted, begrimed headstones of long-dead villagers.

Inside the church he paused, struck by the unexpected beauty of the windows, which glowed with deep hues. Bars of rich color pierced the thick gloom. He looked about for a candle and tinder box but found neither. He passed down the length of the aisle from pools of ruby and violet to shadow, noting the narrow, worn benches, empty candle stands, puddles on the floor, and the plain square pulpit. He stopped before the bare altar and waited for the transporting emotion to take hold as it had under the white light of his vision.

He never discovered how he had come to the *Convento do Desterro* high in the mountains. The nuns would say only that a farmer brought him. He woke in a narrow bed in a plain, white room under a carved wooden ceiling, whose beams he came to know well. Light from a small, stone-framed window bathed a diminutive nun in a black habit.

Her voice like the dawn chatter of birds roused him from days of blankness. When he asked in English how he had come to be there, she shrugged and answered in Portuguese, "When you lose everything, you find God."

After that Sister Luzia came every day, coaxing, cajoling, prodding him to recovery. The nuns gave him a white cotton tunic, trousers, and sandals. As soon as he could stand, Luzia had shown him the ruined kitchen garden. For days he sat in the sun, perplexed by her insistence that the garden would heal him. Then one day, sitting there, he saw tools propped against a ruined wall. He had laughed then, but he'd gone to work rebuilding the walls, strengthening the soil and himself, planting, hoeing, weeding, recovering pieces of his past.

There had followed long luminous days with no room in his heart for anything but courage and love. On one of them he'd had a vision. But when Luzia insisted that the mother superior write the bishop about him, they learned that he had not lost everything. He had a family and a title in

England. He found Richard's grave in Spain and left for home.

Now his wounds ached, his stomach grumbled. His hope that in Rowdene he would escape the staleness of his London life seemed particularly vain in the chill nave of the musty, little church. If he fell to his knees in supplication, would the distant diety answer any prayer of his?

More likely he would soil the knees of his breeches for nothing. The prospect of serving God wakened no more zeal in him than the prospect of serving his mother's idols: wealth and power. Instead Miss Merrifield had roused energies that had lain dormant in his body for months. She had kindled the easy heat of his nature, inspiring unclerical desires before he had performed the least of his duties.

The scrape of a shoe on stone alerted him that he was not alone. He turned from the altar. Dowdeswell's large head emerged from the shadows at the rear of the church.

"Ah, Dowdeswell. Been here long?"

"A few minutes, sir."

Leigh let his gaze circle the darkening nave. "Then you see I'm not using the church for a lover's tryst."

"Sir, I never—"

Leigh lifted a hand, cutting Dowdeswell off. "You may report to my uncle that I didn't debauch any maidens on my first day in Rowdene." He made his way down the aisle past his watchdog servant.

At the door Dowdeswell's voice stopped him.

"Sir, may I report that you came down to the church to pray?"

Leigh glanced over his shoulder. "To pray? You're an optimist, Dowdeswell. Good night."

Rosalind first missed her gloves in the morning when she set out to call on Mr. Taylor, the churchwarden. The empty space in the drawer brought an instant vexing recollection of her gloves lying on the work table in Jane's kitchen . . . Lord Winterburn's kitchen.

A second disturbing image immediately replaced the first—Winterburn holding her gloves in his hands. The unexpected thought sent a hot shiver through her. She grabbed her second-best pair and shoved the drawer shut. Most likely Winterburn's servant would find and return her gloves.

As her second pair was neither new nor warm, her fingers were numb by the time she reached the crest of the hill above the village. She cast a quick, resentful glance at the parsonage. No smoke rose from its chimneys, and she allowed herself a brief moment of satisfaction that she would lodge her protest with the churchwarden before Lord Winterburn left his bed.

Of course, while Winterburn slept, the village folk were up and about. Rosalind exchanged greetings with half a dozen neighbors and merchants along the High Street, knowing someone would inevitably tell Lady Ellenby that Miss Merrifield was going about alone again. There was no help for it.

Lady Ellenby, a baronet's widow, had, on the death of Rosalind's parents, appointed herself Rosalind's mentor. Since then she had endeavored earnestly and unceasingly to raise Rosalind out of what her ladyship considered a deplorable country obscurity. Rosalind, while grateful for Lady Ellenby's concern, had no wish to be constrained by her advice, advice that would have been disastrous for Merrifield.

Lady Ellenby advised Rosalind to spend her days at the pianoforte, her evenings at dinners and assemblies. Her plans for Rosalind allowed no time for visiting tenants, managing a property, or keeping up with accounts. Rosalind did not resent the invitations, however, so much as she resented the attitude that the Fowlers were inferior company. This winter there had been a welcome lessening of Lady Ellenby's interference as her own daughters had made their debut in local society. Rosalind had dined less often at Ellenby Manor and just as much as ever at the parsonage. Or she had until now.

Knowing Lady Ellenby's regard for rank made Rosalind cautious about approaching the parish vestry. They were men of some standing in the village, appointed by the squire with Lady Ellenby's approval. Position was important to them, rank admired. She could not reveal Winterburn's deception without revealing his title, and she did not wish to awe them with the presence of a belted earl in Rowdene.

She planned to catch Mr. Taylor at breakfast. As a grain merchant, he did much of his business in the predawn hours, overseeing the loading of his shiny black delivery wagons. At breakfast Rosalind could explain Lord Winterburn's deception while Mr. Taylor was alone and undistracted by the demands of his business. She was not perfectly sure she could make him appreciate Winterburn's perfidy or his unfitness to be Rowdene's new parson, but respect for Taylor's position required that she start her campaign with him.

One of the black carts stood at the barn's gaping entrance when Rosalind reached the yard. The huge horses blew gusty breaths and lifted their shaggy feet restlessly. A kitchen maid scattering grain to a milling, squawking flock of geese gave Rosalind a sliding glance. From the barn came the rattle of chains as men worked the huge pulley that lowered grain sacks to the barn floor. Mr. Taylor spotted Rosalind as he emerged from his barn, following a man hefting a sack of grain. Taylor hurried across the yard to her, his thin face pinched with worry.

He was a nervous man who succeeded in his business by making countless small transactions through the buying season. Rosalind was sure no fieldmouse counted the grains of its winter hoard more often than Mr. Taylor counted his profits. Yet his impatient energy had served him well as the price of grain fell with the war's end. He had continued to prosper while other men of business failed.

"Good morning, Miss Merrifield. D'ye need some seed?"

"No, thank you, Mr. Taylor." She tried to make

herself heard without shouting over the rattle of the pulley chains and the cackling of the geese. "I've come to talk to you about the new man in the parsonage."

"Nash, isn't it?" Mr. Taylor glanced at his workers. "I've not met him."

"Perhaps I should return later," Rosalind said.

Mr. Taylor's wavering attention came back to her. "Beg pardon, Miss Merrifield. The lads dropped a dozen sacks this morning. Broke like eggs and everythin's at sixes and sevens. Still it's good you caught me. I'm off for Chippenham within the hour. What is it you wish to say?"

Rosalind took a deep breath. There was going to be no privacy and no other chance to speak. "Was the vestry consulted about this appointment?"

"Now, Miss Merrifield," said Taylor, his voice deepening with a note of authority, "the vestry knows its duty. We will work with the new parson whoever he be."

"Of course, Mr. Taylor, as you did with Mr. Fowler, but Mr. Nash is a very . . . unclerical person." Rosalind pressed her lips together. "He's not ordained. He's not married, and he seems most unsuited to be a parson."

The kitchen maid listened openly now, no longer making even a pretense of tending her flock.

Mr. Taylor nodded. "Ah, Miss Merrifield, do not fret. We still have Mr. Vernon to see to services."

"A comfort certainly," Rosalind replied, "but

may I ask you, Mr. Taylor, when you meet Mr. Nash, do consider his dress and manner, his . . . origins, his obvious lack of preparation for the position. I think the vestry will wish to make a protest to the bishop."

Mr. Taylor's brows shot up, and he raised his hands as if to ward off the idea. "Protest to the bishop? 'Tis a serious step yer contemplatin', Miss Merrifield."

"But think, Mr. Taylor. If this man is accepted now, there will be no removing him. He will likely be in the parsonage for the next forty years."

Mr. Taylor shook his head gravely, his narrow brow furrowed. "I don't know, Miss Merrifield. 'Tis tampering with the work of our betters."

"But you are all men of judgment and standing." Rosalind stopped herself from saying more. She knew she had pushed him. Without Mr. Fowler the vestry would be guided by the squire. Still, she hoped they would show some independence of spirit and judge for themselves.

A groom drove into the yard with Mr. Taylor's gig, and the churchwarden looked anxiously at the waiting vehicle.

Rosalind thanked him for seeing her. "I won't keep you from your journey. I ask only that you lead the vestry in thinking about this man. Is he truly the parson Rowdene needs?"

At breakfast Leigh opened the first of the theological volumes his uncle recommended. He read steadily for an hour or more, finding the writer's ideas remote and uninspiring. Then a sentence stopped him. *What we must start with, if we wish to pray, is the certainty that we are sinners.* He straightened and scanned the paragraph again. It was like nothing the writer had said before, and it overturned all his notions. He turned the page eagerly for the first time.

Then a deep bellow from the church drew him to the window. Below him a red-faced gentleman in a clerical collar and black coat was attempting to herd four men in laborer's smocks from the churchyard. The clerical man drove them through the gate into the road with his tirade, but they turned and faced him with a dogged air, hats in hand, heads bowed, like recruits cringing under a sergeant's tongue-lashing. The clerical man shouted on, pacing back and forth, stopping to shake his forefinger vigorously in the face of any man who ventured to speak. It occurred to Leigh then that the clergyman must be Mr. Vernon, the curate of St. Andrew's, who was to perform services at St. Nicholas until Leigh was ordained. He was surprised at a surge of proprietary feeling toward the little church and decided he would go down and see what his assistant was doing.

As Leigh approached, the four laborers shuffled off down the road. Vernon glared after them, his feet planted wide, his elbows akimbo, barring the path to the church. He was a stout man of about thirty with a full, florid face, dark hair and eyes, and a nose made for looking down on his inferiors. He turned at Leigh's greeting and exchanged introductions with stiff formality.

"What's the trouble?" Leigh asked.

"Nothing, really." Vernon's voice was flat and thin. "I won't have drunkards ringing the bells, and so I told them. I've locked them out until they stay sober."

"My man Dowdeswell's a sober fellow. He could ring the bells."

"There will be no bells until the men of Rowdene show a proper respect for the church."

It was a petty, tyrannical edict, but Leigh admitted to himself that he didn't know the circumstances. "I think I may have something to say about that, Mr. Vernon," he suggested mildly.

Vernon stiffened. "As you wish, though you will find the villagers difficult to manage if you give in to them from the start."

"I will keep that in mind." He held the other man's gaze until Vernon looked away.

"Have you seen the church yet, Nash?" Vernon didn't wait for an answer but led Leigh along the path and through the doors. "To be sure, it's not much, very plain. The pulpit's just a box, really." He strode ahead of Leigh down the center aisle.

"The windows are fine," Leigh offered to Vernon's back.

Vernon paused and glanced over his shoulder. "Well, yes, I suppose they are. However, the benches are narrow, and the roof leaks." He pivoted sharply and with the toe of one shoe pointed to a depression in the stone floor where a small puddle gleamed dully.

They were face-to-face. "Is there a supply of candles on hand?" Leigh asked.

"Don't know that one needs too many."

"By my count there are brackets for ninety."

"Ninety! The vestry would never countenance such an expense. Besides, that many candles would be too 'high church' for this parish." Vernon's earlier annoyance came back into his voice with this remark. "These are plain folks, an ignorant, superstitious lot."

"I've been misinformed then. I thought there were some large estates in the neighborhood."

Vernon opened a gate in the communion rail and passed into the sanctuary. "Well, yes, there are a few," he said over his shoulder, unlocking a door to the right. "Most of the gentry attend services at St. Andrew's, of course, but Lady Ellenby and Squire Haythorne do look in at Rowdene now and then."

"Do you lack for company then?" he asked, looking through the door of the little room at Vernon, who had busied himself arranging surplices and altar cloths.

"Oh, no. I'm sure I am welcome in a dozen great houses or more. Lady Ellenby always has a spot for me at her table or for an evening of cards."

Vernon made no mention of Miss Merrifield, and Leigh realized he'd been hoping for some word of her. She must live near the church for she had left the parsonage on foot the day before, and her regard for Mr. Fowler's preaching meant she had often attended services at St. Nicholas.

"You are able to manage the extra duties attached to Rowdene?" he asked.

Mr. Vernon looked up from his task, and his chest swelled visibly as he gathered himself to reply. "I've discharged my duties in Rowdene as if the living were my own. I will be here Sundays and Wednesdays as we agreed."

"Wednesdays, too?"

"Yes. Wednesday's my day for churching mothers, settling disputes, that sort of thing. There's a deal of petty thievery here. One's got to be Solomon to settle things among these folks."

"I could take on some of your Wednesday duties."

Vernon froze. "Before you're ordained? Let me remind you, Mr. Nash, 'It is not lawful for any man to take upon him the office of public preaching, or ministering the sacraments in the congregation, before he be lawfully called.'"

"I know," said Leigh. "Article twenty-three."

Vernon sniffed.

Leigh stepped into the cramped sacristy and tried for a moment to picture himself wearing the white surplice Vernon was holding. He gave up. The garment suggested a degree of sanctity he was unlikely to attain. He picked up a silver plate. "Who's got the care of the church and yard?"

"Oh, the warden sees to that."

"When can I get a set of keys then?"

"Didn't you get them from Mrs. Fowler?"

"Miss Merrifield showed me the parsonage and gave me its keys."

"Miss Merrifield?" Vernon frowned. "If I may say so, Miss Merrifield is an interfering young woman, entirely too independent. She should not be allowed to run about as she does or have anything to say about this church."

"*Does* she have anything to say about the managing of this church?" Leigh remembered her parting remark about the vestry protesting his appointment as curate.

"Of course not. The villagers have some strange notions about her, mere superstitious nonsense. The girl ought to be married. She has no sense of her station."

"Superstitious nonsense?"

"Yes. They're a pagan lot at heart. Think some maiden will save the village when they ought to mind their work and keep from drink."

Leigh wondered what Miss Merrifield had done to offend Mr. Vernon.

Vernon put away the last of the vestments. "Well, Nash, I must get up to the parsonage."

Leigh raised a brow.

"That is," said Vernon, "if you will allow me to continue to use Mr. Fowler's study to meet parishioners. If that's not agreeable, I will arrange for rooms in the village, but in that case I will have to insist upon more than the fifty-five pounds."

It was Leigh's turn to nod. "By all means come up to the parsonage. Use the study. I'll take myself off to look about the neighborhood."

The road beyond the church passed between low stone walls which allowed Leigh to view wide stretches of the bare landscape. The hedgerows were leafless tangles of branches, but the fields were ploughed, the dark earth turned up in

rows. A line came back to him from some Greek
his tutor had admired, "the holy and inexhausti-
ble earth." A faint breeze ruffled his hair and
stirred up odors of soil and animals.

He had not gone far when he was overtaken by
a herd of sheep with a dog. A dust-covered young
man with a shepherd's crook in hand fell into step
beside him. The fellow was lean and moved with
a level, ground-eating stride. A pair of shrewd
blue eyes looked out of a freckled face from under
a wide, flat-crowned straw hat.

"Yer Nash, the new parson, aren't ye?" asked
his companion.

"I am."

"Put Vernon's nose out of joint, ye have, coming here."

"Not intentionally."

"Ah, well, a man can hope." The blue eyes
were full of mirth.

"Did I see you with Mr. Vernon earlier today,
Mr. . . .?"

"Braithe. Jeremy Braithe. Shepherd, sir." He
hefted his crook in one hand. "Like yerself,
different flock is all. And not so fine a coat. Will ye
preach in that coat?"

"I won't preach until I'm ordained."

"And when will that be, if ye don't mind my
asking?"

"A year."

"Then ye've time to learn the business." The
road rose in front of them, but Braithe didn't slow
his pace.

"Of being a parson?" Leigh asked.

"It's a difficult business, ye know."

"Is it?"

His companion gave him a quick glance but not an answer. Leigh waited. He suspected Braithe was used to leading an audience on.

As they neared the crest of the rise, Braithe asked, "Do ye walk on water?"

He had to give Braithe credit. The man's countenance did not betray a hint of jocularity. Leigh laughed. "No."

"Not at all?"

"No."

Braithe shook his head. "I wonder then how ye will make a name for yerself as a parson in these parts."

"Is a miracle required?"

"Generally. There's Trebell that got the bells—"

"The bells that Mr. Vernon has silenced?"

Braithe gave Leigh a measuring look.

"A long time ago at harvest, a great fire had started in the corn, and Parson Trebell rang the bell to call the folk. There was but one bell, ye see, and he rang and rang it. The peals filled the sky. They say the echo reached heaven. A great storm blew up. Clouds black as hell. Smoke thick as night. Thunder rumbling. The fire was nigh on the town and Trebell rang the bell to crack it when the first bolt o' lightning fell." Braithe let him wait. "Well, the lightning struck that bell, and there've been three bells ever since."

They topped the rise and stopped to look down a long stretch of gentle folds of land dotted with farms. The nearest house was a fine brick manor at the end of a long drive. It sat proudly on a flat knoll, obviously the home of some gentleman.

The teasing mood left the shepherd. "In a month," he said, "this will all be green as Eden."

"What house is that, Braithe?" Leigh asked.

"Merrifield Hall."

Leigh could not help a start of surprise. "Who lives there?"

Braithe turned and gave him a sober look. "Miss Merrifield is mistress there now. The Rose of Rowdene."

At the odd title the image of the rose and the wheel flickered again in his mind, and he felt the strange excitement that accompanied the vision. It passed. Braithe was watching him, a knowing look in his shrewd eyes.

"Why is she called the Rose of Rowdene?"

"It's another story," Braithe said.

"Tell me, if you're going my way."

They walked on.

"A long time ago, in a time of war and plague, Coker was parson in Rowdene, a priest of the old church. One day he was walking along this very road, and when he came to this spot, he found a knight with his sword drawn upon a maid of rare beauty. A war of roses in her cheeks, hair red as fire, and eyes dark as night. The knight demanded the girl yield her maidenhead, and when she refused, he struck off her head and rode on. Coker rushed forward and put the girl's head back on her shoulders." Braithe fell silent.

Leigh gave in and asked dryly, "And?"

"The maid lived to be a virtuous wife to a good knight for many years. The village escaped war and plague. So they called her the Rose of Rowdene, and they say Miss Merrifield is the Rose come back now when there's war abroad and trouble at home."

Again Braithe was watching him, expecting something. The story was nothing a man of sense could believe, the product of invention and superstition. Leigh looked back at the house, a handsome structure no more than a hundred years old, hardly the stuff of legend. "You do have high standards for a parson, Braithe. Expect no miracles from me."

"Bread and kindness are miracles enow for most folks, Mr. Nash," he said. "Good day to you, sir." He touched the brim of his straw hat, vaulted over a low stone wall, and set off on a footpath over the brow of the hill.

Vernon was gone when Leigh returned to the parsonage. He had walked a score of miles and trusted he would sleep well for it. In the entry he found a young woman slumped in a chair. She was dressed like a London milkmaid with a bunched-up skirt over a petticoat, a striped scarf around her shoulders, and sleeves rolled up to reveal soft, white arms.

Dowdeswell appeared, a scowl on his heavy features. "She's waited for you all afternoon. She refused to talk to Vernon."

The girl opened bright-blue eyes. "Oh," she said. "Pardon me. I've waited so long. Are you

Mr. Nash?" She had a creamy complexion and golden curls under a lace cap.

"Yes."

"Then will you help me? Mr. Vernon would never help."

"What sort of help do you need?"

The girl looked at Dowdeswell and then at Leigh as if the delicacy of her position would not allow her to speak. Leigh waved Dowdeswell away. "Speak, Miss . . ."

"Polly Rees, sir." She stood, grabbed her skirts, and bobbed up and down in a quick curtsy. "It's my da. He's hurt his leg and he can't work any longer."

"He's applied to the parish for relief?"

"Oh, no, sir, he's a proud man. But I thought I could do you a service, Mr. Nash." She leaned close and her voice became a soft, slow whisper. "As yer new here and not settled proper in yer house, I could help ye." The offer was accompanied by a sultry glance from under lowered lashes which Leigh could not misread. "I'll do anything, Mr. Nash."

"Do you think you could help out in the church? Put some candles about?"

"In the church?" It was ludicrous the way the girl's face fell. Then a cunning look came into her eyes. "Of course, Mr. Nash, if you show me just what you want." She leaned close, her white bosom exposed to Leigh's view, her scent teasingly evocative of sex despite her milkmaid looks. He thought she might fall into his arms if she leaned any further his way.

"When shall I meet you in the church?" she asked in a husky voice.

"Tomorrow morning will be fine," he said.

"Yer sure I can do nothing more . . . tonight?"

Dowdeswell appeared in the doorway again. "Here's your cloak, miss," he said.

Polly gave him a quick fierce glare, but smiled sweetly when Leigh offered to help her don the cloak.

"I'm sure your father needs you more than I tonight, Miss Rees."

Chapter 5

Polly Rees appeared at the church at nine, bright as a new-minted guinea, her golden curls arranged under a dainty mobcap. Not a speck of dust nor a drop of grease marked the white apron that billowed over her striped skirts. Leigh handed her a broom, which she held at arm's length.

"It's not a snake, Miss Rees."

"We're not going to clean this whole church, are we?" she asked.

Leigh began to strip off his coat. "A labor for Hercules."

She gave him a puzzled look. "*You* aren't going to sweep, are you?"

He shook his head. "I'll dust." She gaped at him, but he turned his back.

He picked up a pole rigged with a bundle of rags and began to pass the cloth over the apse windows, brushing away dirt and cobwebs. The tops of the windows were beyond his reach, but Dowdeswell was to scout up a ladder and bring it along to the church. Two of the dismissed bell ringers had also pledged to help when Leigh offered to reinstate them in return for their labor around the church or grounds. Behind him he heard Polly drag her broom across the stones.

He concentrated on balancing the long pole and touching the jewel-colored figures of the saints lightly. He was sure they had been added sometime after the church was built. The only one he recognized was St. George, the ubiquitous patron of the English. Sword raised, foot on the neck of the slain dragon, George made sainthood appear easy. Leigh could not give a name to any of the other faces gazing raptly heavenward though saints' names dotted the map of London. St. Clement, St. Martin, St. James. Who were they?

He had spent little enough time in church in his life and none attending to religious instruction. His family had appeared at St. George's in Hanover Square only when obliged to witness the blessing of some worldly office or alliance. So why was he drawn to this little church? The plain exterior hid no more than simple beauties, stone and glass and line and curve which conspired to lift the eye if not the spirit. A slap of wood against stone and an anguished wail from Polly interrupted his thoughts.

He glanced over his shoulder. Polly's broom lay on the floor while she stood doubled over, clutching one hand in the other.

"What is it?" he asked, putting aside his pole and moving toward her.

She looked up with tear-brightened eyes and lifted her palm for his inspection. A long, dark needle of wood was lodged in the smooth skin.

"Hurts, does it?"

She nodded. He took her firmly by the elbow and led her to one of the candles they'd lit. "Hold still," he said, taking the injured hand in his and turning it toward the light. He bent down to examine the splinter and found it not so deeply embedded as he'd first thought. Her palm was soft and white and violet scented, and it occurred to him that she had never supported her ailing father with such hands. Miss Merrifield's competent hands had done far more work.

With the tip of his nail he felt the embedded point of the splinter and began to ease it out of the long, shallow puncture. "How is your father this morning, Polly?"

"As easy as I could make him, Mr. Nash. He's that pleased I am to help you, sir."

"Has he seen a surgeon?"

"Oh, no. 'Twould be too costly. Rest will heal 'im, sure."

"Sir!" Dowdeswell's voice broke over them with stern reproach.

Leigh glanced up, aware the moment he did so of the proximity of Polly's white bosom and full lips. Her gaze was fixed on him, her lips slightly parted. As a technique it was more practiced than subtle.

"Dowdeswell," he said, "another timely appearance." He bent back to his task, taking hold of the now-exposed end of the splinter and pulling it out. He could feel Polly's breath stir his hair and hear Dowdeswell, hurrying up the aisle, puffing a bit in his haste to prevent a debauch.

"There, Miss Rees," Leigh said to the girl. He stepped back and offered her his handkerchief.

"Thank you, Mr. Nash," she said primly.

Leigh held the dark wood fragment between his thumb and forefinger for Dowdeswell's inspection. "Miss Rees was injured in the line of duty."

Dowdeswell looked at the splinter as if it were the very apple that had corrupted Eve. "Should I take miss up to the parsonage to clean her wound?"

Leigh nodded.

"But I must come back to help you, Mr. Nash," Polly insisted. Her lashes dropped to veil her eyes. "Even if I can't sweep any longer."

Leigh took the injured hand in his again. Polly simpered, and Dowdeswell stiffened his already straight spine. "No more sweeping, Polly. You need to preserve these white hands of yours."

The bells of St. Nicholas rang Sunday morning over Vernon's objections. The windows of the apse shone with jeweled splendor. Swept free of grime, the hard, pure surface of the stone lay exposed. If Leigh knelt to pray, he might not receive an answer, but he would not soil the knees of his breeches. When Vernon stepped into the little room off the chancel to don his robes, Leigh lit the candles Polly had placed in holders, all ninety of them.

The peal of the bells faded and men and women entered the church, lifting their eyes to the bright glow, lowering their voices to hushed whispers. Leigh watched from beside one of the squat columns of the north aisle, consumed with an odd impatience. When Miss Merrifield appeared, stopping just inside the doors, he knew what he'd been waiting for. Her gaze swept the nave, taking in the brilliance of the windows and the lambent play of candlelight on stone. He caught and trapped her glance. Before she could veil it, he saw in her eyes the realization that he had brought the light into the church. The thought caused him a sharp stab of joy.

The elements of his vision—light and stone and the rose—suspended him in the moment until her brief nod of greeting freed him. She moved to take her place on the benches, and he was able to look about again.

He was being noticed. Once the villagers' first interest in the lights had passed, he became the object of covert stares and plain ogling.

Next came the churchwarden with a group of men Leigh supposed were the vestry. He had arranged to meet them after the service, but now they stood at the rear of the church, looking from the candles to each other, talking in grave whispers. Above the murmur of their voices, he discerned the complaining grumble of a large fellow whose frame shook heavily with each gusty breath he exhaled.

Abruptly, the warden detached himself from the others and shuffled to Leigh's side. He was a gray, spare-looking man, who twisted his hat in his hands as he approached.

"Mr. Nash, begging your pardon, sir, the vestry would please to put out the candles, sir."

"Why?"

The warden looked over his shoulder at his huddled colleagues. "Too dear, sir."

"Did the church have candles when Mr. Fowler was curate?"

Again the warden looked to the others. "Ay, we did sir, but we haven't the coin for such a show now."

"I'll bear the expense myself." The words came out loud and hollow sounding.

Silence answered him. The face of the fellow who had been grumbling settled into a deep frown. There were whispers somewhere in the church, but around Leigh only silence that spread like the widening ripple on the surface of a pond. Dozens of pairs of ears apparently strained to hear the next words of the exchange. His gaze met Miss Merrifield's, and he felt there was some message in it that he could not read.

At that moment Vernon came striding down the aisle in his black robes and white surplice. "Neighbors, what's amiss? Why haven't you taken your places?"

"Vernon," said Leigh, "apparently the illumination is more than the vestry can afford. I've offered to pay for the candles myself."

"Ah, Mr. Nash." Vernon shook his head. "Generous, but prodigal."

"It's Easter, Vernon."

"Even so, Nash, to teach extravagance to our flock is unseemly." He turned to the warden and his supporters. "Neighbors, Mr. Nash, being new among us, does not know our ways. Peter Pryke and William Moss, snuff those candles. We'll store them, and Mr. Nash's generosity will serve us for months to come." Vernon nodded to the men.

Leigh raised a hand to stay them. "Wait." For Vernon's ears he said, "I will have light in my church."

Vernon flushed. "Mr. Nash, of course, but may I remind you that the service is about to begin." He spoke in a fierce whisper that probably reached every ear in the silent crowd. "As I am still the ordained minister here, you should have consulted me earlier about any expense. It is unseemly for us to dispute now over a matter that should have been resolved before today."

Someone coughed, and Leigh glanced at the vestry. No one would meet his eye. They stood, heads bowed, hands in pockets, shoulders hunched, cowed by Vernon. If they didn't want light, why should Leigh insist? "Suit yourselves."

The candles were snuffed, the bright glow faded. He gripped the back of the pew in front of him and wished for a sword hilt around which to close his fist. He concentrated on the anger. Under it was another feeling he did not want to examine. He could not explain his desire to light the church. A few candles in a country church, what did they matter?

He could feel the eyes of the small congregation

on him and pressed his palms against the rough
surface of the old wood beneath his hands. His
arms and shoulders tightened. No wonder humility was a seldom practiced virtue. He certainly
had no gift for it. But he could not fight Vernon
publicly. He could not proclaim himself the Earl
of Winterburn and win the confidence of the
villagers.

Rosalind tried to forget Winterburn's presence.
She sat up very straight and concentrated on
Vernon mounting the pulpit, solemnly arranging
the fall of his sleeves, clearing his throat. She
clasped her hands tightly in her lap. Winterburn's
humiliation should please her; instead she felt
wretched. It was as if she had been embarrassed.
Though she sat several pews in front of him, she
could feel the hot anger he was controlling.

It was plain he had no notion of how to get on
with a parish vestry. An absurd bubble of laughter threatened to escape her. He was so far above
his company, he could not see what he'd done.
Ninety candles meant nothing to him. Clearly, he
had never counted the cost of anything.

But, the voice of weakness whispered, Winterburn had made the church lovely. The lights had
lifted her spirits the moment she entered. Even
the windows seemed brighter, the colors deeper,
truer.

Sometime later Leigh became aware that Vernon was preaching, his thin, flat voice twisting
words and phrases into long incomprehensible

strings of sound. Frugality and sobriety were his themes, a morality as constricting as his economics. A man two rows in front of Leigh gave an obvious jerk of the head as his chin dropped to his breast. Miss Merrifield's head, however, was high and steady. She was listening with rapt and respectful attention to Vernon's priggish drivel, and that was suddenly more irritating than the curate's voice with its whining edge.

Miss Merrifield puzzled him. He shifted his position slightly and studied the nape of her neck and the tendrils of deep-red hair nestled in the hollow between the curve of her collar and the brim of her straw bonnet. She didn't like him, and she hadn't wanted him to have the parsonage. She was listening to Vernon as if the man uttered piercing eloquence, but she'd liked the candles. And she had not betrayed Leigh to the vestry. The warden had called him *Mr.* Nash, and even Vernon displayed the same condescension he had shown before. So she'd changed her mind about protesting Leigh's appointment. Why?

The service ended, and the crowd shuffled quietly out of the little church. Whatever chance there had been to stir their souls had passed. It left him feeling flat, cheated somehow.

Miss Merrifield offered her arm to a gaunt, white-bearded old man, supported on the other side by a plain girl in a cap and shawl. The old man was blind, and the two women slowed their steps, allowing him to pick his way over the uneven stones.

Outside the church Vernon hustled to the side of an imposing lady with a pair of adolescent daughters, like a ship of the line with two cutters in tow. Leigh looked for the vestry and found them conferring under a tall elm. He would have to attend their meeting and attempt to win their support.

"Nash," Vernon called. Leigh halted, and the other man scuttled to his side, huffing a bit from his haste.

"Lady Ellenby insists I present you." Vernon looked down his long nose, clearly torn between pleasing the lady and introducing a rival to her notice.

Leigh stuck his hands in his pockets and regarded Lady Ellenby, who nodded regally as the villagers passed.

"Well, come on," Vernon said. "It won't do to keep her ladyship waiting. She'll likely invite you to supper."

"Before I'm ordained?" He glanced at the vestry. They had ended their informal conference, and began to walk to their meeting. Leigh shrugged. "Don't worry, Vernon. I won't steal your place at Lady Ellenby's table."

Vernon gasped. "You're too bold, Nash. There's an order to be preserved here."

"Of course," he said absently.

Beyond Lady Ellenby, Miss Merrifield stopped to speak with Jeremy Braithe. A breeze tugged at her bonnet and pressed her gown against her form. She grabbed the bonnet with one hand,

looking up at Braithe, laughing and smiling. Leigh
had a most unclerical thought.

The eight men of the parish vestry met in an
oak-paneled parlor at the inn. An extra place was
set for Leigh at the foot of the table next to
William Moss, a farmer, and across from Josiah
Sloath, the large man who had grumbled about
the candles.

Leigh's first efforts at conversation were met
with stiff, tight-lipped replies which made him
suspect Miss Merrifield *had* spoken against him,
but even his neighbor Moss could get little from
Sloath.

"Will it continue fair, do ye think, Sloath?"
Moss asked.

"No."

"Fine blunder the Corn Act looks, now Bonaparte's escape has sent prices up again," continued Moss.

"They'll go down soon enough." With that Mr.
Sloath addressed himself to the beef and pota-
toes.

The meal reminded Leigh of dining with his
fellow officers at one of their billets in Spain,
except for the lack of banter.

When the platters were empty, the waiter
cleared and Vernon rose, tapping his glass to call
the men to order. The dull murmur of conversation faded. There was a brief scraping of chairs
and lighting of clay pipes while Vernon arranged
three piles of papers in front of him.

"Now, friends," said Vernon, "there are two items for our consideration this afternoon." He steepled his hands together under his chin. "At our last meeting a motion was carried to provide for the repair of the church roof." He paused. "Let me say that the maintenance of the church itself, as it is the Lord's house, must be a serious obligation upon us." His glance moved solemnly from face to face, skipped over Leigh, and came to rest on the papers. He held one up for their inspection.

"Here, Squire Haythorne sets us a fine example. You will find his name at the top of this list. The squire expects, and I expect, that each man will know his duty and pledge generously." Vernon handed the paper to the churchwarden on his left and pushed an ink pot and pen his way.

The warden had the look of a man about to plunge himself in a cold bath. He picked up the pen with obvious reluctance and then with sudden resolution signed the paper and passed it to his neighbor.

"Well done, Taylor," said Mr. Vernon. "Now then, our next order of business is the squire's proposal to reduce the burden of the poor rate on all. Here are the figures to show how it may be done." Vernon began to distribute more sheets of paper, one to each member of the group.

Leigh watched the pledge list go from man to man. Each had the same hesitation Taylor showed, but each one signed.

"Now then," Vernon said, "you have before

you an account of the squire's calculations, showing how with a modest investment in wool we can turn the Long Meadow Poorhouse into a manufacturing establishment, the profits of which will reduce the cost of maintaining the indigent."

All heads at the table were bent over the papers Vernon had distributed, except Sloath's. The big man had the roof-repair pledge list in front of him, his reluctance to sign clearly great. His large hand held the pen in a crushing grip, his brow contracted in deep furrows. At last he made a hasty scrawl and shoved the paper, pen, and ink toward Moss.

"May I?" Leigh asked, taking up the paper.

Moss nodded.

At the top of the page were several close lines of writing and then, next to a substantial sum written large, the squire's signature. Below were the names of Sloath and the others with a figure beside each name. Leigh read the writing at the top, no longer wondering at the men's hesitation, but at why they had signed at all.

At the head of the table Vernon continued to expound the merits of the squire's latest scheme. "As you see from the account before you, the squire has shown how with a small investment in wool we can teach the boys to twist yarn and the girls and women to knit stockings. This scheme, besides giving habits of industry to the poor, will, in time, realize profits that will reduce the cost of the workhouse. Friends, it needs only your approval to set the plan in motion."

"I beg your pardon, Vernon," said Leigh, rising and holding up the roof pledge. "Isn't there a mistake here?"

Vernon's mouth fell open. "What?"

"The squire has not made a pledge."

"Mr. Nash, what are you suggesting?" Vernon adjusted his collar. "May I remind you that, as you are still a stranger among us, you are unfamiliar with our ways."

"Enlighten me, Vernon. The squire is offering a repayable loan. These gentlemen are pledging gifts." Josiah Sloath grunted, a sound Leigh chose to take as support for his objection.

Vernon frowned. "The vestry is familiar, as you are not, with the squire's regular and generous support of the church. If they have no objections, neither can you."

"But I do."

"Mr. Nash, really." Vernon slapped the paper in his hands against the table. His frame shook. "In this instance the amount required is so substantial and the need so pressing that the squire thought it best to make nearly the whole sum available at once through the means of a loan."

"How is the squire's loan to be repaid?"

"Well, of course, in time . . ." Vernon clasped his hands together.

"You'll forgive me for asking, Vernon. The responsibility of repaying this loan may fall on me as the next curate of the parish."

Vernon's face flushed a dull red color. "Then let us hope, Mr. Nash, that you will come to appreciate the strict economies necessary in a parish such as Rowdene and not waste our substance on vain displays of candles."

Leigh looked around. No one met his gaze. He had made Vernon squirm, but he hadn't won the others to any spirit of resistance. He handed the roof pledge to William Moss and resumed his seat.

"May we carry on, then, friends?" Vernon asked.

The men bowed their heads over the squire's figures. William Moss signed the pledge and passed it to his neighbor.

An hour later, when a motion passed in favor of the squire's workhouse scheme, Leigh left the meeting. To hear Vernon, the expense of the workhouse would ruin them all. The growing numbers of indigent and their demands upon their prosperous neighbors called for strict economies. Those who needed assistance must apply to Mr. Parmenter, the manager of the parish workhouse, and they must be willing to work. There was no serious opposition to the squire's plan. Only Sloath abstained from voting in favor of the measure. Leigh resolved to visit the workhouse as soon as he could.

Chapter 6

Long Meadow, the parish workhouse, was a large cottage with a thatched roof and eight narrow, barred windows, like dark eyes in a white plaster face. Two people stood at the door as Leigh approached.

A man in a fitted yellow vest and a polka-dot neckerchief blocked the opening. He leaned insolently against the jamb, staring out on the world with hard, round, unfeeling eyes.

Facing him was a slim, militantly straight-backed young woman, red curls peeping from under the edge of a plain brown bonnet. Leigh recognized Rosalind Merrifield at once and slowed his steps.

"Mr. Parmenter," Miss Merrifield was saying. "I insist you release Mary Fletcher and her child. I guarantee they will be no further burden on the parish."

"Cannot, miss," Parmenter said. "Mary Fletcher's been here three weeks and must work off her room and board."

"I saw her, Mr. Parmenter. You have not fed her enough to require repayment."

"She's had bread, same as everybody." The man's voice became surly. "Mistress Mary waited long enough to come in."

"And why not? She had a cottage and a garden and healthful exercise and air and light and freedom."

The gravel crunched under Leigh's boots, and both parties looked his way. Parmenter straightened and assumed a less insolent expression. Rosalind Merrifield merely gave Leigh a quick, indifferent glance and returned to her adversary.

"Now, miss," Parmenter said, raising his hands palms out as if to absolve himself of all blame. "I run a good house here. No bawdy house like some I know of."

"How can you say so, Mr. Parmenter, when a woman would sooner starve than come here?"

Parmenter shrugged. "If they be idle, miss, they end here. A man must work for his bread. Woman, too."

"Mary Fletcher has toiled all her life."

Leigh stepped up behind Miss Merrifield. Her contempt was obviously having no effect on Parmenter, but the passionate intensity of the sweet, low voice drew Leigh.

"I beg yer pardon, miss, but where's her man?" Parmenter sneered. "Her with a babe and no husband. Long Meadow is too good for her." A cunning look came into Parmenter's eyes. "But you can get her out, miss."

"How?"

"Just pay what she owes."

It was a deliberate tease, only Rosalind Merrifield did not see it. Leigh opened his mouth to warn her too late.

"How much?" She reached for the small bag on her arm.

"Fifty pounds," said Parmenter.

"Monstrous!" she exclaimed, dropping the little bag. She spun away from the door, and three quick angry strides brought her face-to-face with Leigh. He caught her arm as she reached him.

"Do you have fifty pounds?" she asked. Tears of fury and frustration sparkled in her dark eyes.

"No."

She tried to wrench her arm from his grip.

"But I can get us inside where you may help your friend," he said. She drew a steadying breath and dashed away the tears with a fist. "Take my arm," he said quietly. "Did Fowler visit here?"

She nodded, her eyes questioning, but she took his arm.

Parmenter watched warily from the door as they came back to the house.

"Morning, Parmenter. I'm Nash. I'll be taking Mr. Fowler's place at the church." Leigh could see that Fowler's name had an effect. "I've come to visit your workers."

"Today?" Parmenter glanced over his shoulder as if to assure himself that the house was fit to be seen.

"Now." Leigh lifted a brow and waited, letting no impatience show.

"Her too?" Parmenter looked as if he might object, then stepped back. "Suit yerself."

The interior of the house was a disagreeable spectacle. Wretches, hardly distinguishable as men or women by their rags, huddled in filth, breathing stale air and shaking with steady coughs. The misery was acute, but the hand on Leigh's arm did not falter. When they found Mary Fletcher, he left Rosalind to assist her friend and went back to Parmenter.

Parmenter was lounging in the doorway again, and Leigh understood the reason for it. There was not a breath of fresh air to be had in the house.

"Do you never open the windows, Parmenter?"

"They'd freeze, sir."

"Parmenter, release them from work for an hour. Put a broom or a scrubbing cloth in everyone's hand. Let them draw some fresh water and clean themselves and this place."

"Place is clean enough."

Leigh thought of his sword stored in London. A soldier could run Parmenter through or shake him by his jaunty neck cloth. What could a clergyman do?

He ran his forefinger down one of the windows and pressed a grimy print into Parmenter's yellow vest where his heart should have been. "Parmenter, a man doesn't let his barn get this dirty."

When Rosalind and Winterburn left the workhouse, she could take some comfort in the improvement of Mary Fletcher's circumstances. The babe was clean and fed, and Mary's sleeping corner was as comfortable as they could make it.

Parmenter still leaned in the doorway, but the sound of voices within came from the open windows.

Rosalind had had no idea the place was so bad. She would have to find fifty pounds for Mary, and she would have to speak to the squire about Parmenter. The question of where to get the fifty pounds consumed her. Which of her accounts could spare anything? Economies alone could not produce such a sum at once.

Then she looked up. They were passing between low hills at the west end of the village, and she had the impression Winterburn had spoken.

"Still furious?" he asked.

"I beg your pardon?"

"You set a pace a brigade sergeant would be proud of."

She slowed her steps. "I'm sorry. It's been a long time since I walked with . . . someone else."

"I think I can match your stride, Miss Merrifield."

She looked at him then. One of his dark brows lifted a fraction. His gray eyes were teasing, and the look in them unsettled her. She averted her gaze and recalled Mary Fletcher.

"That a man like Parmenter can deprive a woman of her freedom because she is hungry . . . and keep her a virtual prisoner for want of fifty pounds . . ."

"Who is she? One of your tenants?" Winterburn asked.

"No. That is, she was. Her husband had a

chance for a larger place with the squire, and he took it about a year ago."

"How did Mrs. Fletcher come to Long Meadow then?"

Rosalind thought about it. Bad harvests, weariness, and frustration had driven Dick Fletcher off, but not Mary. "Hope," she said. "Mary's husband, Dick, ran off months ago, and she kept hoping he'd return. It's the sort of hope that blinds one, I think. That's why she stayed so long and didn't ask for help."

"I'll have to visit regularly," Winterburn said.

Rosalind glanced at him. She didn't know what to make of such an unexpected statement. He'd felt no compassion for Jane Fowler, yet he was moved by Mary Fletcher, with whom he would never even have occasion to speak. "That would be good of you," she said quietly.

"If I'm still parson, that is," he added.

She said nothing.

"You didn't tell the vestry about me."

"I did. I went directly to Mr. Taylor."

"But you did not betray me as Winterburn."

She stopped at a narrow lane and faced him. "You brought yourself enough trouble over the candles." She made herself meet that mocking gaze. "The church was lovely."

He looked away, and the breeze ruffled his hair. "I thought you were on the side of that candle-snuffing windbag."

Rosalind laughed, and he looked back. His gaze made her breath catch. "I'm on the side of Rowdene," she said firmly. "There are people here who have only rushlights and hoard them at that. You . . . scared them with your extravagance."

"I paid."

She smiled. "That was most frightening of all. A man so . . . free with money."

"You prefer Vernon? If the man's ever had a generous impulse in his life, he quickly got the better of it."

Rosalind studied him. He was unconsciously elegant from his polished boots to his exquisite gray coat, fitted perfectly to his form. He wore his pride with equal indifference. She remembered his humiliation in the church and sensed how rare it was for him to give in. "I did not think the candles a generous impulse precisely."

"That's plain speaking, Miss Merrifield." A glint of self-mockery sharpened his gaze.

Rosalind looked up the lane. "This is my turning. I've a tenant up this way I must see," she said. "Thank you for what you did just now."

He bowed.

She turned away and strode purposefully up the lane. Then she remembered the gloves. She stopped and swung back.

He hadn't moved. For an instant she forgot what she meant to ask. "Lord Winterburn, did your man happen to find a pair of gloves the other day?"

Winterburn smiled a slow smile she had not seen before. "He did."

"Oh." She swallowed. "Well. I believe they may be mine and . . ."

Winterburn's grin widened. "I hope so, Miss Merrifield. I keep them by my bed."

"What?"

"Are you going to Lady Ellenby's dinner this evening?"

"Yes."

"Should I bring them to you there?"

"No." She felt her cheeks burn.

"Some other time then. Good day, Miss Merrifield." He bowed and turned away.

Rosalind walked on. He was an odious man. The impropriety of teasing her about her gloves! He was certainly unfit to be a parson. Too young, too light-minded. He cared more for making her blush than for relieving the distress of the poor condemned to Long Meadow. Surely the vestry would see how unsuited he was for the ministry and protest to the bishop. Her skirts swished with the rhythm of her stride.

A startled thrush rose from the hedge, and a different thought intruded. He *had* come to Long Meadow. She hadn't even asked him what he was doing there. Certain details of the encounter came back to her. He had felt as she had about the condition of the inmates. He had quickly taken Parmenter's measure and made him clean the place. And Winterburn had promised to return. Her steps slowed. His character was a puzzle. She couldn't quite make it out. Pride, certainly, was the main element, and mockery, but quick perception, too, and something else she could not name.

A twist of the lane brought her to the old

soldier's cottage. Lord Winterburn would soon tire of the small concerns of Rowdene. The best thing to do, she decided, was to ignore him entirely.

Rosalind could see from the moment she entered Lady Ellenby's drawing room that her determination to ignore Winterburn would be tested.

Lady Ellenby's guests were all familiar and likely to offer equally familiar conversation. Squire Haythorne and his wife, their son, and his bride were there. And the Kedlestons and their son and Harvey Berrisford, who had just inherited a pretty property. And, of course, Mr. Vernon, who never missed a dinner at someone else's table. Rosalind greeted the others and made her way to Will Kedleston. A boyhood friend of Gerrie's, he had become a shy man, as devoted to his dogs and horses as Gerrie was to cards. He told her at once that his favorite retriever had pupped, and began to describe the litter.

As Rosalind listened to the merits of each of the new pups, she realized Winterburn meant to deceive them all. He sat with Catherine Ellenby, who seemed delighted to entertain her mother's handsome guest. Catherine repeated "La, Mr. Nash, how droll!" with irritating frequency in spite of stern glances from her mother and regretful ones from Julia, the elder Ellenby girl, who was dutifully cultivating the eligible Mr. Berrisford. Rowdene seemed to rate Winterburn as he presented himself, a curate with a minor living and modest prospects.

She did not see how her neighbors could be so taken in. Everything about him—his coat, his air, his proud glance which noted the pretensions and dullness of the gathering—proclaimed him above them. Rosalind was relieved to go into dinner.

A bit of confusion as they took their places at the table put Leigh between Mrs. Jane Haythorne and Miss Julia Ellenby. He had a fricassee of white mushrooms in front of him and a clear view of Rosalind Merrifield at the opposite end of the table next to Kedleston. The closed expression in her eyes told him she was deliberately ignoring him. He should not notice or care, but the play of emotion in her eyes was far more interesting than the company. On a whim he'd teased her about her gloves, but it had been worth it to see the puzzled half-recognition of their attraction in those dark, ardently alive eyes.

He had been unprepared for her in evening dress. An otherwise unremarkable white muslin gown with raised blue sprigs clung when she moved. The slanting cut of the soft bodice revealed the pale swell of her breasts, high, small breasts that would fit the palm of his hand neatly. In London he would have maneuvered to be in Kedleston's place.

Instead he had allowed the Ellenby sisters' rather transparent tactics to govern the seating. He now had the elder girl as a dinner partner while the younger worked on Berrisford. Both girls had ignored Kedleston, but the man's wit apparently fascinated Miss Merrifield. There seemed a perfect ease between them, no reserve.

Kedleston made her laugh. At what? Leigh wondered.

When the second course appeared, she turned
from Kedleston to the squire, engaging him in
low, earnest conversation. As she spoke, the
squire's expression hardened.

"What's this?" he said, putting his fork down.
"You're not asking me to discharge Parmenter,
are you, Miss Merrifield?" His voice silenced the
others.

Vernon choked and dabbed his mouth with his
napkin.

At the head of the table, Lady Ellenby looked
up brightly. "More veal, Squire?"

The squire shook his head. "Be mindful what
you're about, Miss Merrifield." He pointed a
finger at her. "We don't want the whole village
expecting charity. The poor rate is ruinous
enough to drain us all."

Rosalind Merrifield didn't blink. "The poor at
Long Meadow deserve decent fare." She picked
up a platter of stewed sole and passed it to Will
Kedleston. Will, looking most alarmed, passed the
platter on.

All eating had stopped, and Lady Ellenby cast a
dismayed glance at the dish of sole making its way
up the table. "Well," she said. "We all do what we
can. I'm sure I can't do more at the moment, what
with the girls needing so much now that they're
out." She nodded to her daughter. "Julia, pass the
squire some custard, dear."

Then Catherine Ellenby spoke up. "I think the

poor should not be idle. They should endeavor to deserve our charity."

"How very just, Miss Ellenby," said Vernon. He beamed at her and turned to Lady Ellenby. "Your Ladyship will be pleased to hear Squire Haythorne's plans for Long Meadow Poorhouse have been adopted by the vestry. Long Meadow will soon show a profit."

"It may," said Leigh, "if the residents are offered light and air."

He stunned them. Forks stopped moving again, and Rosalind Merrifield met his gaze with a frankly curious one of her own.

"What do you know of our poorhouse, Nash?" the squire demanded.

"Only what I saw this morning."

"And what did you see?"

"Miss Merrifield is right. Parmenter's an idle fellow with little understanding of his business," Leigh said quietly. He took up his wine.

The squire's face reddened. "What Parmenter understands, sir, is thrift. He teaches habits of industry."

"Such as lounging in doorways. I think you may mistake the man's talents, Squire Haythorne."

He had clearly appalled everyone but Miss Merrifield. Lady Ellenby quickly suggested that the ladies retire and leave the gentlemen to their discussion. Leigh had only one last puzzled glance from Miss Merrifield over her shoulder as she left the room. He raised his glass to her, and she looked away.

Rosalind wondered why he'd done it. It could not help his position in the village. Nothing was said about her own challenge to the squire's views. All the talk was of Mr. Nash. Mrs. Kedleston thought it odd that a young man of such modest means in so dependent a position would confront the squire so consciously. What did he mean by it? Lady Ellenby pronounced it folly. Lady Haythorne declared it an unpardonable affront to her husband. Did Rowdene want such a man in the church? Vernon was better; Vernon understood them and their ways. Still, Rosalind could see that Catherine and Julia were thrilled by Winterburn's daring. Men like Vernon and Berrisford and Will Kedleston never ventured to oppose the squire on even a minor point.

When the gentlemen joined them, it was plain the squire remained displeased. He stalked about the room and grumbled whenever his wife asked him to sit. Lady Ellenby set about at once, smoothing the unhappy rift in her party. First Catherine and then Julia and even Rosalind were called up to play the pianoforte. The coffee tray appeared early.

"Rosalind, dear," Lady Ellenby whispered, "take Mr. Nash some coffee." Rosalind smiled. It was a hint to keep him from embarrassing his hostess further.

Not that the strained atmosphere disturbed Winterburn. He sat a little apart, impervious, self-sufficient.

He rose, all politeness, as she approached, but

the mocking lights danced in his eyes. "Ignored me long enough?"

"I can't make out your character," she said, offering him the coffee. "Is it serious or light?"

He shrugged, taking the cup and pulling a chair near for her.

She hesitated a long moment. To walk away would satisfy her conscience but not her curiosity.

He leaned toward her. "Kedleston's conversation or mine?"

He was wicked to tempt her, but she took the seat he offered, and he sat beside her.

"Did you come to Rowdene to make a joke of your neighbors, Lord Winterburn?"

One dark eyebrow lifted. "Did I make a joke of Mary Fletcher's situation this morning?"

Rosalind could not deny the part he'd played there. "Why were you at the poorhouse?"

He looked away. "Why did you bring up Parmenter at dinner?" he asked. "You must know the squire's views on charity."

She sighed. "I confess I was impatient, but it was only that the table was so . . . full."

"And the impression of Mary Fletcher's circumstances so fresh in your mind."

She nodded. "But your speaking up . . ."

"Drew their fire?" He was watching her intently now.

She wouldn't have put it that way, but she knew what he meant. It was an intimate sensation, having a conversation with someone who could anticipate her thoughts. They sat a decorous distance apart in a drawing room full of people, but he made her feel there was some secret link between them, below the surface, like the roots of trees tangled deep in the earth.

Her mind told her his gray gaze should be cool like stone or mist, but his look made her think he wanted to kiss her. The moment of recognition made her body tight and weak.

She tore her gaze from his. "I must go. The Kedlestons are to take me home."

"Goodnight then." He stood and offered his hand to help her up, a quick clasp and release, at once too much and too little.

She'd just turned her back when his voice stopped her.

"Miss Merrifield," he said. She looked over her shoulder, intent on fleeing his presence. "You should have ignored me all night."

Chapter 7

It rained late on the night of Lady Ellenby's dinner. The storm loosened the earth around rocks of every size. A great boulder tumbled down a hillside and blocked the road to the village for two days. In the fields fat stones lay like a crop ready for harvest. Uprooted, the green shoots withered.

Rosalind had been to Adstrop twice to see her bankers for tenants who needed loans. They must resow their fields, and there must be money to buy seed. Standing surety for her tenants, she could not borrow more for herself. She could not free Mary Fletcher. For her own new seed, she must sell more books. It was a small measure, the sale of a few books, but she reminded herself that small measures repeatedly taken would see her through.

Behind the parsonage she gathered stones that had been washed down into Jane's rose garden. She tidied the paths and restored the wells of earth around the base of each plant. Without a ladder she could not attach fallen canes to the

97

cross pieces of the trellis, but she did not want to knock at the parsonage door and risk seeing Winterburn again so soon.

She had seen him three times at a safe distance, on the road, at a cottage door, and lifting a bundle of thatch to a pair of men on a cottage roof. In such moments he looked as if he belonged to the village landscape, but he was not the curate he pretended to be. His very name, Winterburn, said what he was, cold like frozen ground and hot like a Guy Fawkes bonfire. She had put off tending Jane's roses until she was sure she had subdued her disordered feelings about him.

A crunch of gravel on the walk caused her to start, but it was only Winterburn's man approaching. She stooped to gather another stone, covering the flush in her cheeks at what her thoughts had been.

"Here now, miss, you ought not t' be doin' that."

She stood. "Mr. Dowdeswell, isn't it? Good morning." She cradled a load of stones in her apron. Dowdeswell frowned, his white brows drawn together. He was like a gaunt old watch-dog, his deeply creased face fringed with shaggy russet hair except for brows and whiskers that had gone white. An old dog who would grumble when disturbed but quickly settle down again on the rug. "It's just a bit of gardening," she told him.

"If it's got t' be done, it ought t' be done by Miss Rees from the village. She comes every day and does nought."

"It's no trouble to me, and I promised Mrs. Fowler. I'm not disturbing Lord Winterburn, am I?"

Dowdeswell's frown deepened. "It's Mr. Nash, miss, and he's gone out."

"Then I'll continue." She smiled and headed for the end of the path with her load of stones. Dowdeswell followed.

"Really, miss. It's not right for ye t' do such work."

She dumped the stones in the pile she'd been making. "Would you like to help, Mr. Dowdeswell? Mrs. Fowler kept a ladder in the shed. If you'd unlock it, I want to secure these stalks to the trellises."

Dowdeswell glanced at her and at the crossed poles that made the long covered arbor. He seemed undecided, and she stooped down and picked up a stone she'd overlooked.

"Done, miss."

Dowdeswell proved to be unyielding on the point of her ascending the ladder, but he was patient with the process of untangling the thorny stalks and binding them gently back into place. Gradually the covered walk returned to a condition of which Jane would approve. They had one more corner to repair.

"Thank you, Mr. Dowdeswell. Without your ladder I could not have achieved so much."

" 'Twas nothing, miss."

"I've kept you though for quite some time. Won't Lord . . . Mr. Nash want you?"

Dowdeswell snorted. "Not him, miss. He just works and walks. He has little need of me except to black his boots."

Indignation rose in her, and she pressed her lips together to keep from saying exactly what she thought of Winterburn's callous treatment of his servant. It was good to remember how cold and proud he was and forget the hungry look in his eyes.

Dowdeswell came down the ladder. "Beg your pardon, miss. Ought not to have said so. His Grace, the bishop, sent me here. Ought not to complain." He pulled the ladder away from the top of the arbor and began to lower it.

They turned toward the house, and there was Winterburn. How long he had been standing there, Rosalind could not guess. His eyes were dark as slate, and she felt his look like a hand plucking a taut cord deep inside her and making it hum.

He wore another of his fine blue coats. Her gown, an old fawn-colored, checked muslin covered by a brown apron, and her straw bonnet, with a puppy's nibble out of the brim and a worn ribbon under her chin, now seemed shabby, an obvious sign of her penny-pinching.

His gaze dipped to the V of white lawn at her throat and rose again to meet hers. "Kedleston saw you safely home?"

"Yes, thank you."

He turned to Dowdeswell. "I'm going out."

"Again, sir?"

One of Winterburn's black brows rose a fraction. "I'd like a word with you when I return." He bowed to Rosalind and strolled away.

Leigh's first thought was that it was well she concealed her hair under that old bonnet. Impossible to sit at his accounts while her voice drifted up from the garden. The road was his best escape from unclerical thoughts. Though he'd been out once, he went again.

He had been to nearly every cottager in the village since the storm. Most had made repairs to their homes and fields. Only old Croy with no son or grandson still needed help. Peter Pryke had agreed to repair the roof, and Leigh walked to the soldier's cottage to see how the work was progressing. There he found Croy sitting on a stump, his face turned to the sun, and Braithe, stripped to his waist, his wiry frame reddening and taut, lifting bundles of thatch to Pryke on the roof.

"Seeing to your flock, Mr. Nash?" Braithe greeted him.

"Can't sit in a puddle when I visit Croy." Leigh pulled off his coat and passed another bundle of thatch to Braithe halfway up a sturdy ladder. "Lose anything in the storm yourself, Braithe?"

"Sleep is all." Braithe hoisted one of the thick bundles of thatch to his shoulder and passed it up the ladder. Like Pryke, he had leather pads strapped round his knees. "Bad thing, this storm. Bad time for the farmers."

"Expecting miracles, Braithe?"

Braithe gave him a canny look. "Just necessities."

"Such as?"

"New seed. Most have got t' sow again."

"Did one of your sainted parsons produce seed?"

"Shillings would do."

Shillings were what Leigh didn't have. The candles had been an extravagance. "Can't a farmer borrow to buy seed?"

"Most did already. No coin 'til harvest."

Braithe was testing him. Leigh looked around the little yard in front of Croy's cottage. The vegetable garden had been washed away in the storm. Mud and stones remained. He'd always thought English villages quaint, seen from horseback or from an inn yard. He'd thought them free of the mud and squalor of villages in the dry hills of Spain and Portugal, whose people had won his admiration for their hardy endurance. Now he was coming to see a side of his own countrymen he hadn't known before.

"There must be a way to raise a bit of the ready? Something to sell? What would you sell, Braithe?"

"Wool, if the price weren't down. Mutton, if any were buying. I don't have ought else."

Croy's granddaughter came out of the cottage and set a loaf of brown bread and a wedge of cheese by her grandfather's side. Croy put out a gnarled hand to the cheese, breaking off a morsel. Its sharp smell reached Leigh.

"How many farmers have sheep?" he asked Braithe.

"Most."

"Do they milk their ewes, Braithe?" Leigh

watched Pryke tap the ends of the thatch bundles into line.

"What for?"

"To make cheese."

Braithe, swinging a last bundle of thatch to his shoulder, stopped, lost the rhythm of the work, and let the thatch drop to the ground. "Cheese of sheep's milk?"

"It's done in the East, in Tuscany, too."

"Had such cheese, have ye?"

Leigh nodded.

Braithe shook his head and tried again with the thatch bundle. "It's a thinnish sort of milk."

"Still, it makes a good cheese," Leigh suggested, pulling his coat back on.

Braithe passed the last bundle to Pryke and dusted off his hands. "I don't think ye properly understand the sort of beast a sheep is, Mr. Nash."

"I admit I'm better acquainted with wool."

"Fine wool at that, Mr. Nash," said Braithe with a glance at Leigh's coat. "A sheep is a dumb beast. It lives t' nibble and make dung." He came down the ladder and stopped before Leigh, setting his hands on his lean hips. "Wool and meat are what men see in sheep, but the sheep doesn't help men t' make 'em. It's too contrary. Runs off when it ought t' lie down. Falls and forgets it has feet when it ought t' run." Braithe pulled the leathers off his knees. "A cow has more sense. A cow comes t' milking time every day."

"The sheep doesn't need sense if the shepherd has it."

Braithe straightened, his expression a curious mixture of interest and resistance. He was fighting the idea precisely because it intrigued him.

"Braithe, if I milk one of your beasts, will you?"

In the end Braithe agreed to milk a sheep, a concession that put Leigh in a good enough humor to face the accounts he'd abandoned earlier. He was impatient with the management of pennies, but he understood the cost of the candles better now. The distress in Rowdene was general, and he had no power to relieve it, at least until Ralston found a buyer for Winterburn Hall.

At four Dowdeswell knocked on the drawing-room door and announced, "Mrs. Cole to see you, Mr. Nash." Dowdeswell gave him a pointed look.

Vernon was still in the study, and Mrs. Cole had asked for Leigh. Except for Polly, who called daily with transparent intention, none of the villagers had come looking for Leigh. Now a comely widow was asking to see him.

Leigh closed his account book. "Send her in, Dowdeswell." He stood. "And don't worry. I'm sure Mrs. Cole has no designs on my virtue."

Dowdeswell frowned at the levity and turned stiffly. Leigh cleared the books from two chairs, and Dowdeswell was back with Mrs. Cole, a dark-eyed beauty. Leigh guessed she was near thirty. She had inherited her dead husband's dairy and made it thrive. There was a weary, determined air about her which hardly lessened her beauty. She always arrived late and out of breath for church on Sundays, taking a back pew with her three children.

Dowdeswell hovered in the doorway. "Shut the door, Dowdeswell," **Leigh** ordered.

She accepted the **seat** Leigh offered, but kept her gaze lowered, her hands tightly clasped. He sat just to one side of her and waited. She glanced up several times without speaking, her lips pressed tightly together. Her distress was real, and he felt a fraud in the face of it. He pulled his chair closer.

"Mrs. Cole, how may I help you?"

"I've spoken to no one, ye see, and I wouldn't trouble ye, Mr. Nash, but . . ."

He waited, not entirely sure he was prepared for what revelations would follow.

"It's Shepherd Braithe. He must stop it."

"Stop what, ma'am?"

"Thievin'." She looked up then, her great black eyes hurt, her cheeks drained of their vivid color.

Braithe. The shepherd's astonished grin when Leigh proposed milking a ewe was fresh in his mind. Braithe, stealing from this woman. It made no sense. Braithe was kind, and with his energy and enterprise was as likely to thrive as any man in Rowdene.

Leigh's visitor must have read the disbelief in his expression. "Oh, he can't know how it distracts and bothers me. He plays tricks, you see. Only I do not think he knows . . ." Mrs. Cole fumbled with the tangled strings of her reticule in a vain attempt to extract a handkerchief. Leigh offered her his own. She pressed the linen to her eyes and drew a shaky breath.

Leigh struggled to make sense of her accusation. "Mrs. Cole, have you caught him stealing from you?"

"No," she admitted, but the admission didn't shake her certainty. "It's always when he comes that the butter's missing or a pint of cream."

"Has it hurt your business?"

She blushed, making her rosy cheeks quite crimson. "It's not the pound of butter gone that hurts. It's that I go so distracted, I make mistakes. Butter turns so easy. Ye've got to be that careful wi' it."

"Yet you've not gone to the magistrate, nor Mr. Vernon."

She jumped up at the suggestion. "Oh, no. I would not."

It occurred to Leigh that more than turned butter was bothering the woman. He got her to sit again.

"I mean Mr. Braithe no harm, but he must stop. I've seen ye talk wi' 'im, Mr. Nash. Will ye talk wi' 'im about the butter? Will ye make 'im stop?"

"Mrs. Cole, I'm sorry for your distress." He was feeling his way, unwilling to commit himself to a course that would offend Braithe.

"Will ye make 'im stop, Mr. Nash?"

In the end he promised to do everything he could to stop the butter thief's stealing, but he was damned if he knew how to accuse Braithe of the crime. Damned if he knew how to lead even one of his flock on the path of righteousness, if the fellow had strayed.

After his visitor left, he walked down to the dark church and took a turn around the quiet nave. Miss Merrifield said he wasn't suited to the position. A clergyman must be a tireless worker, a director of souls, a man of true devotion. She angered him with her impossible ideals. She thought he wasn't suited to the position. And she was right. He was carnal and worldly. The most use he'd been to anyone but himself had been as a soldier. He was no match for a clergyman like Theophilus Fowler or one of Braithe's parsons or Miss Merrifield's impossible ideals.

Ideals. His mother had taught him about ideals. At fifteen he'd gone to protest Fanny's dismissal.

He had been home from school one Christmas when he discovered Fanny. She was little older than he and seemed possessed of some joyful secret that made her hum and smile and do the most dull chores cheerfully.

Then one day he had come across her, sobbing, collapsed in a heap on the hall floor, broken china and tea slops around her. It had seemed the most natural thing in the world to put his arms around her. She had turned and buried her head against his shoulder while he stroked her trembling back. The sensation of offering protection and comfort had made him ridiculously happy.

He spent the next days watching for Fanny, offering secret help with her work, coaxing her vanished smiles with sweetmeats and flowers, anything that would get her to look joyful again if only for a moment. One afternoon he'd found her on her knees in his room, scrubbing the hearth. He'd lifted her to her feet and kissed her, and because she'd let him, he'd gone on kissing her until his body ached with longing. The desire distracted him for days, overcame him at the slightest glimpse of her.

Then, for no reason he could fathom, his mother sent him with Fanny to deliver a basket to an aging cousin in Richmond. The closed carriage had offered privacy and acquiescence for a long, heated exploration of each other.

He had never meant to take her virginity. He understood what it meant to a girl in her position to lose that prize. So many times he had stopped short of the step that would mean her ruin until one afternoon when she seemed sadder than ever. Braced on his elbows, he lay kissing and touching her, intending only to make her smile, but she'd kissed him back with such longing that he was soon rocking frantically against her. In the disarray of skirts and limbs, his body joined hers with a sudden plunge.

He bit his lip and raised himself on shaking arms, trying to summon the will to withdraw from her sweet depths, but with a tiny forlorn smile she pulled him close. She was dismissed the next day.

He had known better than to mention love to his mother, but he'd been foolish enough to speak of principles and honor.

"You don't still have ideals, do you, dear?" she

asked. And she'd done her best to see that he was rid of them. "Fanny has served her purpose," she declared.

He had stared at her, uncomprehending.

"She has contributed to your education and is no longer needed."

"Not needed? But she needs a position."

"She's with child."

He had swallowed at the momentousness of it. "I'll marry her."

His mother cast him a sharp, mocking glance. "Don't be absurd. The child is not yours." She bowed her head to the letters on her desk. "Why do you think I chose her to instruct you? Fanny and her beau have been well compensated."

It occurred to him now that, in the absence of ideals, Richard had found duty and Marcus, whatever madness had gone into his building and collecting. Leigh could perhaps find work. Work, motion, action, like a wheel turning. The thought arrested him, and he thrust it aside.

He would concentrate on helping Mrs. Cole if he could figure out how to do it. Her distress seemed out of proportion to the complaint, and yet he did not doubt that she suffered. Perhaps only a woman could understand, and he saw a flaw in the church that so readily put its ministry entirely in the hands of men.

He needed a woman's advice, and his mind, willing to be corrupted, turned instantly to Miss Merrifield. She knew both Braithe and Mrs. Cole and might know how he could approach the difficulty between them. He looked around the darkened church. Even his best intentions led his thoughts back to the temptation he had fled earlier in the day.

He wanted to see Miss Merrifield. It occurred to him that there must have been a terrible tension in the Garden of Eden before the Fall, an unbearable suspense in daily life. To walk by that fair fruit day after day and not reach out and pluck it.

Rosalind knelt in the library. A fire burned in the grate, and cloud shadows passed across the windows overhead. There was room for perhaps two or three more books in the packing case in front of her. She found it more difficult to fill the box this time. For her first sale she had parted with her father's Latin and Greek books. Though they were among the most valuable in his collection, she admitted to herself that she was no scholar and would never enjoy them except as reminders of his breadth of mind. To choose among the volumes left to her seemed impossible.

The first sale had alerted prospective buyers who knew her father's name and reputation. She had culled the books they requested. Did she have a copy of Whitlock's *History of King Alfred the Great?* Oh, yes, she did. She took up the small, red leather volume from a stack of books on the floor and let it fall open in her palms. In the old typeface with its curling letters was the story of King Alfred and the burned cakes. For a moment she heard her father's voice reading to her, teaching her not to disdain the smallest duty. Her mother, with a different manner of teaching, had taken her to the kitchen and given her cakes to watch. She had been tending them ever since.

"Selling your treasures, Miss Merrifield?" Winterburn's voice was lazy, cool.

He stood in the open doors of the library, watching her with knowing eyes. He wore one of the blue coats he favored, while she was clothed in dust and duty, an old cloth tied about her head. She tugged her plain skirts from under her and rose, clutching the little red book to her chest. "What are you doing here?"

"Returning your gloves." He stepped into the room and crossed to one long book-lined wall, moving slowly, examining the titles on the shelves. "Your father's collection?"

"And my mother's." She turned to watch his progress down the shelves. "He loved ruins. She loved gardens."

He stopped at the far end of the room, looking back at her over one shoulder. "You've found collectors who know the value of what you have?"

"Yes."

He started back toward her down the other side of the library, an arrogant, assured stroll. His presence did something to the atmosphere of the room, made the invisible particles of air, which ought to have separated them, a medium binding them together, every move he made sensible to her nerves. He stopped opposite her.

"I've come to ask your advice."

"Not humbly."

A silver flash of amusement lit his eyes. "Humility was not much valued at home."

"It's fairly common in Rowdene."

"I'll try to profit from example."

The exchange seemed to have lessened the distance between them. He was not touching her. There should be no sensation of touch, but her stomach fluttered, like a lily pad bobbing at some disturbance in the water around it. She thought it prudent to recall the reason for his visit. "My advice, you said?"

"On a parish matter."

"Shouldn't you consult Mr. Vernon?"

The set of his mouth revealed his contempt for that course of action. "The question is moral not monetary."

"The vestry?"

He shook his head. "The people involved are known to you." It was not a request any longer. He assumed her compliance.

With a gesture she invited him to sit where a pair of armchairs were drawn up on opposite sides of a library table. The table, a substantial breadth of carved oak, would be a physical barrier between them. Another of the books she had been unable to pack lay open there. *The English Moths and Butterflies*, one of a series in quarto, nearly fifty years old, annotated in her mother's hand. He turned the book to him and studied the open page with arrested attention. A pair of blood-red roses, petals fully opened, stems entwined, filled the page. Her mother had noted the

small oak moth fluttering above them. For a
moment Winterburn seemed to have forgotten
her and even himself in his absorption in the
picture. Then he closed the book.

"Mrs. Cole accuses Braithe of stealing from
her."

"Oh." She could not repress a smile.

His look grew puzzled. "Braithe has no cause to
steal butter."

"No." She put the little red book on the table
and folded her hands over it, avoiding his gaze.

"I thought you could help me to prove him
innocent."

It was awkward to put what she knew into
words. "He's . . . teasing her."

"What?"

Her hands tightened on the little book, and she
took a deep breath. "He wants her to notice him."

"Notice him?"

She pressed her lips together. "He looks at her
in a way that . . . His eyes burn . . ."

As she faltered in the explanation, a change
came over him, and her body answered in kind,
with a shiver like the silent disturbance of a leaf in
a breath of air.

"Familiar with burning glances, are you?" He
knew, and she could not deny it. The oak table
separating them was not so wide after all.

"Familiar with kisses?" His voice was low,
rough. His eyes said he wanted to kiss her, but
something held him back. Something hung in the
balance with his question.

She shook her head.

He stood and moved away from the table, abruptly, aimlessly. Her heart raced, and she struggled to calm its mad tempo.

From across the room he asked, "Will Mrs. Cole have Braithe if he asks for her?"

"He won't ask without some hope. In the world's eyes a prosperous widow with her own dairy can look higher than a poor shepherd."

"Does the world's view matter so much in Rowdene?"

"You must see that it does."

"Perhaps Braithe did not consider the world's view when he cast his indiscreet gaze on Mrs. Cole."

She rose, gripping the table hard. "Don't mock him."

He came back to her then and with deliberate care put the hand with the gloves on the table beside hers. "I wouldn't dare."

She stood her ground. He was taking Braithe's courtship seriously, small as it was, a matter far beneath Winterburn's notice.

"Do you want him to win Mrs. Cole?" she asked.

"Yes." He lifted his hand from her gloves and placed it over hers. Heat and power burned her flesh.

She pulled back instinctively, but his hand held hers pinned to the table, while she fought to maintain her hold on sense and indifference. "Tell her she must catch Mr. Braithe in the act. She must invite him in some morning and sit him by the fire with a full tankard."

"And?"

"The butter will melt."

Rosalind, however, felt that she would be the one to melt. Her will dissolved in his gaze, her resistance escaped like a wisp of smoke, drawn up the chimney, blown apart in the breeze. She held her hand and her back steady and met his heated gaze. Her throat and lips were dry, and she swallowed to free the needed words. "He hides it in his hat, you know."

He laughed and lifted his hand from hers. "In his hat?"

"Yes, a boy's trick."

"Thank you, Miss Merrifield." He stepped back. "You've likely saved me from ruining my first chance to help a parishioner in distress."

Chapter 8

A week of bright sun ended. Heavy dark clouds sagged above the village, oppressing Leigh's spirits. He had not persuaded the squire to do anything about Parmenter. His theological books had no power to hold him, and the prospect of a morning within earshot of Vernon drove him from the parsonage. He took the south road out beyond the first hills toward the cottage where the blind old soldier lived with his granddaughter.

It would be one of his shorter rambles. He had walked every day since he'd come to Rowdene, getting to know the landscape on intimate terms and wearying his body beyond restlessness. He was rapidly ruining a fine pair of boots, but it was satisfying to see Dowdeswell labor to repair them each night. Duty was a language he and Dowdeswell could both speak, an uncomplicated tongue, with a reserve that suited them equally.

And he'd discovered a duty with which Vernon would not interfere: visiting the poor. As he tramped through mud to distant cottages, listened to impenetrable accents, and watched for signs of acceptance and trust in faces like stone, he was inclined to agree with Jeremy Braithe. Bread and kindness might do for miracles in Rowdene.

The blind old soldier, Sergeant Croy, was the first to invite Leigh into his home. Only a blind man would, Leigh supposed. In the village as in the church, his appearance drew stares and giggles. He'd seldom worn a top hat since Portugal; now he gave them up entirely, but he refused to give up his London coats.

The old man's granddaughter fluttered around the cottage, trying vainly to find Leigh a cup that wasn't chipped, until the soldier told her to give it up.

"Da, he be used t' the finest things," she protested, glancing at Leigh. "Ye've never seen the like of his coat."

"Gel, he be used t' cracked heads and mud. Go." Croy rapped his table. "Won't ye sit down, sir. We were t' talk of Badajoz today."

Badajoz, where Croy's youngest son had perished and where Leigh had learned the meaning of war. He pulled the rough stool he'd been offered closer to the old man, and began to recount his experiences there.

Leigh had joined the regiment with reinforcements from England after the Battle of Ciudad Rodrigo. Until Badajoz nothing opposed them. The regiment moved like a bright dragon, brilliant with fiery color and flashing scales, winding sinuously over the winter landscape, exhaling a flaming breath from which the enemy fled.

Then, under a clouded night sky, the Fourth and Light Divisions made their attack on the French-held fortress. Three times men swarmed down into a deep trench and attempted to scale a sword-studded slope under murderous French fire. Three times they were repulsed until the ditch was filled with the dead and dying, and the men were consumed with sullen rage.

Leigh studied Croy, letting the bloody images fade. With his spine curved, his head tilted, the old man seemed to become a thin ear, a fixed point of attention, drawing the story deep into himself. His gnarled hands rested on his knees. Ridged veins gathered the spare flesh into dark cords like the roots of an old tree. Leigh kept his gaze on those still hands as he finished his tale.

At Badajoz he had watched soldiers despair of all hope as they flung themselves against the French defenders, watched them show no mercy to a defeated foe when they finally entered the city. He had become a man of the sword.

For a time duty filled his days. The possibility of death absolved him of all responsibility to the future. He had made a perfect escape from his mother's plans.

Later, much later, he realized a man did not possess force; it possessed him. It intoxicated him or destroyed him. Only Wellington seemed to understand how to avoid the intoxications of force.

Richard had agreed. "Hookey? He calculates his forces as nicely as any London miss rates her wares. Never overextends himself."

They'd laughed then, but Richard had forgotten his own wisdom. In a skirmish in the Pyrenees, the fleeing French had been too much of a temptation. He'd led his men far beyond the main force of the regiment. Alone, in the vanguard, he'd been slaughtered. Leigh, trying to reach him, had been cut down.

"Best go now, Mr. Nash," Croy said when the story was done. "'Twill rain within the hour." He lifted a knobby knee. "Can feel it here."

"Your knee tells the weather?"

"It does. I work for Miss Merrifield, ye know. I be her weatherman."

Leigh looked at Croy's granddaughter, who nodded. "He does. Miss comes ever' week. Says da's her oracle."

The rain held off until Leigh was just a mile or so from the western end of the village. One minute the road through the hills stretched before him, the next a flash of lightning and a crack of thunder split the clouds and released a torrent that blotted out the landscape. He pushed forward blindly, his hair dripping. If he could make the inn, he could wait out the storm in comfort. Then he stumbled and realized he'd left the road. He would soon be soaked and lost. A shadowy shape loomed dark in the gray blur of the landscape, and he made toward it instinctively.

When he reached it, he found a yew and an oak grown so close together they appeared to form one massive trunk. The yew's dark-green branches made a thick canopy nearly touching the ground at the base of a slight slope. He ducked under them and found a place where he could stand upright, stripped off his cravat, and dried his streaming face and hair. He could see nothing beyond the screen of branches. The rain had imprisoned him as completely as walls of stone. He had to laugh. Vernon had the snug parsonage and he, the mud. With the toes of his boots he scraped together dry leaves and dead ferns around the base of the yew trunk.

He had just settled himself to wait for a break in the storm when a cloaked figure hurtled into the dry space under the yew. Miss Merrifield halted, exhaling bright puffs of breath. She lifted her head, threw back the hood of her cloak, and froze. "You."

Her expression wary, she retreated a step, fumbling with the hood of her cloak. He came to his feet and grabbed her wrist. "Don't be a fool. You'll drown out there."

"Surely not." She tried to shake free of his hold.

He yanked her up against him and said evenly, "You'll step in a ditch and break a bone. You can't see three feet in this."

"I know my way." Her gaze locked with his.

"You know your weather, I'm sure." He released her wrist. "This sort of rain carves crevices in roads and washes crops out of furrows."

"Very well, Lord Winterburn. It's Noah's flood."

"Welcome to the ark, Miss Merrifield." He offered her his cravat, and when she only looked at him, he said, "To dry your face and hair."

Her cheeks flushed crimson, and in answer a familiar flash of heat swept him. She pressed the fabric to her face.

He averted his gaze. "How long do you think the storm will last?"

"Not forty days and forty nights."

"You'll wait then?"

She returned the cravat without meeting his eyes or touching his hand. "It may let up in a while."

"Noah's neighbors said the same."

She turned from him and shook water and mud from the hem of her cloak and skirts.

He watched that feminine concern for skirts with a hungry fascination. They were plain wool skirts, brown and unadorned, and her attention to them was not vanity nor even concern for comfort but care of things entrusted to her. Her little task done, she looked around at the narrow space under the sloping branches. A stir of the air brought him the sweet scent of her. He gestured to the pile of leaves he'd made at the base of the corded trunk, and she settled down with her back against the yew. She drew her knees up and folded her arms across them, her eyes on the storm. It was a girl's pose, innocent, careless. The tilt of her head exposed the curve of her throat. He estimated her chances of escaping unkissed at zero.

He scraped together another pile of leaves and lowered himself to the ground on the opposite side of a gnarled ridge of yew root. Mere inches separated their shoulders. The rain drummed on the ground beyond their shelter, and his blood drummed awareness of her in his veins while she seemed utterly composed, patient, unmoved. He supposed it was another twist of divine irony to strand him with such temptation, to show him what he was. Before breakfast he'd been reading theological text. Now, before dinner, he was planning to steal a kiss or two from his neighbor.

"Ignoring me again, Miss Merrifield?"

"What?" She turned her head.

"I won't go away."

She must have recognized something of his thoughts in his eyes, for her gaze skittered off. "Of course not," she said tightly.

Her fingers tightened around her elbows, and he guessed no one flirted much with Miss Merrifield. He had no experience with virgins himself. Even Fanny, the maid his mother had bribed to seduce him at fifteen, had been with child by one of the footmen.

"What were you doing out on a day like this?" she asked.

It would not occur to her that he had been doing anything as decent as his duty. "Visiting old Croy, your tenant. A valuable man."

"He is. He—"

"Tells you the weather."

She looked at him over her shoulder, clearly trying to understand him. "You walked?"

"I walk everywhere, Miss Merrifield."

"It cannot be what you are used to."

"Yet I've been doing it for nearly thirty years."

Her gaze slipped to his muddy Hessians. "In

those boots? That pair was made for the paving stones of Bond Street."

He laughed. "First my coat and now my boots offend you."

"Sergeant Croy could feed his family for a year from the profit of selling your coat to a second-hand clothes dealer."

So she knew about secondhand clothes dealers. And she collected dependents like Croy and Mary Fletcher. *Generosity*. A quality his mother rated slightly above imbecility.

Tendrils of her bright hair had escaped their confinement, and she pushed them off her brow absently. In the dim green light of their shelter, with the wall of gray water beyond, the copper brilliance of her hair was like a palpable flame. He wanted to warm his hands in it.

She caught his glance and asked in a shaky voice, "What did you find to talk about with Sergeant Croy . . . Lord Winterburn?"

"Mr. Nash."

"It is your title."

"Not always. I was a soldier once."

"Where?" Plainly she doubted him.

"The Peninsula." He shifted his position slightly, and the brush of their shoulders distracted him. "You do knock my vanity, Miss Merrifield."

"I beg your pardon. I had no idea."

She turned away to stare at the invisible landscape. Lightning flashed, a blaze that did not so much illumine as consume the light, leaving them in a brief blackness. Rain filled the silence, stuffing their ears with sound, pelting the road, swishing against the branches of their tree, rushing down some nearby spinney. The cold air seeped through the damp layers of his clothes and set his old wounds aching. He had not been warm since he left Spain. Now he craved warmth.

In a black moment she spoke again. "I thought you would have left Rowdene by now."

"Why?" he asked the darkness.

"A clergyman's life can't interest one such as you."

"What do you know of me?" he asked, but he feared she knew too much.

The sky lightened to gray again.

Her look was steady, frank. "You do not seem suited for the church."

"Not pious enough for you?" He snapped a twig between his fingers and tossed it aside.

She took a deep breath. "Do you pray?"

He looked away. "Beyond my capacities, you think?"

Her voice turned imploring. "Rowdene needs someone who will work hard and direct souls, and show a real devotion. You could appoint someone like that. You have the power."

He had to laugh. He should tell her how broke he was.

She came to her knees, her feet tucked under her, her hands curled into fists. "Why do you stay? What do you want here? What can Rowdene have to offer you?"

"What does Rowdene offer you, Miss Merrifield?"

"Everything I want."

It was an innocent's answer. She was not indifferent to him, but she didn't feel the ache of longing.

He seized her chin in one hand. "You haven't begun to know everything that can be wanted," he said fiercely. He let the moment last, let her see his hunger. She rocked back, wrenching out of his grasp.

After a moment, she said, "You are lucky you found this spot. There is no other shelter between here and the village."

"A curious pairing, these two trees."

"Yes. It is said . . ."

She broke off as she realized that he was watching her intently. In the green gloom her eyes were wide with recognition of the feeling between them.

"It is said . . ." He prodded.

"That they are man and wife." She paused. "When we were younger, my brother and I carved our initials in the oak."

"There's a story in every corner of Rowdene."

"Yes."

"There's a story about you. That you are the Rose of Rowdene, the maiden who will save the village. They say you must never leave."

He'd confused her, and she looked away. "Where did you hear that?"

"The shepherd, Braithe."

"Mr. Braithe is full of stories. No one believes half of them."

"You've never left Rowdene."

"I don't want to."

He studied her profile with the straight nose and sweet curve of the full lower lip. Generosity. Frankness.

"Or, you can't." All that he'd seen and heard about her made sense. "Your brother has wasted your fortune."

Proud color flared in her cheeks. "You've been listening to gossip, Lord Winterburn."

"I've been listening to you, Miss Merrifield. You walk everywhere, keep no horses or carriage, and count the cost of candles."

She rose, struggling to pull the hem of her damp cloak out of her way. "It's not letting up. I'm going."

He stood, too, and she backed away abruptly, catching her hair in a low branch of the yew. She twisted her head, further ensnaring her hair, and reached up, tugging futilely at the tangled strands.

"Don't move. Let me."

He stepped close and pulled off his gloves. She went dead still, so that he hardly thought she breathed. He felt his heart change its rhythm and his nerves hum with longing. He shoved his gloves in his pocket and lifted his hands to her hair. Lightly, he pulled the tangled strands free of the stiff branches, a contact intensely unsatisfying. A tremor passed through her, and he paused.

Then he cupped her bright head in his hands and tipped her face up to his.

Rosalind searched his gaze for mockery and found only longing. It pierced her like a sudden gleam of sunlight on a winter day.

"Don't," she said.

Only the rain replied.

He rested his lips against hers. A brief unde-manding touch, no more disturbing than a leaf settling, but she clutched his arms for balance. Every other touch she'd known had involved a hand or a shoulder or some part of her person, not the whole.

He made a low sound in his throat and kissed her again, pressing his mouth to hers. She tasted him, the familiar mockery, the deep hunger, the unexpected generosity, and could not stop tender blades of feeling from pushing up in her heart, green and new and sweet.

The subtle movement of his lips against hers coaxed her to respond to him. She kissed back, allowing him to taste, too, as she knew he would, her willingness.

The kiss changed, grew ragged, consuming breath and will, and her body arched to his. The press of their bodies made her breasts ache and draw tight. He seemed to sense the feeling in her. His hands brushed aside her cloak, found her waist. He drew her closer, turning her slightly, placing a hand to her breast, brushing the tender bud of sensation with his thumb. She could think only of being joined to him, like the two trees of their shelter. She broke the kiss and pushed away.

Then she was free. She took a quick shaky step, pulling up her hood, unable to look at him. She quelled the urge to flee. She could not leave him stranded in the storm. "It's but a mile to the inn," she said, conscious of her altered voice. "I can show you the way."

"Take my hand."

"No, I'll be fine."

"I won't." He held out his hand.

She looked at his hand then, just his hand. If she took it, she would be tempted again. She was. She reached out and his fingers closed around hers.

The rain washed away the landscape. It streamed down Rosalind's face and plastered her clothes to her body. Every step required her to drag the tangle of clinging skirts forward. Mud pulled at her feet or sent her slipping giddily along. She breathed rain and tasted it on her lips and tongue. But all the rain in the heavens could not wash away what they had done.

The hour spent under the yew had been excruciating. The moment he'd touched her wrist, he had altered something in her, stirred a painful longing to move closer. The desire both humiliated and fascinated her. It was as undeniable as it was unsuitable that this man should exercise the mysterious pull that drew her to him. Not even her knowledge of his deception seemed to temper the effect he had on her.

In character they were completely at odds. Even her errand separated them. She had gone to arrange the sale of her father's books where no one would care or comment. He would burn ninety candles in an hour. She had been counting pennies for so long, she could hardly think in larger sums. He would consume whatever he was offered freely and without counting the cost.

He seemed to know her secrets, and his eyes promised to reveal the mystery to her if she'd let him. She could not enter the inn with him without revealing her foolishness to all of Rowdene.

When they reached the inn yard, she stopped and allowed him to come up beside her so that the pull on her hand slackened ever so slightly.

"There," she said, pointing to the inn.

He leaned forward to see, and she wrenched her hand from his grasp and flung herself from him, running for Merrifield Hall and safety.

Chapter 9

Three visitors were waiting in the parsonage drawing room when Leigh returned from his walk. He stopped in the doorway, and the breath of air that entered with him—fragrant with meadowsweet and grass and Rosalind Merrifield—faded. It was London air he would breathe in the company before him. Five years earlier he and half of London's dissolutes had vied for the favors of Lucetta King, the demimonde's reigning beauty. His friends Harry Hunt and Alex Frimley had wagered on his success. He felt as if he'd stepped back in time. Rowdene had changed him. He needed to make a subtle shift in his inner balance to face these friends who now occupied his modest drawing room.

Frimley, tall, sturdy, and golden-haired, saw Leigh first. "Nash, hallo." He strode to Leigh's side, pumped his hand, and thumped him on the shoulder. Turning to the others, he announced, "He's here, Harry."

Frimley and Hunt. At Eton they'd been dubbed "the twins" for their similar blond looks. Together with Leigh they'd been formidable on the playing fields: Frimley as wicket keeper, throwing his body in the path of every pitch that escaped a batsman, Hunt as a cunning bowler, and Leigh as a batsman who could hit fours and sixes at will. He'd not seen his friends since his return from the Peninsula.

Harry Hunt, the slimmer of "the twins," looked up from toying with Lucetta's hand. "Frimley, you blockhead." Hunt paused. He never forgot the distinction of rank. "It's not 'Nash,' it's 'Winterburn.'"

Lucetta gave Leigh a cool glance while Frimley worked to correct his understanding. "Right. Forgot the title, Winterburn. Sorry."

Leigh returned Frimley's grip. "Nash will do," he said. "Winterburn sounds too much like Marcus."

"Right." Frimley grinned and gave Leigh another energetic thump, propelling him into the room. "Snug place you have here, Nash."

Leigh stopped in front of Lucetta. She'd lost none of the sultry dark looks that had drawn would-be protectors to her. A pocket Venus, petite and voluptuous, with big dark eyes and a sinful mouth. Lucetta's lips had been the talk of the clubs, and Leigh knew exactly what they could do.

A pale apricot gown barely covered her breasts. A single pearl set in gold filigree winked in the folds of each satin sleeve. Lucetta was in funds. With the slightest hesitation she lifted her free hand to Leigh.

"You're in sporting company, Lucetta." He knew Hunt couldn't afford her and Frimley avoided clever women. "Have these gentlemen thought to offer you any refreshment?"

"Would have," Frimley said, "but you've gone Methodist on us, Nash. Had to send to the inn for a bottle of claret. Your man should be back with it."

Lucetta studied him. "We heard you were wounded terribly in Spain."

Her glance was as soft as her hand in his, but he wasn't taken in by it. She had a keen eye for a man's weakness.

"I survived." He released her.

"Right," Frimley added. "Nursed in a convent. Lucky devil, always finds a woman. I mean, think of it. The only thing in pants in a convent." Frimley's blue eyes were wide with possibilities. "Are they . . . were they . . . I mean, was there a sister who . . ."

Leigh shook his head. He could not blame Frimley for thinking he would seduce a nun. At sixteen he'd led Frimley and Hunt into the exclusive London brothel his father favored. It was his second visit there. Frimley's money, Hunt's tact, and Leigh's experience got them past the intimidating bruiser at the door, past the affronted patrons, and into the arms of some of London's most sophisticated courtesans. They'd gone up to Oxford with their reputation for carnal indulgence assured.

"Frimley, enough," said Hunt, coming slowly to his feet. It was said at Eton that what took

Frimley three minutes took Hunt three hours. "Where's that man of yours, Winterburn?"

"Right," said Frimley. "Sent him off an hour ago for the wine."

"He must be here then." Leigh opened the drawing-room doors and produced his uncle's trusty spy, stiff with offended propriety, tray in hand. It was something like a magician's trick. Hunt raised a brow, but Frimley strode forward, taking the glasses and passing them around.

"We ought to have a toast," he proclaimed. "To your new . . . home, Nash." He thrust his glass in the air, sloshing the wine dangerously. Hunt and Lucetta made a less hearty salute.

Leigh raised his glass. His visitors fell silent, exchanging glances as if they needed some private conference. He took a seat opposite the sofa where Hunt and Lucetta lounged, but he looked straight at Frimley. "What brings you to Rowdene?" he asked.

Frimley opened his mouth, glanced at Hunt, and shut it. Leigh took a swallow of his wine.

"Sit, Frimley," Hunt ordered.

"Right." Frimley drained his wine, looked around, and dropped into a chair near the window.

"You didn't come to see us in London," said Lucetta. "We had to come here. To show you we did not resent the slight."

He had to give her credit. She had always been cool under fire. Five years earlier, when his mother had been pressing him to make a match with a pale, witless heiress, he had pursued and won

Lucetta with enough scandal to scare away the heiress and her fond parents. But he'd left Lucetta for Spain a few weeks later.

"Came to cheer you up," said Frimley. "Must be dashed dull here."

"My God," said Hunt. "First we heard you were wounded, then you come into the title, then you disappear." He swirled the wine in his glass in lazy circles. They were all looking at Leigh—Lucetta sullen, Hunt distant, Frimley confused. The strangeness of their traveling together struck him again.

"Right," said Frimley. "Had a time finding out where you'd gone. Couldn't figure what you'd want with being a . . . parson."

"Escape."

Frimley's brow cleared. He slapped his thighs. "Don't want to marry, eh? Can't blame a fellow for that." He glanced at Lucetta and Hunt as if to say "I told you so. Can't just give up one's freedom."

Leigh experienced a jarring sensation. He had not named the thing he was escaping, yet Frimley assumed it was his mother's plans for him. "My mother thinks freedom a small price to pay for the right bride," Leigh suggested.

"Well, a mother always wants a fellow to set up his nursery. Takes that sort of thing seriously."

Leigh examined the contents of his glass. "Does my mother have someone specific in mind?"

Frimley opened his mouth and clamped it shut.

"Frimley, you blockhead," said Hunt.

"Right." Frimley looked rueful. "But damn, secrets aren't my rig. If Lady W. wanted to make spies of us, she ought not to have sent me. She knows me well enough."

They'd been bought. His friends and his vengeful ex-mistress. By his mother. The signs were unmistakable when he considered it. She had picked the most expedient means of confronting him with his rakish past.

A cold, impotent fury swept him that she could reach him in Rowdene. *You don't still have ideals, do you?* He waited, letting the rage subside.

He raised his glass to Frimley. "Who's my mother got in mind for my bride?"

"Sally Candover. Twenty thousand a year. Not a beauty but close enough. And she knows what's what. She'd give you your heir right and tight and you could go your way."

Leigh understood how his mother had persuaded Frimley to go along with her scheme. "Tempting," he said.

"It should be," said Hunt with a trace of asperity. "The girl's been out three years and spent them fending off smitten suitors."

"Less tempting," said Leigh with a level glance at Hunt. "Why should she yield her twenty thousand pounds to me?"

Lucetta leaned forward, an imperceptible adjustment of her spine lifting her breasts. "Because women want you." It was a calculated stroke of the male ego, like the stroke of a familiar hand along a cat's back. Lucetta plainly expected the cat to arch.

"There you have it," said Frimley.

A knock at the door interrupted them. Polly Rees entered, in her billowing milkmaid skirts and a low-cut bodice which revealed her snowy bosom. Frimley stood up, transfixed.

"Mr. Nash, will ye be wantin' anythin' more today?" Polly asked. Her gaze took in the elegantly dressed males and fixed coldly on Lucetta, who appeared to be considering her nails.

"No, thank you, Polly," said Leigh. Polly bobbed a curtsy, dropping her lashes, sliding a glance up Frimley's tall frame.

When the door closed, Frimley grinned broadly at Leigh. "No wonder you're here. You've got your own covey, a private preserve. Is she hot?"

"I don't know."

Lucetta rolled her eyes.

"Right!" said Frimley, comprehension dawning. He rubbed his hands up and down his thighs with undisguised anticipation.

"Frimley," said Hunt, "you goat. Take Lucetta up to the inn, and go chase the girl. I'm sure the two of you can come to some arrangement."

Lucetta looked sulky. "I won't go just so that Alex can nose about that tart."

Hunt rose and extended a languid hand to Lucetta. "You'll go because I say so, and because I'm holding our purse. I want a word with Leigh. You'll get your turn, I promise."

Lucetta held out for a moment, matching Hunt's stare, then she gathered up her skirts and stood. Frimley stepped forward and thrust an impatient arm her way. She glanced coldly at Hunt. "Neither of you has an ounce of subtlety, and if you . . ."

Hunt cocked his head to one side, his look daring her to complete the threat, but she had control of herself again and allowed Frimley to lead her away.

When they had gone, Hunt returned to his seat on the sofa. He put aside his wine and looked about the room, a leisurely perusal that took in its unpretentious dimensions, sparse furnishings, and clutter of books. Slowly he brought his gaze back to Leigh. "Is this what you want?"

Leigh returned his friend's look. Hunt had neither birth nor fortune behind him, yet he contrived to stay in the game. He showed the world effortless charm and unruffled poise even when the duns were at the door. To throw away power and position as Leigh was doing would be incalculable madness in Hunt's eyes.

Leigh thought perhaps he had been a little mad, as Marcus and Richard had been. "I chose it."

Hunt leaned an elbow on the arm of the sofa and propped his chin in his palm. It was the pose he always adopted when something genuinely puzzled him. "What do you *do* here?" His free hand made circles in the air. "I suppose there's a hunt, some intelligent society?"

Leigh thought of Vernon and Lady Ellenby and Squire Haythorne. "Not to speak of."

"Your mother thinks there's a woman."

Leigh was not deceived by the apparent casualness of the words. "Are you supposed to reveal your employer's views?"

"I have no loyalty to your mother. I'm merely taking the purse she pressed on me."

"No scruples either."

"Can't afford them." Hunt watched him closely. "Is there a woman?"

"You saw Polly. She's doing her best to interest me."

Hunt gave a short, sharp laugh. "Rustic bliss? Hardly your style, Winterburn. Polly would never get you in bed."

"You think Lucetta will?"

A flicker in Hunt's eyes said he regarded the prospect with some regret. "This time?" he asked quietly. "She'll have a go at it."

Leigh stood. "You came to bring me down then, not back."

"You won't last." Harry came to his feet with indolent grace. All indifference vanished from his expression. "One day, Winterburn, you will want money."

It seemed to Leigh then that, in spite of his mother's interference, Hunt had come because Leigh's choice overturned his view of human nature. Greed, power, lust, Hunt could understand; ideals baffled him.

"I may fall, Harry, but you won't be the cause."

"That eases my conscience. I'll just stay to watch and reap whatever rewards your mother's handing out." He stretched lazily. "Join us for dinner at the inn tonight?"

"No, thank you."

"Can't tempt you with good company, good wine? We've ordered the best the house provides. Your mother's paying, of course."

Leigh shook his head. "Harry, I'll not invite you here."

There was a little check in Hunt's easy stride. "Won't matter. I daresay we'll see you about."

"Sir," said Dowdeswell, lifting the cover on the fish. "Did you not find supper to your liking?"

"It was fine." Leigh turned over a leaf of the book he was reading.

"But you did not touch the fish, sir."

"The soup was enough."

"There's a meat pie, if you'd care for it."

"No, thank you, Dowdeswell. You may clear."

"Any difficulty, sir?"

Leigh looked up. Dowdeswell's concern seemed genuine.

"Just another day in Eden, Dowdeswell."

Leigh saw his friends everywhere but in church. And everywhere they went, they brought the air of his mother's London with them, its lust for worldly power, its precise attention to place and wealth, and its chief game: dominating others. Leigh thought Lucetta likely to win.

Frimley had a smart curricle as well as a couple of hunters with him and was immediately in the squire's favor. They passed Lucetta off as Miss King, a cousin of Hunt's and brought her to dinner at Lady Ellenby's. Whether Frimley and

Polly Rees had come to some understanding Leigh didn't know. Polly appeared at the parsonage as usual, wandered about idly with a dust cloth or a stack of linens, and departed. Leigh did not want to dismiss her, for to his amusement she kept Dowdeswell in a state of perpetual alarm.

When it rained, Frimley trudged up to the parsonage for a day of cards, and Leigh didn't have the heart to turn him away. Frimley, at least, wasn't taking money from Lady Winterburn. But when Hunt and Lucetta turned up for luncheon, Leigh discovered their campaign against him was working.

They had heard about his milking Braithe's ewes, so he made a tale out of it, as he would in London. A story about a close encounter with a silly reeking ball of dank wool, the round drops of dung swinging from her rear, the feel of the teats, everything but the satisfaction of filling a pail with milk that might be cheese, that might feed a child in the village. In their company tales were to amuse and silences for wondering who was sharing whose bed.

Hunt and Lucetta had only to look at one another and images of their coupling filled Leigh's mind. It was the sort of idle speculation that filled evenings in London. And Lucetta knew it. Her eyes were full of the mockery of it.

The following day it cleared, and Frimley insisted the others accompany him to a wrestling match a dozen miles away. For the first time since his friends had descended on the village, Leigh was free. He turned to his studies and found them dry. A sentence that a week earlier had seemed to go to the heart of his spiritual struggle now seemed incomprehensible, even on a third reading. He shut the book.

He was applying Miss Merrifield's tactic, trying to wait out his friends, counting arrogantly on his indifference to Lucetta and his desire to escape his mother's plans. But his approach wasn't strong enough. He did not expect to be saintly. No one could expect that of a man of his experience and temperament, but he could be dutiful and more generous than Vernon. Even that aim was threatened by his friends' presence.

He'd made up his mind to go out when Jeremy Braithe called with a round of sheep's-milk cheese. They laid it on the kitchen worktable and cut a slice. It was just dry enough to crumble lightly, tangy and mildly nutty, and Leigh found himself returning Braithe's very wide grin.

"It's good," he told the shepherd. "You've made cheese before?"

Braithe regarded the cheese closely and brushed the crumbs into his hand. "Mrs. Cole had a hand in it."

"How is Mrs. Cole?" Leigh asked, studying the cheese.

Braithe eyed him levelly. "Ye told her I'd the butter in my hat."

"Blame Miss Merrifield. It was her advice."

"I had to explain myself with butter runnin' off my chin."

Leigh laughed. "You must have done some fine explaining if she helped you with the cheese."

"Ye think ye did me a . . . *favor.*" He laid particular emphasis on the word. "Mebbe. Mebbe I'll do ye one. Let's take our cheese up to Miss Merrifield."

Leigh stiffened. "*Your* cheese."

Braithe gave him a steady look. It was a look Leigh was coming to recognize, very different from the sizing-up sort of look his London friends gave a person. It was a look asking if one couldn't do better, do more, expecting it even. "If Miss Merrifield will milk her sheep, her people will milk theirs. Mrs. Cole thinks that if we can milk near a hundred ewes twice a day, we might make twenty-five pounds of cheese a week."

Leigh turned away. "Good. I think you should take the sample up to the hall."

"Ye'd best come wi' me. Miss Merrifield is like to think 'tis one of my stories if I come alone with sheep cheese."

Braithe grinned, and Leigh found himself wanting to be persuaded. He had not seen Miss Merrifield since his London visitors arrived, and they were miles away. They would not know he'd made a visit to the hall.

The countryside was green now, the sky clear and blue, with a brisk, cool wind that drove patches of cloud westward, so that shadows chased each other over the green ground. Not far from the village, Leigh and Braithe came upon Mr. Awdry, a farmer, kneeling beside his wagon, its right rear wheel sunk in a muddy ditch.

"A toff in a fancy rig drove me to the side a bit

ago and the shoulder gave way. Fair mired I am,"
he explained.

While Awdry's horse cropped the grass of the
verge, they gathered around the sunken wheel
and considered strategies for freeing it from the
steep lip of the ditch. The ground was soft and
churned to mush under Awdry's efforts to extract
the weighted wagon. The plan on which they
agreed at last was to lay a path of sticks over the
mud in front of the sunken wheel. They searched
for stout sticks until they found enough to lay
nearly a yard's width. When the sticks were in
place, Awdry went to the horse's head, and
Braithe doffed his jacket and secured the wrapped
cheese in his upturned hat in the shade of a gorse
bush. His blue eyes sparked with the flicker of
humor Leigh was coming to appreciate.

"Need an invitation to enter the ditch, Mr.
Nash?"

Leigh regarded the filthy, scum-covered water,
a cloud of insects hovering over it. "The miracle
was walking *on* water, not *in* it, Braithe."

"It'll be easier than milkin' a sheep."

"Milking sheep cost me a pair of breeches."

"This'll likely cost ye another."

Leigh returned Braithe's grin. "But I refuse to
lose a good coat."

He shed his coat and for good measure his
waistcoat and cravat, feeling the sharp breeze
press his thin shirt to his body. He followed
Braithe into the ditch. The cart loomed above
them against the blue sky, and their feet sank in

the muck of the ditch. They braced themselves, Braithe with his back to the rear of the cart, Leigh with his shoulder to the right end. As the scum closed over the top of his boots, he smiled to himself. Dowdeswell would be scraping and polishing this night.

At Leigh's signal Awdry set his sturdy horse in motion, and Leigh and Braithe strained against the weight of the wagon. The big wheel rose a few inches and hung stubbornly on the curve of the first stick. The wagon clung to the edge, unmoving, a precarious balance. They had to push more, but Leigh could not move a step for better purchase in the soft ground.

"Turn, damn you." He cursed the wheel, straightening the last bend in his knees, pushing upward with his shoulder from some well of strength he didn't know he had.

The stubborn wheel trembled, lifted, then rolled onto their makeshift ramp, snapping sticks like the merest twigs. The effort raised Leigh a fraction from the muck. He turned to Braithe, heard Braithe shout his name, and felt a blow to his head.

Chapter 10

❧

A chunk of flying wood the size of a man's arm caught Nash squarely on the side of the head. As he crumpled, Jeremy charged through the mire. He caught Nash about the waist, dragged the fallen man up onto the road, and laid him on the grass.

"What's happened to 'im?" Awdry asked.

"Caught a clout in the head from one of our sticks."

"Best put som'at cold to his head then."

Jeremy had already removed his neckerchief. He slid back down into the ditch, stirred away the surface scum, and dipped his rag in the muddy water. He scrambled back up and pressed the wet cloth against the nasty bump forming on the side of Nash's face.

Nash didn't stir. He was covered in slime from his boots to his waist, his body cold, his face white. Jeremy rocked back on his haunches. Where he'd pressed the cloth to the side of Nash's head was a scar he'd not noticed before. Jeremy

145

pushed aside the thick black hair that ordinarily covered the spot and considered the wicked pucker of skin.

He looked up to find Awdry staring. "Must've taken a sword or a bayonet in the wars." Awdry's head bobbed wisely. "Old wound like 'at. Won't bring 'im round soon."

Jeremy stood. "I can't leave 'im here."

"Load 'im on my wagon."

Jeremy glanced from the wagon with its sacks of seed to the unconscious man. A trickle of muddy water ran off Nash's brow and disappeared in his black hair, just the way the first warm trickle of butter had run down Jeremy's face by Catherine Cole's fire. He recalled the look in her dark eyes when he'd decided to stop playing and speak plainly. He had a favor to return.

"Thank ye," he said to Awdry. "We'll take 'im to Merrifield. It's just over the rise. Miss Merrifield's people will tend 'im."

At the door to the hall, Awdry balked. "Ye can't bring 'im into Miss Merrifield's dripping mud."

"Help me with his boots then," Jeremy demanded. His plan required quickness.

A round-faced young housemaid named Nan answered the bell, and Jeremy gave her his most persuasive smile. "I've brought your mistress somethin', Nan. Will ye run and fetch her?"

"O' course, Mr. Braithe." She peeked at Awdry holding Nash, and her eyes grew big. "Miss is in the garden, sir."

"Run then, Nan," Jeremy said.

Nan darted back through the house, leaving the

door open, and Jeremy resumed his half of the burden of the unconscious man. The fine old hall offered no couch or table on which to lay Nash. Gerald Merrifield's ways had stripped the mantel and walls bare, and reduced the furnishings to a painted cabinet, two old chairs, and in the center of the room a small table with a vase of flowers.

"By the grate," Jeremy advised Awdry. They lowered Nash to the white and black marble tiles, Awdry muttering that miss would not like her floor sullied. Jeremy hurried Awdry out the door, snatched Nash's clean clothes from the wagon, and wadded them up under his head. The horse's harness jingled as Awdry turned the wagon, but Jeremy concentrated on removing Nash's muddy shirt and breeches, stripping the unconscious man to a pair of linen drawers. He left the muddy boots by the door and the soiled clothes in a heap at Nash's feet.

"Ye'll thank me later," he told the unconscious man. He dropped the cheese on the table beside the flowers and dashed out of the hall, sprinted up the drive, and pulled himself up on Awdry's wagon.

Rosalind gripped the door frame hard, Nan's incomprehensible message suddenly clear. Winterburn's still form lay on the marble tiles as cold and white as an effigy knight in a tomb. She thought her heart stopped.

"Is he dead, miss?" Nan whispered at her shoulder.

He couldn't be. Rosalind crossed the hall, tearing off her hat and gloves, and dropped to her knees at his side. She touched him and felt his chest rise and fall under her hand. "No, he's not dead."

She looked for his injury and found the swelling on the side of his head and beneath it, in the tangle of black hair, an old scar. He had received a blow to the head and been soaked and stripped— why or how she couldn't guess.

"Why did Mr. Braithe strip 'im?" Nan asked.

"Did he?" It seemed peculiar behavior on Braithe's part.

"Must've. 'E had 'is clothes on when they dragged 'im in."

"Nan, we need linens, a blanket, and water. Quick."

The girl nodded and hurried off.

Winterburn was a wonder, all clean-limbed elegance and smooth muscle. With the mocking eyes closed, his face was solemn, as if in prayer. Along his shoulder and across his ribs were two tight ridges of skin. He'd been a soldier, but she'd thought him a parade-ground hero in a fine coat. She'd not guessed he'd have such wounds, wounds that would ache on a cold, damp day as Croy grumbled his wounds did. Winterburn's wounds made her want to weep.

"Miss?" Nan's voice brought Rosalind back to what must be done. The girl had linens and a basin of water.

"Thank you, Nan. We must wrap his feet and dry him." Rosalind stood and reached out, but Nan clutched the blankets to her, staring at Winterburn, her round, pink face worshipful. "He's wicked beautiful, miss."

Silently Rosalind agreed. She tugged firmly at a blanket, and Nan yielded her hold on the linens. Rosalind knelt and tucked one end of the blanket around Winterburn's icy feet, unfolding the other end for Nan to tuck about his waist. It seemed peculiarly intimate to touch his feet. The moment stretched while she arranged the blanket.

When she looked up, Nan was staring frankly at Winterburn's sex, ill-concealed by the fine fabric of his damp drawers. "Nan, cover him," she said sharply.

Nan started, lifted the blanket reluctantly, and paused. "Don't you wonder about it, miss?" She did not take her eyes off the unconscious man.

Rosalind shook her head, an instinctive denial, and stopped. It was a lie. She had wondered ever since Winterburn had come to Rowdene. She felt a hot rush of color in her cheeks.

"They say if ye stroke it," Nan whispered, "a man's root swells like a toadstool after rain, and he'll be wantin'—"

"Enough," Rosalind said sharply, as much to herself as to the girl. She came around to Winterburn's side and pulled the blanket over him herself. "We must keep him warm and dry."

At Rosalind's sharp tone Nan looked so downcast, Rosalind berated herself. Hadn't she giggled at school when Sally Candover talked of such things? "He's to be our parson, Nan," she said gently. "We can't be . . . be thinking carnal thoughts about him."

It was an unconvincing reprimand. Winterburn was the least clerical parson in England, with his black hair, fine coats, and the way he kept Rosalind's wits on edge, her body vibrating like the taut strings of a harp, her limbs jelly.

Nan gave her a sly look. "Polly Rees told Josephine at the inn that he's not a parson at all, but a rich lord and a rake."

"A bit of gossip musn't make us forget what's proper, Nan."

"But, miss, a girl never gets a chance to see a man . . . naked."

"Some do, and you know what happens to them, Nan. A girl must wait for her bridegroom."

Rosalind took a linen towel and dried his right arm and shoulder with quick, light movements, while Nan, with a heavy sigh, began to work on his left side. They covered him up to his chin and laid a damp cloth across his forehead.

"He'd make a lovely bridegroom, miss. Makes me think of smooth white satin, he does. Makes my stomach flip like a fish on the bank just to look at 'im."

Rosalind laughed. Nan made her uncomfortably aware of the man. "Then you'd best go on about your work, Nan, and let me sit here till he wakes."

Nan stood and shuffled to the door, then paused and looked over her shoulder. "Ye could kiss 'im, miss. T' see if it wakes him."

"Nan, you're incorrigible. Go."

The door closed behind the girl, and Rosalind was alone with Winterburn and the wicked suggestion. She needn't do anything but wait. He would wake on his own. Patience, she counseled herself. She leapt up and stirred the fire, then sat and tucked the sheet more closely around him. Still he didn't wake. She took the cloth from his forehead, freshened it in the cool water, and put it back. His mouth was finely drawn, his lips slightly parted. What would happen if she pressed her lips to his?

She had promised to dislike him. He had taken Jane's house without a thought for the home lost. He mocked himself and Rosalind at every turn. He made her cares seem a matter of dust and pennies, her desires petty and circumscribed. He kissed her.

He had filled the church with light, and now he lay naked on her floor, his frailties and his courage exposed, tempting her beyond endurance. She took his hand from under the sheet and held it between her own, chafing it lightly.

Leigh woke to a throbbing head and knew he must not open his eyes. He concentrated on the sharp beat of pain, learning its rhythm, waiting for a lull. Somewhere, far from the hammering in his head, his body lay cold and still. Then he felt a warm, light touch on his right hand. He opened his eyes and for one confused moment saw Rosalind Merrifield bending over him, her eyes closed as if in prayer, her bright hair framing her face. He had a fleeting recollection of the rose and the light and the wheel, then his lids fell, and the pain mastered him.

An indefinite stretch of time passed before he opened his eyes a second time. The ache was now a dull constant, permitting his wits to work. A fine ceiling stretched high above him. A fire hissed and snapped nearby. A cold floor pressed against his back.

"Where am I?" he asked.

Her eyes opened, and she smiled at him. "At Merrifield. Jeremy Braithe brought you."

Her hand started to slip away from his, and he caught it in a firmer grip.

The curve of her cheek blossomed with extraordinary pink delicacy. "What happened?" she asked in a strained voice.

"Awdry's wagon was stuck in a ditch."

"You went into a ditch to help?"

He would have laughed at her surprise, but his head would not allow it. "My boots must be muddying your floor." The words made him conscious of his feet, bare and warm, his body's nakedness. There was a wet cloth on his forehead, and he released her hand and brushed the cloth away.

She pressed her hands together in her lap, staring at them. "Jeremy Braithe removed your clothes," she said. "I fear they're ruined."

"How long have I been here?" He could feel his bare chest, his damp drawers clinging to his loins. He was naked on his back with Rosalind Merrifield. Heaven certainly mocked his pretentions to be a man of the cloth. "Braithe brought me here?"

She nodded. "Nan and I covered you."

"Observed the proprieties, did you?"

He'd made her uneasy, and her gaze shifted away from him. "We were trying to bring you round."

"You were waiting again, Miss Merrifield." He liked the way she stiffened, offended at his tone. He wanted to kiss her in spite of his aching head. "You did not think to wake me with a kiss?"

She took a quick breath. "You heard."

It was a slip, not the full admission he wanted. He turned his head carefully to the right. "You thought about it."

"No." Her mouth was a firm, tight line of denial, but her eyes betrayed her.

His chin was just below her knee. It was an odd position for a man considering a seduction, even a minor one. Her skirts smelled of crushed grass and lavender. "Think about it now."

Her glance, wary and fascinated, flickered over him once.

"There's no need now. You are awake."

"There's more need now." He struggled to raise himself on one elbow and stopped, dizzied by the effort.

She lifted her hand and gently pushed him down, a sturdy competent hand, brown from the sun, the palm lightly calloused from work. His heart beat madly in answer to the touch. "A mistake, Miss Merrifield," he whispered.

She knew it. Her eyes grew big with the knowledge. Her fingers curled against his chest. She was tempted, so tempted. He spoke before she could gather the strength to break away. "You could find out what more there is to want."

Rosalind withdrew her hand from his chest. It was unbearable not to know. He made it unbearable. He offered a mysterious knowledge beyond all the knowing of her familiar world, an understanding of the deepest mystery of herself.

"Why you?"

"Why not a sensible choice?" He guessed her thought. "Why not Vernon, who takes his duties seriously?"

A wry smile crossed her face. "Well, not Mr. Vernon." She lowered her gaze briefly and raised it again. "There was a naval captain once, and a young duke who invited my parents to explore his ruins," she confessed.

"Why not one of them?" His throat felt tight. He did not want to answer the question as it had been answered for him in his father's favorite brothel years before. *Because love is an illusion. Because we are base creatures ruled by lust.*

A moment passed. He ought to speak to warn her, but she was simply looking at him with open curiosity.

"It makes me so impatient not to know. Does it make you impatient?"

"You have no idea."

Rosalind leaned forward. He lay dark and unyielding, his face marked by lines of mockery, his gaze heated. Her senses played tricks on her. She thought she saw generosity in his mouth, veiled hope in the depths of his eyes.

She touched with permission now. The smallest details of his person required her attention. A hollow under his lower lip invited the tip of her

finger. The smooth gleam of his cheekbone and
the rough, dark edge of his jaw drew her palm. As
she studied him, she grew self-aware, conscious
of a tight pull in her breasts, the heated surface of
her skin, a dizzying plummet somewhere deep in
her person.

She braced her hands on the cold marble tiles,
bent lower, and pressed her mouth to his. His
pent breath, released, mingled with hers, a recognition of wanting. His lips parted and hers
opened in response. He pushed up, compelling
her acceptance of their openness to one another
with all its lack of reserve, its danger and exhila-
ration. It led her on. She moved with him, following his lead, finding the fit between them. His
hand came up and slid into her hair, binding her
to him, ensuring the union of their mouths.

Then his tongue touched hers, a taste of undreamed intimacy, wicked knowledge. She would
have drawn back, but his hand at her nape held
her to him. At her faint hesitation he made a low,
aching sound in his throat and withdrew his
tongue. She regained her courage. His warm
mouth on hers stirred the consuming impatience
to know more. His hand slipped from her neck
down her shoulder to cup her breast, his thumb
brushing the peak, sending aching spirals of
longing through her. A tiny gasp escaped her. As
if in answer, he reached up and pulled her down
to him so that she lay along his length.

His hands trailed down her back and locked
around her waist, while he raised tiny kisses to
her brows, her eyes, her chin. Her limbs melted

against his without resistance, and he claimed her
mouth again. Then some realization seemed to
take him, and he slid from under her, releasing
her. She pushed herself up, conscious of the
disorder of her senses and her person.

Leigh had confused her by breaking off their
embrace. She sat, perplexed, breathing as hard as
he, her eyes dark with wakened sensuality and
something else that eluded him when her glance
slipped away. He had been unable to slow his
response to her. Looking cool and untouched as
the moon, she had roused him far beyond the
bounds of her experience, his will subject to the
hot tide of sensuality she stirred.

But her kisses had been wholehearted, unguarded, and he who had known Lucetta's clever
manipulations had been about to lead her to a
knowledge of passion that would disillusion her.
Still, he ached from letting her go. He reached up
and traced the sweep of one full brow, and a
tremor passed through her. She jumped to her
feet, the keys at her waist jingling sharply.

"I'll bring you water and dry clothes," she said,
and she was gone.

A round-faced maid in an overlarge cap
brought him the clothes and water, staring curi-
ously until he sent her on her way. He thought
then that Miss Merrifield would not return, but he
misjudged her. He had just managed to get his
boots on when he heard her voice at the door. He
called out, and she slipped inside the room, her

hand still on the knob. She saw him and turned away to hide a smile.

"What?" he asked.

"Your face," she said. "My father's shirt and breeches are not to your liking?"

"They were made for a man with thinner legs and shoulders," he said stiffly.

"Should I send for your tailor?"

"Irony, Miss Merrifield?" He watched her. "You suffered no lasting harm then from our kiss?"

She studied the floor, but the cowardly impulse passed and she looked up again. "I wanted to know. Now I know. It needn't happen again."

"Then I'd best leave you now."

He heard the quick indrawn breath, imagined her tight grip on the doorknob.

With slow deliberate steps, he crossed the room to the little table where Braithe had left the cheese. "Before I go, Braithe and I have a proposal for you."

She watched him warily. He recognized the vulnerability of senses newly stirred.

"Have you ever milked a ewe, Miss Merrifield?"

She shook her head. He told the tale again, surprised to find it undergo a transformation. He heard himself describe the softness of the ewe's wool, the fluttering beat of her pulse, and the satisfying weight of the full pail.

"And this is the cheese?" she asked, relinquishing her stand at the door.

He opened the cloth that Braithe had wrapped around their sample, inviting her to taste it.

She was within his reach again, but he held

himself easy and let her crumble a morsel of the cheese, watching it disappear between her lips.

"You and Braithe made this?"

"Mrs. Cole helped," he said, looking at her significantly.

A slow, happy smile drew up the corners of her mouth. "The butter melted?"

"It did." If it was difficult to resist Rosalind Merrifield when she was solemn, it was impossible when she was pleased at something he'd done. He reminded her of the proposal.

"You want me to milk my sheep?"

"Braithe says your tenants will do as you do. Mrs. Cole has cheese presses to spare."

"And what will you do with the cheese?"

"Sell it at the next fair, or feed it to hungry children."

She was looking at him as if he were a puzzle she could not work out. "You've done something good."

"Be careful," he said. "You'll be wanting to kiss me again."

"Never," she said.

Rosalind tucked her bundle under one arm and knocked on the parsonage door. She would show Leigh Nash she had not been rendered witless by a few kisses. She would thank him for his idea about sheep's cheese and tell him that a few of her tenants were willing to milk their ewes. She would return the breeches that she and Nan had laundered.

The door swung open at her touch, and Mr.

Vernon appeared. He jammed his hat on his head and began yanking on his gloves, his face red, his frame quivering. "Miss Merrifield, whatever are you doing here?"

"Good after—"

A tall, golden-haired young gentleman in muddy boots and grass-stained breeches skidded into the hall from the drawing-room. "Interfering Methodist sneak," he shouted, glaring at Vernon.

"Corrupter of youth," Vernon retorted.

The blond gentleman strode to the door waving a limp, mud-caked bladder, the sort the village boys used in their games. He shook it under Vernon's nose, forcing the curate out onto the porch. Rosalind stepped aside. "Right," said the blond man. "At least I don't hide in hedges to prick a fellow's bladder and spoil good sport. Lads ought to kick your high hat around." He gave another shake of the popped bladder. "Hypocrite."

Vernon clutched his hat. "Tell Nash I hold him accountable for this outrage. Idle sport and beer on a Sunday. The bishop will hear from me." He turned and descended the steps, then stopped and looked at Rosalind.

"Come, Miss Merrifield. This house is no place for a lady."

"Hallo," said the blond man, smiling at Rosalind. "Don't listen to him. He's sour as vinegar. Come to see Leigh, have you? I'm Frimley." He dropped the bladder and nudged it aside with the toe of his boot, wiping his hands on the sides of his breeches and offering her a hand.

"Miss Merrifield," Vernon said, "I cannot answer for your virtue if you enter that house."

Rosalind reminded herself that Vernon meant no offense. "Mr. Vernon, thank you for your concern, but *I* must answer for my virtue whatever house I enter."

Vernon whirled and stalked off, and she turned to Mr. Frimley.

"Let me take your bundle, Miss Merrifield," Frimley said. He took the folded breeches from her and drew her toward the drawing room. "Nash, you have a caller," he announced.

Rosalind's first impression was that she had interrupted a party, but she saw in a moment that Winterburn had only two other guests, a dark beauty and another blond gentleman, almost a double for Frimley. They lounged on Jane's comfortable chintz sofa, sipping dark wine from tall glasses. Their elegance surpassed anything Rosalind had seen in Rowdene and made her feel positively rustic. That was all she saw before her gaze met Winterburn's.

One look and she understood herself better. Whatever excuse had brought her to the parsonage, she had come to be kissed. It was an awkward moment for such an insight. The couple on the sofa rose, and she was conscious of their tooknowing glances, as if they'd guessed her intention before she realized it.

Winterburn crossed to her, interposing his body between their stares and her heated face. He took her hand, his expression as cold and hard as slate. The strangers seemed to bring back all his icy pride. "Miss Merrifield, you've caught us in a dispute over the merits of sport." He spoke lightly. "Will you allow me to introduce my friends to you?" She nodded, mastering herself, and he turned her to meet the others. "Frimley, you've met. Miss King and Mr. Hunt, acquaintances of mine from London."

Miss King nodded. Hunt put aside his wine, took her hand, and held it. "How is it, Miss Merrifield, that we've not met you at Lady Ellenby's or Squire Haythorne's?"

"I live a quiet life, Mr. Hunt."

"Just a visit now and then to my friend Nash at the parsonage." His eyes glinted mockingly at her, and she felt Miss King's stare.

She hesitated a moment, unsure what to call Winterburn before these people. "Mr. Nash has been good enough to interest himself in our sheep, and I've come to thank him," she said.

Miss King stepped to Winterburn's side and slid her arm through his. "Our Leigh is good, isn't he?" Her body leaned into his.

Mr. Hunt cast Miss King a quick hard glance, and Rosalind struggled to think what she could say to dissolve the terrible tension in the room, but it was Frimley who spoke first.

"Miss Merrifield brought you something, Nash."

Rosalind turned as Frimley held out the pair of breeches she and Nan had rescued from the mud. The cord around them slipped, and one pant leg unfolded, revealing the nature of the garment. Rosalind felt the color rise in her cheeks. Frimley groaned and fumbled to refold the dangling pant leg.

"Is she your laundress, too, Leigh? Such devotion. I don't believe I ever laundered your breeches for you."

Winterburn's hand shot out and caught Miss King's arm in a tight grip.

Rosalind did not have to look at him to know the truth of his association with the woman at his side. It should hurt. It would hurt, but a surprising feeling had taken hold of her—anger at Miss King's meanness. It coursed through her unchecked.

She plucked the breeches from Frimley's fumbling hands and faced the dark beauty. "You never showed Mr. Nash any kindness then, Miss King."

"Kindness was not what he wanted from me."

Rosalind shook her head. "You must not know him very well, after all. He is kindness itself in Rowdene." She paused to restore the neat folds of the garment. "Our mud seems to bring that out in him."

She set the folded breeches on the tea table. "Thank you again, Mr. Nash, for your suggestion about the sheep's milk. Good day." She turned on her heel, brushed past Frimley, and was out the door before any other feeling could take hold.

Leigh released his grip on Lucetta and carefully moved away from her before he could give in to the desire to hit her.

"Sorry, Nash," said Frimley. "I didn't mean . . . what a tigress Miss Merrifield is."

"In defense of her lover," said Lucetta.

Hunt took Lucetta's arm and strode to the door, dragging her in his wake. "Come, Lucetta, I think we've pushed our host far enough. There's a quaint hypocritical custom that Winterburn might be willing to revive just for you." He leaned to speak in Lucetta's ear. "Whipping a whore behind a cart."

Lucetta stiffened. "Have I been naughty, Harry? You punish me."

"Frimley, take her," said Hunt.

Leigh heard her protests as Frimley dragged her away. He picked up his wine. He must show nothing. Rosalind Merrifield was vulnerable to them, to their malice and their capacity for scandal. He had made her so. "She's nothing to me," he said.

"Prove it." Hunt gave him a bitter smile. "Bed Lucetta."

Chapter 11

〜 ⌒᠊᠊○○⌒ 〜

S ydney Barton raised a steaming cup of tea to his lips, held it there, and drew in the brisk, clean fragrance, blotting out the sour odor of his guest. Gerald Merrifield slumped over the sporting news opposite Sydney, apparently inured to his own stink. Barton lifted the cup a fraction closer to his nose and thought of the handsome house in Wiltshire that would be his if he could endure the close proximity of sweat and vomit a bit longer. Barton's man, Crumb, set a platter of liver and eggs before Merrifield, who swept aside the sporting news and picked up a fork.

"Damned decent of you to take me in, Barton." Merrifield forked liver onto his plate in hearty portions. "Damned duns. Must know I'm not good for anything until quarter day."

Sydney moved his cup slightly closer. "Impatient lot, the duns. I suppose you'll have something for them then?"

"Got to give the hall a visit. Never seen such a run of bad luck." Merrifield sliced a piece of liver, exposing the pink inside of the meat. "I'll get

Hinkson to take some silver or something. Damned thieving cheat, diddles me out of a fair price every time."

Crumb opened the window at Sydney's elbow a blessed crack. "Such a bother to dash off like that every time you need a bit of the ready, Merrifield. Just mortgage the place and get a sum you can really use."

"Thought of that." Merrifield spoke around a piece of liver. "My father's man never follows through, damn him. No head for that sort of thing myself."

"Sell the place."

For a minute Sydney thought he'd blundered. Merrifield had that stupid, uncomprehending look he got whenever he lost at cards or the races. He simply could not conceive of circumstance or fate going against him.

"Thought of that." He shook his head. "Never get what it's worth. Men of business always get the better of a gentleman in a deal, don't you know." He started in on his eggs.

Sydney made himself swallow a sip of tea. Merrifield's use of the term "gentleman" roused his temper. A hall in Wiltshire, not any refinement of mind or taste, made Merrifield count in society, while Sydney with all his elegance, his discernment, depended on the convenience of the great hostesses. He was invited to make up the numbers, paired with a dowager or a spinster, never with a marriageable daughter of the house. Not in twenty years on the town had he been eligible. A hall of his own would take him from the fringes of society to its center.

"And there's my sister." Merrifield's voice recalled Sydney to the present. "I'd have to get her off the place, get her settled."

A sister. It was the first time Merrifield had mentioned the girl. If he got her married off, he'd no doubt dip into his new brother-in-law's pocket, and that might delay Sydney's plan. He had made careful inquiries into Merrifield's situation. The estate was not entailed, and Merrifield was bent on gaming it away as fast as he could.

Sydney stared at his guest. A bit of egg fell from Merrifield's lips to the limp linen around his throat, his stained neckcloth a record of his coarse, careless life. The image of a feminine version of Merrifield occurred to Sydney, and he shuddered. He lifted his gaze to a row of fine architectural prints on the wall above his guest. The spare, clean Palladian lines restored his calm. Merrifield would never exert himself for another's comfort.

Merrifield rustled the newspaper. "Damn, this fellow from Hill's looks promising. If I had something to put down on him against Nat Temple, I could make a quick recovery."

"That's the pity of your situation, Merrifield. You find yourself strapped when an opportunity arises. You need to make use of that house of yours."

Merrifield looked up from pushing the last piece of liver through the grease on his plate. He wore the dull-witted expression that most annoyed Sydney. "Make use of my house?"

Sydney lowered his cup to the table. "Host a private card party." He spoke slowly to allow Merrifield's less than agile brain to grasp the idea. "High stakes. Select players. Choice amenities. We'd be the bank."

Merrifield's expression improved at once, becoming if not precisely intelligent, at least cunning and eager. "A chance to win big for once. Who'll we get? Revelstoke? Sherrard? Davies?"

Sydney nodded. "And Maitland and Crawley."

Merrifield slapped the table with an open palm. "By God. I'd like to see Crawley lose for a change."

Sydney freshened his tea from a pot Crumb put beside him. "Yes, he always struck me as winning a bit too much, too easily."

Merrifield's grin collapsed. "The hall's in no shape for a party. Sold the beds."

Sydney waved a careless hand. He'd anticipated this. "Well, of course we'd have to invest a bit to make a go of it."

Merrifield shrugged, spreading his hands in a helpless gesture. "You're forgetting, Barton. The duns are at me night and day. I'm at low tide, haven't a feather to fly with."

"But I have, my friend." It was irksome but necessary to apply the term to the stale creature in front of him, and he could endure it a few weeks longer. "I can make you a small loan. Mind you, it would be a loan. I'm a fellow of modest means, but I'd take your voucher."

"Damn generous of you, man." Merrifield shoved his plate away and wiped his mouth and chin carelessly with a napkin. "What's the game then? Faro, Macao, hazard?"

"Faro for Sherrard and Revelstoke. Hazard for Maitland, Davies, and Crawley."

"We need tables." Merrifield seemed to think he'd had a brilliant insight. Sydney nodded. "Chairs, wine, food. And tarts. Crawley never plays unless he can squeeze a handful of tit between games. Maitland has to have champagne. Sherrard has to have a leather chair." Merrifield continued listing the eccentricities of his fellow gamblers. Each one had some peculiar requirement for food or drink, lighting or seating, or clothes. High stakes and willingness to cater to such whims, not affection for their host, would draw them to Merrifield's house party.

That, too, was part of Sydney's plan. He could not think of anyone who cared much for Gerald Merrifield, though probably no one found him as offensive as Sydney did, except Crawley. Crawley objected to Merrifield's stupidity. Every guinea that Merrifield won at cards or on some sporting wager affronted Crawley. But Merrifield wasn't stupid. Gaming was his opiate. The only thing that could distract him at play was another wager. Barton had developed a tacit partnership with Crawley. More than once he had offered the sort of suggestion that distracted Merrifield enough to allow Crawley to win.

Now Crawley owed Sydney a little help. Sydney's carefully hoarded treasure would buy the wine and women, hire the furnishings and servants for the party, and Crawley would ensure that Gerald Merrifield lost all, and when he did, he would owe it to Sydney Barton. By quarter day he would be Sydney Barton of Barton Hall, Wilts.

Sydney surveyed the length of the pale-green drawing room. It was a handsome room with just the touches he admired most. The paneling and molding were in excellent condition, and though Merrifield had sold the original furnishings, his sister had had sense enough to preserve the collection of fine bone china in the coral display cases. Nor could he fault her housekeeping. The rooms were fresh with lemon and wax and lavender, no hint of dust or mildew.

He and Merrifield had decided on three gaming tables, which the drawing room accommodated as easily as one of the clubs. Along the outside wall was the low couch where Crawley's tarts were to sit. Sherrard's leather chair was in place, as was a table for Maitland's champagne. Lamps had been hung from the ceiling and branches of candles arranged to suit the needs of the guests. Sydney himself had overseen the dipping of the wicks in spirits to ensure quick lighting. Once play began, no one would leave the room for two days.

The sound of a carriage on the drive drew his glance to the window. Seven guests had arrived already. He liked the bustle of their servants moving about. When the hall was his, he would fill it with discerning visitors. Though the party had grown beyond their original conception, it was not beyond Sydney's control. He had directed Merrifield in the necessary purchases and seen to the hiring of a few discreet servants from town.

Sydney had never allowed himself to spend such sums in rapid succession. It was almost dizzying. He had gone beyond his own stash and borrowed from the moneylenders. But with each advance to Merrifield, Sydney had felt his power grow. He and Crawley had come to an easy understanding, and with Merrifield's vouchers in his pocket, he was certain of his future ownership.

His proprietary vision dissolved as Gerald Merrifield entered the room. Merrifield had a feverish, impatient look, his face flushed, his movements rapid and abrupt. His linen was clean for once, but his waistcoat was askew, the buttons not properly fastened. He paused at one of the tables, straightening a chair, and moved on restlessly, touching the card box on the faro table, fingering a stack of markers.

"Looks ready." He paused at the couch. "Think two whores will be enough?"

"They seem an accommodating pair," said Sydney. He had sampled the brunette's wares, and she'd satisfied him as well as her sort ever did. He liked to dominate women, but there was no triumph in dominating professionals who were accustomed to cringing and fawning, not as there would be in having the Countess of Winterburn under him. "There's a girl at the inn who might be willing to join us."

Merrifield rubbed his hands together. "It's my lucky night. I can feel it."

"Gerrie." Miss Merrifield strode into the room, her skirts rustling. She had proved surprisingly difficult all week with her ring of keys at her waist as if she owned the hall. She marched right up to her brother. "I will not allow you to wager mother's pearls."

"Can't stop me, Roz. Got to have a stake to start off."

"I will stop you. I'll tell the other gentlemen they're my pearls."

Merrifield's restless movement stopped. "You shouldn't, Roz. Shouldn't come downstairs at all tonight." He shook his head at the girl. "Tell her, Barton, gentlemen's party."

Sydney stepped forward and offered his arm. At first she had welcomed his civility. "Miss Merrifield, your brother's quite right that you should not appear among his guests tonight. Spirits and cards bring out the worst in some men."

The girl's eyes sparkled dangerously. "Then I had better speak to the guests now. If you'll excuse me, Mr. Barton." She started to pull away, and Sydney caught her arm. She looked at her brother.

"Be nice to Mr. Barton, Roz. He holds my vouchers."

That roused a satisfying flash of alarm in the girl's eyes. She straightened. "This is the friend you told me you borrowed from?"

Merrifield nodded.

"And if you lose tonight?"

"I owe Mr. Barton a sum I can never pay." Merrifield flung his arms in an expansive gesture, stumbling as he lost his balance briefly.

She twisted her arm, trying to escape Sydney's grasp, but he tightened his hold. She gave him a cold look and turned to her brother.

"He wants you to lose, Gerrie," she said. "Can't you see it? He has encouraged every step of this folly, the ruinous expense of it."

"No, Roz. Barton wants me to win, to win big. We've planned it." He gave Sydney a wink.

"I think your sister should be encouraged to keep to her room," Sydney suggested. The girl was smarter than her brother, and he would not have her spoil his plans.

"Locked in, you mean." Gerald nodded. He snatched at the ring of keys at Rosalind's waist and snagged them.

"Gerrie," she yelled, trying to wrench them away from him.

Gerald staggered away from her, panting. "Take her up. It's the southeast corner."

"Locked in? In my own home?"

"My house, Roz."

The girl looked stunned. Plainly she had no idea of the hold gaming had on her brother.

"Gerrie," she said, her voice patient, firm. "We belong to the house as much as it belongs to us. We guard it and keep it and pass it on."

"The key, Merrifield," Sydney said.

"You." The girl turned on him in a fury, and he clamped a hand over her mouth and twisted her arm up behind her back. He pushed her out the door, down the hall, and up the stairs. Her feet tangled in her skirts, and she stumbled and fell against the polished steps. Tomorrow she would be covered with bruises, but Sydney hauled her up each time, compelling her upward, jerking her body against his.

In the room he pinned her against a wall. Her hair was down, the bodice of her plain gown twisted, revealing the smooth tops of her breasts. The heat of her struggle had released a sweet fragrance from her skin. Sydney drew in the scent of her, as fresh as her brother was stale.

Her resistance stirred an unexpected surge of sexual desire in him. She was of the class of women who held themselves above the Sydney Bartons of the world. Perhaps he would marry her after the hall was his. An offer from him would look magnanimous and make it impossible for Merrifield to balk at relinquishing the hall to Sydney. She was not the Countess of Winterburn, but he could still have the countess in his bed. He thought it would pique Lady Winterburn's appetite to know he was plowing a young bride.

"Miss Merrifield, I like the way you writhe under me." She stopped instantly. Her breath came in short pants.

"Mr. Barton, your airs don't deceive me. You prey on my brother. You are no gentleman."

He wanted to hit her, but Merrifield appeared in the doorway, holding the key. "Barton, let's get Roz locked up and show the guests about."

Sydney pushed away from the girl. She steadied her balance and glanced at the door. He stepped next to Merrifield, blocking any escape attempt.

The girl looked at her brother. "Gerrie, you don't need to lock me up. I can leave the hall for the night."

"Where would you go?" Merrifield asked.

"The parsonage."

Sydney caught Merrifield's eye and shook his head. No telling what the girl would say to the neighbors.

"Sorry, Roz."

She lunged forward, but Sydney caught her and flung her back onto the bed. He backed out, and Gerald closed the door, inserting the key.

"Don't worry about the pearls, Roz. Tonight I can't lose."

Rosalind stared out the window at the loveliness of the gardens in the fading light. She'd been in her room a night and a day. She guessed it was now near ten on Saturday night, and still they gambled in the rooms below hers. Sometime in the night, while she'd dozed, the door had been opened and a tray of food left on the floor. Since then no one had come near her.

It was a long time to wait, a long time to consider how blind she'd been. A week ago she had welcomed Gerrie and his guest, Sydney Barton. Barton's civility, orderliness, and interest in the house had made her think he was the kind of friend Gerrie needed. Then the green baize tables had arrived.

She had reasoned and argued and pleaded and prayed. Her first mistake. Nothing had swayed Gerrie. Her own servants had been sent away and Barton's hirelings installed. Food and wine and furnishings had arrived by the cartload, and then the women had come from London. In no one had she found an ally. Gerrie had moved about in a restless ecstasy of anticipation, ordering the arrangement and rearrangement of furnishings and lamps, tasting the wine, testing the beds with one or the other of the tarts.

She had not turned to Mr. Vernon or Winterburn. Her second mistake. She had waited. *You were waiting, Miss Merrifield.* She heard Winterburn's voice in her head over and over. Truly she had been waiting for three years, thinking Gerrie would soon tire of London and return to his responsibilities, while in her secret heart she had not wanted things to change, was secretly proud of running Merrifield without a man.

She had thought herself like King Alfred. But now the story of Alfred and the cakes came back to her, and she understood it differently. The king had had to learn to wait and watch the cakes, but he had known how to act, to fight to save his kingdom. She had been taught only half of what she needed to save her home.

She turned from the window to her wardrobe and took out her nightdress. Waiting three years did not seem as long as waiting one day to hear whether her brother had lost their home. She did not let herself dream that he would win big, as he claimed he would. Only once or twice in three years had Gerrie come home a winner, stuffing banknotes in everyone's hands. He liked to up the stakes as a game went on, to risk ever-increasing amounts.

Tomorrow the game would end, and when it did, she must act accordingly. She shed her shoes and stockings, her dress and chemise, and slipped into the cool nightdress. Her man of business could arrange a mortgage that would allow them to pay Barton and reclaim Gerrie's vouchers. But if she paid Barton and Gerrie went on gaming, he would drain the hall so that paying the mortgage would be impossible. It might be wiser to let the hall and receive rent, but rent would be useless if Barton demanded the whole sum at once. She could sell off some more of the property and perhaps the entire library, but not in time. Her room was the least of the traps in which she was caught.

The key turned in the lock, and she slipped to the door, positioning herself to escape if she could. The door swung in, and Gerrie sagged against the wall, blocking her way.

She moved as close to him as she dared. He stank of wine and urine. "Is it over? Have you won?"

He pushed himself up against the wall and grinned at her. "I was up twelve thousand. Twelve thousand. Took it off of Crawley."

"You didn't lose the pearls?"

The question seemed to fog his brain. "Pearls are for dowds, Roz. You need diamonds. Fellows downstairs can buy you ropes of them. You have to be a good sport though." He wagged a finger at her.

"A good sport?"

"Come along, Roz." He reached out and clamped a hand on her arm. His hand was slick, and she slipped free of his grasp, backing into the room. He staggered toward her and knocked her against the wardrobe. Her head hit the edge with a sharp crack, and for an instant black dots danced before her eyes. He grabbed her again, twisting her arm behind her back and pushing her before him.

"Gerrie, where are you taking me?"

"Drawing room."

"Why? You wanted me to stay away." She tried to brace herself, but her bare feet could get no purchase on the hall carpet.

"Need you now, Roz. Got to stay in the game."

"But you won twelve thousand."

"Last night. Down tonight. Down eleven. Got to stay in the game. Need a new stake."

"Gerrie, I don't have anything for you to wager."

They reached the stairs, and he half dragged, half pushed her down them. The drawing-room doors were just ahead.

"Gerrie, I'm in my nightdress. I can't go in the drawing room with your guests."

"Better that way, Roz. Fellows will see what you've got." He shoved her forward, and she staggered into an open area between two green baize tables. The room was hot and smelled of wine and bodies. The carpet was sticky under her feet. Pools of light illuminated the tables but left the rest of the room dim. Men gathered around each of them, staring intently at cards and markers. She had thought Gerrie strange, but she saw now that he fit in his world. The others had the same feverish look. One had his sleeves rolled up, his neckcloth tied about his head. Another wore his jacket inside out. Still another had a green shade pulled down over his forehead. No one spoke, but as if her presence disturbed the concentration, heads turned her way.

A man sitting on the couch, fondling the breasts of one of the London tarts, looked up from the woman and slipped her off of his lap. He stood and came toward Rosalind. "Merrifield, what's this?"

More men stopped their gaming to stare. Her body felt on fire with shame. A man in the far corner of the room looked at her over his shoulder while he continued to make use of a piss pot.

"Gentlemen, the Rose of Rowdene," said Gerrie.

Sydney Barton stared at Merrifield. The man was mad. What did he mean, bringing the girl into it now, frozen in the light, her hair down, her feet bare, the filmy gown revealing the shadow at the apex of her thighs. Crawley had spotted her right away.

"There's a spot for her here on the couch, Merrifield," Crawley suggested.

Merrifield shook his head. "No, no. Virgin."

Every man who had not yet turned did now. Barton looked them over. They were a very

drunk, very select crowd. Most were true gamblers with the singlemindedness of the breed that
left no room for affection or chivalrous nonsense
when there were cards on the table. Only one or
two might object to Merrifield's actions.

"She's a treasure. The Rose of Rowdene. Worth
her weight in guineas. My stake," Merrifield said.

The girl lifted her chin and looked around the
crowd. "I am not a stake in anyone's game."

Only a slight quaver in her voice suggested fear.
Sydney would not want her himself if Crawley or
Maitland had her, but if one of them did, she'd be
in no position to oppose Sydney's plans for the
hall.

"We are all a stake in somebody's game," he
said. "'As flies to wanton boys are we to the
gods.'"

"A fine literary conceit, Barton." The speaker
was Hunt, a fellow not on their original guest list.
He'd come over from the inn for the second night
of play. "But I'd prefer that Mr. Merrifield have
ready money if he wishes to continue play."

"I agree," said Davies. "The girl says she's not
willing."

"I'm not," she said.

"What virgin is?" asked Crawley, drawing a
laugh from the crowd.

There was a restless stir in the room. They'd
been too long from their cards and their wine.
Sydney had to turn them back to his purpose.
"Gentlemen, I respect your scruples, but may I
remind you that virgins of birth and breeding are
auctioned off every season. You all know the price

a man pays: a settlement of ten thousand and his freedom. Let's allow Merrifield to set a fair price on the girl and get on with it."

"Who is she?" asked Maitland.

"My sister."

"Well, I won't hold it against her," said Crawley. "Name her price, Merrifield."

"Five thousand."

Chapter 12

Rosalind turned to the door. Only Gerrie was between her and the opening, and he was looking not at her but at the round table at the far end of the room, hungrily, impatiently. She measured her chances of escape. She could run, but her legs were weak, shaking. She would stumble, and they would be on her. She drew a steadying breath. If she waited . . .

Gerrie lurched forward and patted her on the back. "Don't look so down, Roz. I won't lose. Can't lose tonight."

She hated him for saying it, for believing it.

"What's your game now, Merrifield?" the man from the couch asked.

"Faro," said Gerrie. "Come along, Roz."

He pulled her over to the far table and placed her hands on the green surface. She pressed them flat to conceal their trembling. In a few minutes the game would absorb the guests. Perhaps then she could . . . could what? Her brain seemed unable to conceive of the simplest action to save herself.

Men closed around the table, frankly staring at her breasts, her body. The man on her right nudged against her, his leg and hip rising against hers, pushing her gown up. She squeezed closer to Gerrie, and his knees buckled. He caught himself and pushed her away. She clung to the table edge to keep her balance.

"Got to have room to place my markers," Gerrie mumbled. "Who's got the box?" he asked.

A gentleman at the end of the table answered, and Rosalind watched him place a deck of cards face up in a box with a slit up the side of it. She had never seen the device, but it had an ominous closed look. A two of spades appeared on top, and around her men studied cards of their own. There was a flurry of silent activity as the players put down cards and placed markers on them. Rosalind had the feeling that she had entered a different world where everyone knew the language but she. Gerrie played two cards, one with a black hexagonal chip in addition to the ivory markers.

When the bets were laid, the man with the box discarded the first card and, with his finger in the slit, popped the next card from the box. It seemed like a child's game to her, looking for pairs that matched, but Gerrie patted her back. Then the dealer took a stick like a miniature rake and began gathering in markers. Rosalind tried to comprehend what had happened. The dealer's stick shoved an equal pile of markers toward each of Gerrie's cards.

Gerrie picked up his own cards and chose again, laying the double stack of markers on his new choices. "You bring me luck, Roz," he whispered.

The dealer slipped his finger up the side of the box again, exposing another card. Rosalind looked round the table. They were guessing, each man was guessing the rank of the card that would turn up in the box. She watched the dealer. His movements seemed efficient, indifferent, but there was a little pause each time before his finger pushed a card from the box, a heartbeat's hesitation that acknowledged that men were staking their fortunes on the turn of a card. Rosalind's own heart seemed to pause in those moments. How long before Gerrie started losing?

Gerrie won again and again. He stopped doubling his bets because the stack of markers tumbled over. When the last few cards were visible in the box, the gentlemen deliberated slowly and made adjustments to their bets, drawing out the procedure. Gerrie placed three cards down and stacked markers on all of them. Rosalind held her breath. Her legs felt stiff and unsteady. Clearly he was betting all. He would lose now.

But again, miraculously, he had a match. The dealer pushed triple stacks of markers his way. Rosalind stared.

"Gerrie, you've won," she whispered. "You could quit now, ahead."

He stared at her blankly and drained a glass of wine offered by a footman. "Next box," he called, counting in a low mumble, stacking the markers with clumsy fingers so that the piles kept tumbling down.

The dealer started to shuffle a new deck. Rosalind felt her legs shake. She gripped the table hard. Few men were watching her so intently now that the game was in progress. She had to think of some escape. Someone tapped her shoulder, and she turned. The fair-haired London woman stepped between Rosalind and Gerrie.

"Gerrie, love." She pressed her breasts against his arm and whispered something in his ear.

Gerrie continued to fumble with his markers, his eyes glittering bright. "Take her then. Bring 'er right back."

The woman turned to Rosalind and slipped an arm under hers. "Call of nature, miss, come along." She winked.

Rosalind clutched the offered arm and willed her unsteady legs to take a step. The door looked so far away. She glanced about for Barton, who would stop them, but she didn't see him. She saw Winterburn's friend Hunt, his back to them, engaged in conversation with another man. Somehow they passed through the door and down the hall to the morning room. The other woman, a brunette, let them in and put a glass of wine in Rosalind's hand.

"Drink up, sweetheart. 'Twill give ye strength," she said. They led Rosalind to a chair.

The room seemed to have been turned into a large closet with women's clothing and toiletries strewn about. The brunette nodded approvingly as Rosalind sipped the wine. Then she knelt and took one of Rosalind's feet and began to tie on a slipper. "Got to get you out of here, miss."

The blonde came around behind her and slipped a cloak over her shoulders. Tears stung Rosalind's eyes. Their kindness, the kindness of strangers, was so welcome after her brother's cruelty.

"Now, none of that, miss," said the blonde.

Rosalind brushed away the tears with the back of one hand. "Why are you helping me?"

"Just protecting our profits, miss." The blonde took the wineglass. "Can't go losing customers when we've come all this way."

"Hush, Jenny," said the brunette. "A girl's got a right to sell herself." She tied the cloak strings under Rosalind's chin with brisk efficiency. "My da sold me, and I said never again. I sell myself now and make 'em pay good money to have me."

"You do the same, miss," said Jenny, pulling Rosalind up from the chair. "You get yourself a good protector."

They hurried her to the window. Jenny pushed up the casement and held it, while the brunette went to the door.

Rosalind swallowed the ache in her throat. "Thank you." She gave Jenny's hand a squeeze.

"Go now. Mr. Hunt will delay your brother a bit, but you'd best go quick. Hunt says you're to go to the parsonage."

Rosalind hitched up the cloak and gown and swung one leg over the sill. For a moment she clung to the window frame, one foot in the

morning room, the other dangling above the
ground. The cool night air sent a shiver through
her, and the sharp edges of the facing bricks bit
into her thigh. She quelled a sudden devastating
thought that her home was lost and eased herself
out the window, stretching to touch ground.

A shout erupted in the hall, a roar from Gerrie.
Rosalind slipped, falling, her arms outstretched,
her leg scraping across the rough bricks. The
window slid closed above her, and she crouched
on the damp earth, biting her lip, holding the
pain of the raw scrape inside her.

She heard the door of the morning room bang
open and Gerrie shout, "Where is she? Got to find
her. Got to find my luck."

Jenny's voice crooned a soothing reply, then
something crashed.

"She's gone to fetch her slippers," shouted the
other girl. "Upstairs, ye cursed sot."

"Upstairs," mumbled Gerrie. "Got to get my
luck."

Rosalind ran.

Leigh plucked Lucetta's note from the tray of
cold supper Dowdeswell had left him. *Hunt's
away.* The message was clear. She was alone and
expected Leigh to take advantage of the fact. It
was his chance to prove his indifference to Rosalind Merrifield. Whether he went or stayed away,
he would betray her.

He rose and crossed to the drawing-room fire,
picking up the poker and stirring the coals to life.
If he went, Hunt would be satisfied that Rosalind

Merrifield meant nothing to Leigh. The scandal would be all his and Lucetta's. He would not be ordained. His mother would win, a nasty prospect at best.

Still, it would be less sinful to go to Lucetta than to allow himself to be ordained, knowing he was poor material from which to fashion a clergyman. The lustfulness of his nature was far from dead, as each encounter with Rosalind Merrifield proved. Neither prayer nor sermons rose easily to his lips. And he could not, as Vernon did, condemn folk for their pleasures. Vernon had written to Uncle Ned over the matter of the burst bladder. The bishop had sent Leigh a pithy note, reminding him that there must be no "fatal error," no "disabling improprieties" if he wished to be ordained. Ordained. The mockery of it. A man who couldn't pray.

He wandered over to the sideboard and filled a glass with wine from the decanter. He lifted the wine to his lips. So why was he so reluctant to have Lucetta? Why did it seem less a betrayal of his own aims than a betrayal of Miss Merrifield, a girl he'd kissed once, a girl with a mistaken notion of his goodness. Her first assessment of him had been more accurate. She'd thought him heartless and self-interested, and she'd been right. No thought of the widowed Mrs. Fowler had crossed his mind when he'd taken the parsonage for himself. It was Rosalind Merrifield who held him back. He would cynically profess the required faith and be ordained, except that she still had ideals.

He set down the wine and wandered to the window, looking out at the dark outline of the church below. He wondered if he *could* pray.

A shadow moved, and his eye followed it. Something white fluttered along the path from the road. He pressed his hand to the window and peered out. It was the white edge of a woman's gown as she came up the parsonage walk. The light step was familiar. He was at the door in a minute.

What he saw first was the stark expression in her eyes. *Dear God*, a fleeting thought, hardly a prayer. He knew that look of loss and disillusionment, had seen it on the faces of young soldiers. Her fists clutched a cloak around her, and muddy white skirts clung to her legs above a pair of soaked slippers. She opened her mouth to speak, and a violent shudder seized her. He reached for her, but she stepped back, shaking her head at him.

"You need help," he said.

She nodded, her body still shaking.

"Come in."

She seemed frozen, unable to move for the trembling. He stretched out a hand, but her fists only closed more tightly in the folds of the cloak. She pressed her lips together and blinked away tears.

"Should I carry you?" he asked.

"No." The word came out on a watery breath, but she took one limping step toward him and then another.

He nodded, backing toward the drawing room,

resisting the urge to touch her. "You are outdoing me, you know. I had to be carried into your hall."

Her eyes seemed to see him then, and he felt foolishly glad for that spark of life. He led her to the sofa and, with a brief touch, compelled her to sit. In the light he saw blood on her skirts.

He dropped to his knees and lifted one of her slippered feet. More blood on the ankle strap. Gently he pushed up the muddy gown. Her shin was a mass of bruises, her inner calf scraped raw. Trivial compared to wounds he'd seen in Spain, but unthinkable injury to the flesh of this girl.

"I scraped my leg climbing out the window," she said, her voice flat, numb.

"I'll take care of you." Words beyond his intention or his power, and yet he could not stop them.

He rang for Dowdeswell and knelt again at her feet, working the laces of the muddied slippers. Her silence worried him. Something ugly had happened to send her fleeing her home. "Your brother is giving a house party tonight. My friend Hunt is there."

"It's a card party."

He paused, his fingers suddenly stiff. Gaming, of course, her brother's passion. He pulled off the first slipper and worked at untangling the ties of the second. "There's drinking," he suggested.

"Gerrie is very drunk. He's losing." Her voice was faint. There could be only one thing for Gerald Merrifield to lose.

As the second slipper came off, Dowdeswell came to the door, and Leigh sent him for water, linen, and brandy.

There were no more revelations for a time. He dried her feet with his neckcloth, rubbing gently. He sensed her mind working its way back to some pain that must be faced, some act that had sent her from her home in the night.

Dowdeswell returned with a basin of water, halting abruptly at the sight of her wounded leg. Water sloshed onto the floor. Leigh took the bandages and brandy from the older man's unsteady hands.

"Make up a bed and some tea to warm her," he ordered.

Dowdeswell steadied himself. "Best to give her some laudanum, Mr. Nash. She'll not sleep else."

Leigh nodded and turned back to his patient. He tended her leg with warm water and brandy-soaked cloths, dressing it in fresh linen. Though the brandy must have stung, the pain drew no sound from her.

Dowdeswell returned and left a tea tray. As Leigh finished, her breath came out in a long shudder. "Thank you."

She looked around as if she were just recognizing her surroundings. He handed her a cup of tea with the laudanum, and with a confused look she let go her hold on the cloak.

"May I stay here?" she asked.

"You must," he said, hoping to spark some spirit in response to his tone of command.

A little resistance flared in her gaze but faded instantly. She gave him a small, sad smile. "Yes, I must. Gerrie's lost the hall." Another sigh escaped her, and she sipped her tea, lost for a moment in reflection. She was not telling him everything.

A powerful feeling mastered him. He wanted to hit Gerald Merrifield, a man he'd never seen, didn't know, who'd done no more than dozens before him, throwing away their substance on the turn of a card, beggaring their dependents. But he had no right to such rage. How little it had cost him to dismiss his home when Marcus lost it. Then, to suit his convenience, he, too, had put a woman out of her home.

He waited for some sign that Miss Merrifield was aware of him again, and when it came, he spoke. "Village gossip said your brother was coming home with a large party, hiring town servants, buying up wine and all the choicest cuts of meat. I thought he had repaired his fortune."

She stared at the dregs of her tea. "I believe he meant to. That was the idea behind the party. He explained it all to me, how there were to be three tables, how the odds favored him, how he knew the quirks of every one of his fellow players. He meant to win."

She lowered the teacup to her lap as if it had suddenly become too heavy for her, and he took it from her loose hold.

"He loved the hall when he was a boy. We . . ."

She fell asleep on the thought of a childhood companion who no longer existed.

He untied the strings of her cloak and lifted her from the couch. Her body seemed to curl into his. Her head found his shoulder. Her hair brushed against his jaw. The cloak fell open, revealing her white nightdress. The sweetness of her person filled his senses. As he carried her up to the chamber Dowdeswell had prepared for her, he imagined he was carrying a bride.

He laid her on the waiting bed and pulled the counterpane over her. He understood why the adventuring prince had fallen in love with the sleeping beauty. The world contracted to this point of strength and sweetness in Rosalind Merrifield's face.

But Dowdeswell stood at the door, and Leigh turned from her.

"Keep watch over her, Dowdeswell."

Leigh headed down the stairs.

Dowdeswell looked surprised, then knowing. "Going to the hall, Mr. Nash?"

"In the morning," said Leigh, halfway down the stairs.

"Plant Mr. Merrifield a facer," Dowdeswell recommended, coming down behind Leigh.

"Just what I had in mind." He found his coat and hat and pulled the entry door open.

"Where are you going now, sir?"

"To the inn, Dowdeswell."

A furious glare was the man's only reply.

Leigh smiled. It wouldn't do to let Dowdeswell think him heroic. The old fellow might let down his guard.

A country inn on a Saturday night, even at the early hour of midnight, did not offer the same company one found in the haunts of London at all hours, day or night. Still, there were a few customers in the taproom, enough to see him and note that he stayed below, drinking the night away. With any luck the innkeeper would gossip, and no one in Rowdene would connect their new curate with Rosalind Merrifield. He had just settled himself with a pint when he heard a familiar voice.

"Mr. Nash." Polly Rees came out of the shadows and settled her buxom self on the bench next to him.

Chapter 13

❧❧

Dew was on the grass and Squire Haythorne's gig at the door when Leigh entered
Merrifield Hall. It was a fine morning for knocking a scoundrel down, but he was cheated of the
satisfaction.

Gerald Merrifield lay sprawled at the foot of his
grand staircase, his neck broken, his sightless eyes
gazing heavenward. Leigh paused in the entry,
Rosalind Merrifield's words fresh in his mind.
Gerrie is very drunk. He's losing. She had fled the
hall before her brother died.

However Merrifield had died, the squire, as
magistrate, had been summoned to investigate.
Haythorne stood over the body, noting in a small
leather book the comments of a second gentleman. Leigh started toward them, and at the sound
of his footsteps they turned, neither pleased to see
him. It gave Leigh a little jolt to discover the
second man was Sydney Barton. He'd last seen
Barton paying court to Lady Winterburn.

Haythorne frowned at Leigh, and certain

heated conversations they'd had about candles and the poorhouse came to Leigh's mind.

Haythorne introduced Leigh and Barton.

"We've met." Leigh nodded to the other man. Barton had a pinched expression, as if he smelled some foul odor.

"Ugly business here, Nash." Haythorne turned to the dead man. "Gerald Merrifield's gone and broken his neck, and Miss Merrifield's nowhere to be found."

Leigh looked at Barton but saw no obvious uneasiness. The man had the self-possessed, indifferent air of a London gentleman. If he didn't know where Rosalind Merrifield was, she had not trusted him.

Haythorne checked his notebook and pointed up the stairs. "Now, you say, Barton, that Merrifield fell from the landing there."

Leigh glanced up. Sixteen polished oaken steps. "A sober man could slip on those stairs," he said.

"Merrifield was hardly sober," said Barton.

"According to witnesses?" Leigh asked. It was time to let Barton know there might be a different side to the story. "Miss Merrifield's at the parsonage, squire."

Both men turned to him.

"Well, why didn't you say so?" Haythorne looked impatient.

There was no change in Barton's bored, gentlemanly stance, but just for an instant there was a flicker in the cool stare.

"She should be sent for," Barton said stiffly.

"Squire, would you send your gig for her?"

Leigh asked. "She'll need a few things. Is Nan around?"

"No servants about," said Haythorne.

"None?" Leigh shifted his gaze to Barton. "Did they leave before or after Merrifield's fall?"

"Got that all here," said Haythorne. He tapped his notebook. "Barton's man, Crumb, found the body."

"And then the servants left?" Leigh asked. "There was a card party in progress, wasn't there?"

"Just so," said Haythorne. He looked down at the dead man and shook his head. "Drink and deep play did Merrifield in."

Leigh looked at Barton. "How much was Merrifield down?"

"As I told Squire Haythorne, Gerrie was distraught over heavy losses. He left the room, saying he was going to find his stake. When he didn't return, I sent a servant after him, and this is what he found."

"When?"

"Midnight? One?" Barton shrugged. "It was early yet."

There was a grain of truth in the account, Leigh was sure, but it did not explain Rosalind's flight. "Where are the other guests?"

Barton stiffened and glanced at Haythorne, who was studying the body and making further notes.

"Gamblers don't stay where the luck is bad," Barton said.

"Then Merrifield had no friends among them?"

"We were all friends."

Leigh raised a brow. "Yet no one closed Merrifield's eyes."

"See here, Nash," Haythorne said, slapping his notebook shut. "This is my investigation. It's a plain case. Don't muck it up. Get Miss Merrifield's things, while Mr. Barton and I conclude the business."

Leigh stepped over Gerald Merrifield and headed up the stairs. When he reached the landing, he looked down and caught a very different look on Barton's face, a look of extraordinary self-satisfaction. Leigh asked, "Which room is Miss Merrifield's?"

"Southeast corner," Barton said absently.

Leigh gripped the bannister hard and forced himself to keep climbing. He had no proof at the moment that Merrifield's death was other than the accident Barton described. No proof that Barton had anything to do with Rosalind Merrifield's flight from her home. But he meant to go on asking questions.

When he came down, the squire was shaking Barton's hand. "Word of a gentleman, of course. Don't want to make too much of this business. Would look bad for Miss Merrifield. Girl will inherit nought but debts as it is."

Barton looked a bit surprised, as if something unwelcome had occurred to him.

Leigh took a few minutes to write Rosalind Merrifield a note and dispatch the squire's man with the gig. Then he spoke to the squire about removing the body to a position of more dignity.

With the help of Barton's man, Crumb, Leigh was able to lay Merrifield out on one of the green baize tables in the drawing room. Crumb was hardly a talkative fellow, but Leigh kept up a string of questions about the party, the winners and losers, the staff, anything he could think of. The stiffening of Crumb's manner at certain questions hinted at what Barton had to hide. Hunt, too, would be able to tell Leigh more.

Rosalind Merrifield looked stronger in the morning light. She still limped, and there were shadows under her eyes, but she had abandoned the cloak for her usual clothes, and her gaze did not falter when Haythorne told her her brother had died. "He fell coming down the stairs."

Her glance followed the stairs up to the landing. Then she turned to Leigh. "Where is he?" she asked.

"In the drawing room." He offered his arm, and she took it.

At her brother's side, she reached down and closed a button gaping open on his waistcoat. "Leave us."

As Leigh closed the door, he saw her kneel and bend her head. She knelt as easily and naturally as she did everything, and he had no doubt that her prayers rose as easily and sincerely from her lips.

Gerald Merrifield was buried on an unseasonably hot, dry day in May. When Leigh returned to the parsonage, he found Hunt stretched out on a sofa in the darkened drawing room, eyes closed.

"What brings you here, Harry?"

"My deep interest in your tangled affairs, Winterburn."

Leigh raised an eyebrow. Dowdeswell brought them ale, and Leigh settled in a chair across from Hunt.

"Were there any mourners for the poor bastard?" Hunt asked.

"Miss Merrifield and Barton." Leigh did not mention Braithe, who had watched from a distance.

"I hope Miss Merrifield didn't weep."

"She didn't."

"Is she alone in the house?"

"I sent for a friend of hers, a widow, who will keep her company."

There was a stir from Hunt, nothing so definite as a movement, just a change in the quality of his languor. "Do you prefer her in black or in the white nightdress?"

Leigh refused to answer. "Hunt, what happened at that party?"

Hunt opened his eyes. "She didn't tell you?"

Leigh studied the beads of moisture on the ale cup. "Should I shoot Barton?"

"Lord, yes, on general principles, don't you think? He's going to take her house from her." Hunt's dangling hand settled on the rim of the ale cup on the carpet. "You are forgetting, though, that you are a man of the cloth. Turn the other cheek, that sort of thing."

"I may forget entirely."

Hunt pushed himself upright, propping his chin in the palm of one hand. "If I didn't know you so well, I'd suspect you of noble sentiments."

"Tell me what happened, Harry."

"Merrifield was badly dipped. They were about to bar him from play. I've never seen a man as mad for the table as he was. He brought the girl down in her nightdress before them all, called her 'The Rose of Rowdene' or some such thing, set a price on her."

It stunned him. He remembered her hands clutching the folds of the cloak around her, the same hands closing the gaping button of her brother's waistcoat. Merrifield sold her, and she forgave him. It pierced him. She had too much goodness in her nature.

Hunt was watching him, and Leigh recalled the thread of their conversation. "No one stopped him?"

"He insisted he couldn't lose." Hunt shook his head and took a draft of his ale.

"How did she get out?"

"I arranged a little assistance for her. After the first box at the faro table."

"Faro!" Leigh left his chair and paced the dim room. Betting on the turn of a card, no skill involved, just dumb luck between his sister's honor and ruin.

"Alice and Jenny—Crawley's tarts from a

house on Norris Street—were more than willing to help."

"Then you left? Before Merrifield fell."

"Yes. I thought it best that Barton not connect me with her escape."

"You say Barton's going to take the house from her? I thought Crawley was the big winner against her brother."

"Barton didn't need to win. He fronted the money for the party."

Leigh could see the cleverness of Barton's scheme. How easy to offer Merrifield money for a card party to recoup his losses. Then the vouchers Barton held would have court recognition as debts of honor did not.

Hunt was watching him from lazy, heavy-lidded eyes. "Lucetta's offended. Incensed."

"You didn't really think I'd go to her, did you?" He wanted to show nothing but indifference.

"Perhaps not. But to go to Polly Rees?"

"I didn't."

Hunt just looked at him. "A half dozen unreliable, gossiping witnesses saw you leave the common room with Miss Rees. Others saw you enter the humble cottage she shares with her father. It's the talk of the village."

"The final irony. Damned for what I didn't do." Taking Polly home had been the only way to rid himself of her company that night. "I suppose you'll go back to London to collect your reward."

Hunt unfolded his length from the sofa, rising slowly to his feet. "Soon enough." From the doorway he looked back at Leigh. "Winterburn,

Miss Merrifield needs money, a great deal of it, and soon."

Leigh saw the bitter satisfaction in his friend's face.

"Money," Hunt repeated. "You won't be able to save her without it."

A scowling maid in a ridiculous cap led Sydney Barton to Miss Merrifield's drawing room. It was his third call on the girl. He had not counted on Merrifield's death or the girl's resistance to his plans. Even before the funeral he had been forced to move to the inn, an inferior establishment, where his chief consolation for the discomforts of damp sheets and greasy food had been his energetic couplings with the village slut, Polly Rees.

It did him good, though, to be back in the house. Each visit stirred his imagination about what could be done with the rooms, and he had begun to think of a livery for his servants which would fit the style of the place. Miss Merrifield had removed the hired furnishings, but the drawing room retained its quiet elegance. His prints would do very well above the balustrade carving of the mantel. Miss Merrifield had drawn together a pair of comfortable armchairs and a table in the light from the tall east windows. There she sat with the Widow Fowler.

Sydney concealed his irritation as he crossed to them. His mother had been just such a widow, wasting away in black gowns too large for her frame, making herself useful to a series of relatives, taking whatever corner she could find for herself and her son. He had wanted to rage at her then, to goad her into defiance just once, but he never had, and she had faded away entirely, once her relations had paid his Cambridge fees.

He greeted the ladies and rang for a chair, which he pulled up at Rosalind Merrifield's side. The widow had a dry, sweet scent, like a faint sachet in a drawer, and he wanted to keep about him the earthier odor of Polly Rees.

"Mr. Barton, you will be paid," said Miss Merrifield.

"Miss Merrifield. You must not imagine that I call on you today merely to collect a payment like some dun. You must not think I am lost to all finer feelings."

"But I do, Mr. Barton." She smiled sweetly as she said it and reached across to the widow, whose hands had stopped their motion. Miss Merrifield gave the other woman's arm a squeeze, and the woman collected herself, came back from whatever past scene had claimed her, and smiled warmly at Miss Merrifield.

Sydney changed his tactics. "Your drawing room remains elegant, Miss Merrifield, even without furnishings. Did you ever have a pianoforte in the room?" He glanced at the widow. "Mrs. Fowler, does Miss Merrifield play?"

Mrs. Fowler looked up in surprise, as if she'd forgotten she might be addressed. "Oh dear, yes," she said. "There was an instrument here once, wasn't there, Rosalind?"

The remark drew another smile from Miss Merrifield for her friend. "There was. Mother was the accomplished musician of course."

"Well," said Sydney. "I think you should have an instrument again, Miss Merrifield. Perhaps your mother's instrument might be recovered. Did your brother sell it? Through that man Hinkson?"

Miss Merrifield gave him a contemptuous smile. "You will be paid, Mr. Barton."

He leaned toward her. The scent of his sexual encounter with Polly and the fragrance of Rosalind Merrifield mingled nicely in his nostrils. "We need not have any bitterness between us. Your brother made meticulous plans to recover from his losses in town, and as a friend I could do no less than support him every step of the way. Tragically, his plans miscarried, but that very tragedy has brought us together—two who appreciate this house as he never could."

"Do you believe your own lies, Mr. Barton?"

The widow looked up, and Sydney rocked back. "Miss Merrifield, conciliation would be a wiser approach in your circumstances. You may not fully understand the nature of your brother's debts, but I assure you your man of business does."

"You will be paid."

"So you say." He could be patient. The girl would come around. He had made his position clear to her man of business. "I would ask you to consider another arrangement between us. In exchange for this house and property, I am prepared to settle your brother's other debts and to provide a reasonable dowry for yourself. I have friends in London who would be pleased to sponsor you for a season or longer until you make a match to your liking."

"Until you sell me off to the highest bidder?" Miss Merrifield leveled her gaze at him. "No, thank you, Mr. Barton."

He looked away. She would make him lose his temper. He watched Mrs. Fowler's progress at her sewing, and thought again of his mother's wretched humility. Rosalind Merrifield should learn some meekness. He stood slowly, letting his gaze slide over her, a reminder of her humiliation in this very room.

"You are sure, Miss Merrifield, that we can't deal together in some way?"

"Very sure."

"Then you leave me no alternative. By law this house will be mine by quarter day."

"Unless," she said, "you receive your money."

"Of course." He bowed and showed himself out.

Leigh went to Rosalind Merrifield in the late afternoon on the day after the funeral and waited impatiently in her sitting room. He had planned to keep his distance from her, to let her mourn her brother, and to allow any gossip that might arise from his sheltering her at the parsonage to die. But Hunt's information changed everything.

Hunt woke Leigh from the dream of playing parson, just as battle had once wakened him from the dream of playing soldier. He had become a thorough fraud, visiting the poor, arguing with the squire, lighting a few candles, all while seeking Rosalind Merrifield's kisses. The part he had played in her life had been ungentlemanly, contemptible.

He could not explain it to himself. After months of indifference to women, he had seen Rosalind and wanted her. He had lied to himself, pretending he could resist her when every encounter proved he could not. Nothing could excuse him. His nature had been clear to him from his youth.

Now she was going to lose her home. The only decent thing he could do was to offer her the one he had taken from her friend. He would ask her to marry him. He realized the idea had first occurred to him when he'd carried her, like a swooning bride, to his bed. The plan had everything to recommend it, he thought. The parsonage was not the hall, but she was fond of it. They would deal well together in bed, and he would encourage her to lead her life as freely as she now did. He would invite her to bring Mrs. Fowler with her. And if Rosalind accepted him, he would be free to kiss her without restraint.

She entered the sitting room and closed the door behind her. Even the late-afternoon shadows in the room and her gray mourning gown could not dim her brilliance. He took hold of the back of a nearby chair to keep from moving toward her. He meant to resist temptation until he made his proposal.

She caught the movement of his hand and cast him a questioning glance.

"How are you?" he asked.

"I'm not giving in to despair," she said, her brown gaze steady. "Will you sit?"

"In a moment," he said, watching her take a seat, her hands smoothing her skirts. His proposal stuck in his throat. "How is Mrs. Fowler?" he asked. He had been shocked at the shrunken figure of a woman he had called for at the coaching inn in Adstrop.

She seemed to read his thoughts. "She's better today. Thank you for bringing her to me."

"She's plainly suffered. Do you blame me?"

Her quick forgiving glance made his heart leap. She shook her head. "The loss of the parsonage was hard, but her brother is more to blame for her present state than you are. He makes her feel her dependence so much that she's afraid to eat or speak or even rest in his house. She's exhausted."

Her words raised a real doubt about his plan. Rosalind Mérrifield did not like dependence of any sort. He crossed to the mantel and leaned an elbow on it, looking down at her. "But I brought Mrs. Fowler to help you," he said.

She looked up. "That's the cure, you see. Jane will improve rapidly, just knowing she's a help to me. I'll keep her busy in the garden."

It was what Sister Luzia had done for him. He

straightened and pushed away from the mantel. "Hunt says Barton is going to take this house from you."

"What?" She jumped up and strode to the window.

"Is it true that you can't meet your brother's debts to Barton any other way?" he asked, sick to be pressing her for an answer.

She stared out on the green sweep of Merrifield land. "I won't let Barton have the hall."

"How will you pay him?"

She looked back over her shoulder. "You don't have a few thousand pounds to spare, do you?" she asked.

He tried to read her expression, to gauge how serious she was in asking. Hunt's words came back to him. *Someday, Winterburn, you'll want money.* "I haven't, you know," he said. "Not even fifty pounds to free your friend, Mary Fletcher." It was one of the saddest things he'd ever said.

He left the hearth and strolled toward her place at the window. "I came to Rowdene because I had no money. My brother, Marcus, like Gerald, had a passion that ruined him. Us. The living at Rowdene was one of the few things left."

He stopped opposite her, his gaze fixed on hers. Her eyes, which might have scorned or condemned him, seemed full of quiet understanding. He clenched his fists to keep from touching her.

She seemed to sense his temptation and turned away, moving around the room, touching things as if to reassure them of her care. He cleared his throat.

She halted at a little round table and looked up from straightening its clutter. "Thank you for telling me. I have judged you unfairly."

He let a short harsh laugh escape him. "I think not."

"Yes, you are generous and kind."

He wished it were true. He lost himself momentarily in eyes that made him believe it was true. But what he felt was maddened lust. In fact, his splendid proposal no longer seemed worthy of her. What was it but lust and selfishness? What did he offer but dependence?

She moved again, and his eyes followed her straight, sweet form. "Since you've no money to spare," she said, "I must find my own way to pay Barton, for I cannot let him have the hall."

Her own way. She had been finding it for years without him. He admired that self-sufficiency in her.

"I am expecting Mr. Harwood, our family man of business, this afternoon. He will advise me." She offered him a brave smile. "I still have hope, you see, that something can be done. It must be done."

Leigh swallowed the last illusion that his proposal was for her good. While there was a chance that she could save her home, he could not tie her to him. "Then I should take my leave," he said, but a shaft of light caught her hair, and he lost the will to act on the words.

"Yes." She, too, had a lost look.

"I came to kiss you, you know. I tried to cover it in polite, clerical concern for a grieving neighbor, but you should not be deceived." He crossed to the door and grasped the handle firmly. "I have been lusting after you since I came to Rowdene, Miss Merrifield."

Rosalind offered Mr. Harwood tea and biscuits while he laid out papers for her perusal. She was still reeling from Winterburn's unexpected confession of desire. He had come and charged the atmosphere of her life, and she was left waiting for the storm that would clear the air.

But now she must think of Merrifield. The terrible thing was that Sydney Barton had the power to deprive Rosalind not only of her home but of her power to do good. If she lost the hall, she could not offer shelter and comfort to anyone who needed her. Unless Mr. Harwood had seen some way out of her situation. She watched him as he laid out documents. He had the same calm, unruffled air she had always appreciated in him. She could not imagine Mr. Harwood shouting or running a hand through his very neat hair or leaving his buttons unfastened. She poured them both tea.

"Thank you, my dear," he said absently, laying out the last of several papers. He glanced up then and adjusted his spectacles to the proper place on the bridge of his nose. And then he simply looked at her, quietly and without speaking for a minute.

She put aside her tea, reading in his expression the news she feared to receive. He beckoned, and she came around and stood beside him, looking at the trail of papers.

"You can't win, my dear," he said. He pointed to the first paper. "Here is the sum of Mr. Barton's claim."

She looked at the staggering amount.

"Here is all of the ready the estate can produce by quarter day."

Rosalind sighed. It was more than she had expected and so much less than what was needed.

Mr. Harwood's finger moved to a third page. "Here is the figure of other outstanding claims against your brother, excluding gaming debts. Mr. Barton explained his willingness to discharge these under certain conditions?"

"Repellant conditions."

"Just so. Well, then." Mr. Harwood drew his handkerchief from his pocket and polished his spectacles. "Here's what we can get from a mortgage." He pointed to an encouraging sum. "And here's what we might be able to get from an appropriate tenant."

It was not enough. She could mortgage the estate and pay off Barton, but she could not then meet the mortgage and the demands of other creditors. The papers formed a neat box around her hopes.

"You cannot save the hall, my dear," Harwood said quietly. "You must think of saving yourself." He put an arm around her shoulder and gave her the lightest squeeze, an uncharacteristic gesture, and like the kindness extended her by the London tarts, it threatened her composure. She took a deep, steadying breath.

"And how shall I save myself?" she asked.

Mr. Harwood looked at her in surprise. "Why, marriage, of course. You must have thought of it sometime these three years. It is a gentlewoman's surest provision from want."

"Ah, Mr. Harwood." She smiled at him. "I have not been besieged by suitors."

"That, my dear, is because you've hidden yourself in the country."

"So, you think I ought to go to London and sell myself on the marriage mart?"

"Sell yourself? My dear, I only meant you should find a decent husband, a man of property and integrity."

"Do you know any, Mr. Harwood?" She was teasing him now, but he removed his spectacles again, giving them an unnecessary cleaning, giving her question serious thought.

"I believe I do," he said, readjusting his glasses on his nose.

"And do you think I could find a husband among them by quarter day?"

"You are teasing me, miss," he said. "But I shall put my mind to it." He took up a pen and made a solemn note. "A husband for Miss Merrifield by Midsummer Quarter Day."

"Make him very rich," she said.

"Very rich," he added to the note.

"Now, then," he said, "there's one more thing I think you ought to do for yourself." He took up another of the papers. "Bonaparte is going to meet Wellington in the next few weeks. It's inevitable. And I think you should have some money in the funds. When the battle comes, hold on, ride it out, and you will have your own dowry. What do you say to that?"

"Fine."

They were back to the unhappy truth of her situation. Mr. Harwood began to pick up the papers and pack them in his case. "I will settle with Barton whenever you wish me to," he said. "We can hold out for perhaps another fortnight."

"Mr. Harwood, I'm willing to give Barton money, but not the hall, never the hall."

Chapter 14

A light evening breeze fluttered the long red pennants on the supper tent of the mid-May fair at Adstrop. Rosalind coaxed Jane up the dusty track filled with country folk headed toward the tents and booths and pens of animals. People offered greetings, children dashed around them, and a huge man in a shepherd's smock swung Jane over a muddy ditch which crossed the road. While the fair lasted, everyone present seemed to feel the links that bound them together and to the land.

Rosalind had not thought to go this year. She'd come to Adstrop to arrange the sale of more of her father's library. The library shelves were emptying fast, and she was but a few guineas closer to paying off Barton. For the moment, however, she refused to think how far she truly was from the required sum. The fair beckoned.

And Jane had agreed to take tea and supper there, a victory for Rosalind over her friend's still weak appetite. At the supper tent, however, militiamen in scarlet coats lounged on benches, talk-

ing of the expected battle between Wellington and
Bonaparte. As Rosalind entered, their conversation lapsed, and one of them called, "Sweetheart,
here's a spot to rest easy." He slapped his thighs.
Rosalind shook her head and urged Jane out of
the tent. "We'll come back for supper."

A row of booths stretched up the meadow,
enticing fairgoers to purchase trinkets or play
games, and Rosalind steered Jane toward them.
Rosalind was wondering if Winterburn could be
somewhere in the crowd when Jane tugged her
sleeve. "I think I see Mr. Braithe, Roz."

Rosalind followed Jane's gaze, looking out over
a sea of bobbing hats to a straw one with a black
band. She could not be sure it was his. Jeremy was
more likely to be at the pens where sheep and
cattle were auctioned off, but she said nothing.
Jane's notice of the hat meant she was not lost in
visions of the past.

Rosalind fixed her gaze on the man in the straw
hat and pushed forward through the jostling
throng.

"There's our straw hat," she said to Jane. "Just a
bit further."

"Ladies," a barker shouted, stepping into their
path, and startling Jane, who clutched Rosalind's
arm. "Do ye care to see a wonder?" He tried to
induce them to enter a booth displaying a two-
headed snake, and the crowd shifted, bunching
up around him to hear the outrageous particulars
of the freaks on display inside. In the space that
opened Rosalind could see the straw-hatted
man's booth clearly. He stood before it under a

painted sign which showed a round of cheese with one wedge cut out. Mrs. Cole waved from behind the counter, and Rosalind remembered Braithe's scheme to make sheep's cheese.

The man in the hat looked their way, and even as he did so, she knew it was not Braithe at all. Her stomach took a sudden turn like a goose on a spit. The hat suited Winterburn.

The setting sun played tricks with her vision, showing her not the arrogant lord, but the neighbor and friend whose kindnesses were as plain and unexpected as his hat. Only his eyes reminded her of his mysterious pull. Some feeling transformed their grayness into dazzling silver.

He doffed the hat and greeted Jane, drawing a smile from her and engaging her in undemanding talk while Rosalind stood silent, too aware of him for easy speech. Mrs. Cole joined them until her two little girls appeared, demanding cheese and bread. Jane laughed at seeing the girls and asked about their brother. Two sheepish faces confessed that they'd abandoned him. Mrs. Cole was alarmed, and Jane offered to go with the girls to find the boy.

In the blink of an eye, the whole scene changed, leaving Rosalind and Winterburn alone in the midst of the fair. Jane followed the children. Mrs. Cole became absorbed in her cheeses. Dozens of people moved and talked and laughed about them, caught up in the ordinary and familiar. No one remarked on them, frozen, gazes consuming each other, freed by the indifference of the crowd to look their fill. Rosalind was incapable of feeling any other presence but his. He'd come to kiss her, and she saw the unfulfilled intention in his eyes. He was not more than an arm's length from her, and she clasped her hands together to keep from reaching out to him.

He moved then, a quick step to the side, putting his back to the crowd, shielding her from it. "This is an impossible situation." His breath came out in a rough gust. "I can't kiss you here."

Rosalind clasped her hands more tightly and pressed her lips together. She looked at the ground, trying to fix herself firmly in the real world. The gray skirts of her mourning dress stirred the dust and straw. She raised her head.

"How are you faring?" He watched her eyes.

It was a terrible question. She was tempted to tell him how afraid she was, how desperate, how unable to conceive that she might lose the hall. If she told him, if she let go of the burden for a minute, she did not think she could take it up again. "I'm managing," she said.

His eyes said he did not believe her, and she looked away.

Beyond them she could see her bailiff, Mr. Symonds, going among the laborers offering themselves for hire. They stood in their smocks, tools in hand signaling their availability for harvest work later in the summer. For the first time in her life, men from Rowdene stood in the crowd, waiting to be hired away from Merrifield. Families would be pulled apart, sweethearts separated. And when Barton took possession, things would be worse. Croy would lose his cottage.

Winterburn followed her gaze. "Did Harwood have a solution for you?"

Her throat contracted. "I won't let Barton have Merrifield. Only money, only what he's owed."

He looked at her with sudden intensity. "Listen," he said, "Barton may have cheated your brother. If we talked to the guests—"

He was interrupted by a shout. They were facing the horse pens where a man had mounted the auctioneer's block. A score of buyers hung on the rails of the pen, examining the horses inside. A trainer brought out a chestnut mare and led her around the pen.

"What am I bid for this three-year-old mare?" the auctioneer asked. "She's sweet-natured and smart."

"She's lame," shouted a man from the crowd.

The auctioneer ignored the heckler. "Pretty, too, and she knows her paces."

The buyers, all farmers Rosalind knew, seemed to focus an unwavering attention on the gentle mare. A man's hand went up, and the auctioneer caught and shouted his bid. Then another and another, so that the numbers ran together in the rippling cadence of the auctioneer's speech until he shouted, "Sold!" Rosalind blinked. The coaxing of the auctioneer had driven up the mare's price to an astonishing figure in a few minutes. She watched as two more horses were sold.

It was a far different process from the haggling she did with Hinkson or the buyers for her father's library. Here the advantage seemed all to the seller. She wondered if she should not arrange an auction of her father's remaining books.

She turned to Winterburn and saw that he had anticipated her thought.

"What will you auction?" he asked.

"My father's books and perhaps—"

"What's wrong with cow's milk, I ask ye, Mrs. Cole?" a deep voice asked.

They both turned to the cheese booth.

"Why, nought's wrong wi' it, Mr. Sloath, but nought's wrong wi' sheep's milk either. Ye've got to try it." Mrs. Cole gave him a sweet smile, and the man accepted a morsel of cheese, tasting it with a skeptical frown. More customers gathered around the big man. A woman demanded a sample, and Winterburn undertook to persuade her of the wholesome properties of the cheese.

Rosalind stepped aside, whispering to him, "I see your sales have less to do with the quality of the goods than with the charms of the sellers."

She watched the continuing auction, wondering if Mr. Harwood could arrange such a thing as she had in mind.

When she turned back to Winterburn, Lady Ellenby and her daughters had claimed his attention.

"Sheep's cheese is such a strange idea, Mr. Nash," said Catherine Ellenby. "So eastern. Makes one think of harems."

She gave Winterburn's arm a flirtatious tap. Her mother frowned.

Winterburn slanted Rosalind a glance. He knew

he was being flirted with. "Taste it with some good English bread, Miss Ellenby. You'll find it less exotic."

From the booth Mrs. Cole handed him a slice of bread topped with a thin layer of cheese. Catherine exchanged a look with Julia and both tittered.

"We heard, Mr. Nash," said Julia, "that you milked the sheep yourself."

He turned an amused gaze to her but kept a straight face. "An experience I've no desire to repeat," he said.

The girls refused the offered cheese, dissolving into unconcealed laughter. Rosalind watched them, thinking of Sally Candover and how they had giggled in their school days at the slightest attention from a handsome man. Winterburn, it seemed, could melt the brain of any female who came near him.

Just then a young woman shouldered her way between Lady Ellenby's girls into a little space before Winterburn. Her bright golden hair was escaping its pins. Her striped skirts were soiled, and her pretty face was flushed with anger. Rosalind recognized Polly, the girl who cleaned at the parsonage. She came to a halt, breathing hard, and planted her clenched fists on her hips.

"Mr. Nash," she cried, "I must speak to ye."

The giggles stopped. Polly's tone caught the ears of several bystanders, who turned to watch whatever drama would unfold.

"What's wrong?" Winterburn asked.

"Ye lied to me," she said, taking hold of his coat sleeve and giving a sob.

He stiffened. "Lied to you?"

"Ye told me I wouldn't get in any trouble, but now I have."

"What trouble?" His voice was low and cold, the words distinct in the hush that had fallen around him.

The girl sobbed again, her shoulders shaking. "Ye must know, and ye must own to it. Ye've given me a belly full of child."

Lady Ellenby gasped. Catherine and Julia gaped unabashedly. In a blink the indifferent crowd was watching closely. Rosalind saw staring eyes in every direction. From somewhere Mr. Hunt and Miss King appeared. Whispers rippled back from the edge of the crowd, which seemed to press in on the girl and Winterburn. Only Winterburn's friend Frimley stood back a little, looking sick.

Winterburn removed Polly's arm from his sleeve. His face betrayed no surprise. Rather, he looked as if he'd expected the accusation all along. "Who wants you to say this, Polly?" His eyes were colder than Rosalind had ever seen them.

The girl backed away from him, then her chin came up at a defiant angle. "I say it myself."

He let them wait, let her wait, all staring, hungry for some further revelation. Rosalind did not believe it, yet she could not breathe, waiting for his denial.

Then he spoke. "It's a lie." The reply was so calm, so indifferent, so dismissive, it seemed to take away Polly's breath.

She let out a long wail. More sobs shook her. "There's those that saw ye walk me home from the inn, Mr. Nash."

"A walk through the village, nothing more."

"Ye won't own to knowing me, Mr. Nash, because yer a fine lord, but ye've known me all the same." She looked around at the crowd, making sure she had all eyes on her. "Ye know him as Mr. Nash, but that's not who he is at all. He's Winterburn. Let him deny that, too."

"Winterburn?" said Lady Ellenby, affronted, stiff with outrage.

"Yes." The word came out as a hiss from Polly. She spun around, facing the crowd. "With fine airs and London friends."

"May not a highborn man serve as our parson?" Rosalind inquired quietly. His bleak gaze found hers briefly.

"High is as high does, miss." Polly sneered at Rosalind, then twisted and pointed at Miss King. "There's his London whore." Miss King smiled wickedly, and Polly's pointing finger swung toward Rosalind. "And there's a high and mighty miss who's had her time in his bed."

Rosalind felt all the color drain from her. Her stomach contracted painfully. Her limbs froze.

Lady Ellenby drew herself up and sent Rosalind a withering glance. "See what comes of your foolish independence, miss." She glared at Winterburn. "Vile seducer, deceiver, we will have you out of that parsonage." With a haughty toss of her head, she beckoned her gaping daughters and pulled them from the circle.

Winterburn grabbed Polly's arm in a cruel grip. "Lie about me, but not about Miss Merrifield." He looked at the crowd. "I have not seduced anyone."

Polly looked wildly about. "Liar!" she shouted, writhing in his hold. "Don't I know yer body? Don't I know the scars? The one that starts just there on yer shoulder and curves down across yer breast, and the one that starts low on yer ribs and goes up 'em. Wicked scars they are. And yer a wicked man to show 'em to a girl and deny it."

Rosalind felt the sick knot in her stomach twist more tightly at the mention of his scars, the scars that had moved her to pity him.

Winterburn searched the faces of the crowd, and Rosalind knew what he saw: doubt, distrust, even hatred. Mrs. Cole hung her head, not looking at him or offering any support.

"I do deny it." He flung Polly away and turned, but the girl launched herself at his back, clinging and clawing, as if mad with rage and betrayal.

Hunt stepped forward swiftly and pulled her off his friend. "Miss Rees," he said sharply, "come away. You do not help your case with this outburst." He gave Winterburn an ironic look.

"You stayed to see the fall, Harry," Winterburn said.

Polly cast one last despairing glance at Winterburn and allowed herself to be led away.

Rosalind looked at him. He was changed again in her sight, the gray of his eyes as cold and hard as stone. He looked as he had when the candles were snuffed in the church, empty and enraged.

"The show is over," he said tightly to the cluster of onlookers still standing about, waiting as Rosalind was for more of his denial, for something that would alter the balance in his favor.

He bent to pluck up the straw hat, which lay on the ground, then stopped and simply walked away into the dusk.

The crowd began to murmur at once, and Jane appeared at Rosalind's side, tugging urgently at her sleeve. "Come away, dear. Come away."

Rosalind yielded to the plea in Jane's voice, and they hurried down the path out of the fair, colliding with a burly man in a smock, who grumbled at them. Somewhere a horse squealed in fright. The crowd suddenly seemed weary and cross.

Jane's worried murmur in her ear kept Rosalind moving, but her thoughts tumbled crazily through the scenes of the afternoon. His eyes haunted her, silver and stone. She stopped abruptly, feeling that she had left something behind, something so precious, she could hardly do without it. A sob escaped her.

"Don't stop, dear. Don't stop," Jane said.

But Rosalind could not move. The sky was dark, and she understood what had been lost at the fair. For Winterburn, for her. Joy. That had been the transforming light in his eyes, and it was gone.

Chapter 15

Leigh put out the lamp and let the darkness close around him. Tonight his studies had been without purpose, an act of habit. His books lay open on the dining table, the wisdom they offered inaccessible to his dark mind and soul. He had been playing at parson, a sinner who couldn't pray.

He had underestimated his mother, thinking she would be powerless to interfere with his life in Rowdene, but she had sent Hunt and Frimley and Lucetta—and hired Polly. Sure of his resistance to Polly's obvious lures, he had missed what she really was, his mother's tool. If he had recognized Polly's cunning, he would have noted the signs. She had known who he was even that first day. At the fair she had not wanted justice for herself or aid for the unknown babe. She had wanted a scene, the sort of scene a poor girl could not afford in a small village. He doubted there was a babe, wondered how much Polly had been paid, and imagined that Trevor had been obliged to hire the girl. That was the way his mother worked.

He had had an odd moment of clarity at the fair, standing before his neighbors, accused of sins he had not committed, punished surely for all those he had, for the very sinfulness of his nature. He had been fifteen when his mother arranged his first lessons in self-knowledge through the embraces of a pregnant housemaid. Then because he had claimed to love Fanny, his mother had arranged a further lesson for him. Their father had taken Leigh and Trevor to an exclusive brothel, where, in the arms of two practiced courtesans, his body's desires made a mockery of his heart.

He had not had time to recover his wits after the excesses of that night when he had been summoned to his mother's boudoir. She sat at her writing desk in a silk wrapper, her hair down, an unmistakable sensuality about her. He would not have recognized it before, but then he did.

He faced her in his crumpled clothes, his breath stale, his head aching, his body ripe with the scents of his own sweat and seed and the perfume of whores.

She put down her pen. "Well," she asked, "have you a bit more wisdom this morning than you showed me last week?" There was no sympathy in her gaze. His schoolmasters were more lenient with his faults.

"I loved her," he said doggedly of Fanny, who had been his lover for a few glorious days, but it seemed a dream and he could not believe his own words any longer.

"You fancied yourself in love. Now you will judge such feelings more accurately."

He wanted to protest, but recollections of his own acts in the brothel stilled his tongue. He felt exposed, his pretensions to be anything fine and good stripped away.

"You have a carnal nature. It's an advantage if you use it well. Women will fall in love with you."

He opened his mouth to protest, but a gesture silenced him.

"A carnal nature can also be a weakness," she warned. "Do not let it mislead you into making extravagant sacrifices for the use of a woman's body." She took up her pen and returned to the letter she was writing.

He decided then that, if he was carnal, he would be unabashedly carnal. Within a week he had taken Hunt and Frimley back to that very brothel and astonished the denizens of the place with his appetite for indulgence of every kind. It had been years before he stopped. His affair with Lucetta King had been his last defiant assertion of his carnal self.

In Portugal and Spain he thought the blood and terror of war had washed away his old self. At the *Convento do Desterro* he had filled his days with work, letting his wounds heal. Wheels turned everywhere in the village: the huge, screeching wheels on the carts, the waterwheel below the bridge on the river, the humming wheel in the village potter's shop, the wheel in the church tower. Somehow his wounded head had taken in the wheels and made a vision. It was what he had told Sister Luzia, his friend in the convent kitchen. She had laughed at him. "You understand nothing." She had tapped his chest, like a bird pecking at seed. "Not even who you are."

Today he had remembered who he was. Rosalind Merrifield's wounded eyes were just the mirror to reveal him to himself.

He turned away from his books and went up the parsonage stairs in the dark. At his bedroom window he stood looking down at the church, a darker shadow in the night. It seemed farther away than ever.

"Sir." Dowdeswell's voice came from behind him in the dark.

He looked over his shoulder.

"Best to come away from the window, sir."

He started to ask why, but a noise made him turn back to the window. Lights moved in the darkness, a dozen or more torches held above a loosely formed crowd coming up the road from the village. He cracked the window open.

"Sir." Dowdeswell's voice was sharp with alarm.

The crowd came on, banging pots, shouting, screeching a song he did not recognize. In their midst was some odd bundle carried aloft on a hurdle.

"What is it, Dowdeswell?"

"A country custom, sir." Dowdeswell's voice sank.

The flicker of the torches showed two figures grotesquely entwined, a woman with golden curls and striped skirts about her waist, a man with black hair and a straw hat, the hat he'd left at the fair.

The crowd reached the parsonage walk and spilled through the narrow gate, fanning out over the lawn, silent except for whispers and grunts of exertion. They set the hurdle on the lawn, and someone unfurled a banner across it. Then the banging began again.

Leigh leaned closer to the window, but Dowdeswell touched his arm.

"Don't show yerself, sir," Dowdeswell whispered.

The torches were bunched together now, illuminating the figures clearly. The ugly word on the banner was plain. The crowd began shouting. A hail of objects thudded against the house. Somewhere below a window shattered, and the reek of ordure and rot rose up to Leigh's nostrils.

"Fornicator!" they cried.

Then the crowd receded like an angry tide, tumbling back over the gate.

"Will they hurt the church?" Leigh asked.

"No, sir, 'twas meant for you."

"Then they've done. Good night, Dowdeswell."

The library of Mr. Harwood's London house had become Rosalind's refuge. Though it had not the grand scale of the library at Merrifield, it had the same air of timelessness and calm. The vast, continuous bustle of the city, its noise, its smells, its concerns, seemed distant in the library. And it was the one room Mrs. Harwood had not filled. Every other room had its corners stuffed with chairs and tables, cushions and porcelain figures. After the spareness of the hall, Rosalind felt cramped in the well-furnished rooms of the Harwoods' house.

Rosalind sipped tea and watched Mr. Harwood

lay out his papers, papers that would soon free her and Merrifield from Barton. She had been with the Harwoods a week, and Mr. Harwood had astonished her with the refinements he'd made to the idea she'd brought him.

Her first thought as she and Jane stumbled from the fair was that she must leave Rowdene, must distance herself from this pain. If Jane had not clung to her arm, she would have gone into Adstrop and taken the first stage as far as she could go. But she returned to the hall and made sure Jane was comfortable. Then she went up to the library. She had the thought that she could go to Mr. Harwood to arrange an auction of her father's books, but the empty shelves mocked her. There in the dark she remembered the little mare in the ring and the cries of the eager buyers, and knew that she had something to sell after all.

Mr. Harwood had tied Barton's hands with some legal maneuver, giving them time to arrange an auction, and he had built undreamed of safeguards into every step of her plan. She would not be paraded through a pen while men shouted bids for her. She would be auctioned from this very room, her future and the future of Merrifield secured by contracts of the most binding sort.

"Now, my dear," said Mr. Harwood, straightening the last paper. "All is in order." He beckoned her to him, and she put aside her tea. "Let's consider your course again."

He settled his spectacles on his nose and pointed to the first document. "Here are the names of the men of substance and property who have indicated an interest in our auction." Rosalind was now familiar with each name. His hand moved to the second document. "Here is the contract all participants must sign."

Rosalind nodded. The men had pledged to protect her reputation with silence.

Mr. Harwood's hand shifted to a third paper. "Here is the marriage contract your husband-to-be must sign. It puts Merrifield in the hands of your trustee."

Rosalind had discussed these arrangements before, but she knew he was proud of them and allowed him to continue.

"The device of the trustee keeps the property in your name when you marry and insures that you may return to it at regular intervals and at such times as the management of the estate requires your attendance."

He paused before moving to the final paper. "Here is a special license granting you the right to marry when and where it is convenient."

"Thank you," she said.

Mr. Harwood shook his head. "No gratitude yet. Perhaps I've overlooked something." He peered at the papers as if they offended him in some way. Then he turned to her and took her gently by the shoulders. "You could stay with us, my dear. Indefinitely. Mrs. Harwood and I are fond of you, you know. You could have your pick of suitors. Choose from among these very men, I daresay. In a more conventional manner."

Rosalind felt the ache in her throat that had troubled her all week. The Harwoods were kind and generous. They had fitted up a little room in the back of the house overlooking a small walled garden, a thoughtful arrangement that only served to remind her of how far she was from Merrifield. Merrifield, enclosed in its own green garden as far as the eye could see. Even if she could bring herself to let Barton have Merrifield, she could not remain in the city, and she could not endure a courtship.

She could not marry for love. Her heart had shrunk to a dry and withered thing. She had seen Polly rail and cry and had known that she, too, would howl if she had given herself to Winterburn and he'd betrayed her. To marry another man for love when her heart was empty was impossible. To pretend would require powers of deception she did not possess.

"Thank you, Mr. Harwood. Your kindness . . ."

He stopped her, lifting his hands from her shoulders and waving away her thanks. "If we gave Barton just the hall, we could still provide you with a measure of independence through a trustee. And you could choose a husband, instead of allowing a husband to choose you."

She got hold of herself, returning Mr. Harwood's earnest gaze calmly. "But how could I choose among them? All men of substance and integrity, men of sterling qualities." She hazarded a small smile.

"Just so. But that does not mean, my dear, that

in the . . . intimacies of marriage all would be equally agreeable to you." Mr. Harwood's face wore a most unexpected shade of pink. He made a small adjustment of his glasses on his nose.

"They are all respectful and respectable men?" Rosalind asked.

He nodded.

"All have agreed to sign the terms?"

He nodded.

"You haven't chosen any ill-favored gentlemen or any gamesters?"

"Heavens, my dear. No." Mr. Harwood removed his spectacles for a quick cleaning. "But they are not . . . young men."

"They are not so old that they do not want a wife. How could I choose among these paragons if they came to court me?"

"With your heart, my dear."

Rosalind shook her head. "No." She turned away from him. She had loved Gerrie and begun to love Winterburn. "I have an untrustworthy sort of heart. Better to let one of them choose me."

"Well, then," said Mr. Harwood, "we will proceed." He began to gather the papers. "There is just one more thing, my dear." Rosalind turned. "Mrs. Harwood would like you to have a dress, a wedding dress."

"Oh, Mr. Harwood, I don't think . . . it's not going to be . . ."

"It is going to be your wedding, and she, we, would like you to have a dress." He drew himself to his full height, looking at her almost fiercely.

Rosalind blinked hard, holding the tears at bay, and nodded.

Sydney had hoped to find the Countess of Winterburn alone. Instead, he found her on a dazzling couch of turquoise silk, tête-à-tête with her son Trevor and Harry Hunt, no servants in attendance. Gilt caryatids arched their golden breasts to support the sofa ends, and above the lady, the curves of a reclining nude echoed the back of her couch. The nude's knees coyly concealed what her smile seemed to offer.

Sydney crossed the room slowly, inhaling the scents of opulence: wax and polish and underneath them the heavy, rich metallic scent of gold.

"Barton, back from the country?" The countess offered her hand, and he bowed over it. She smelled exotic, a mélange of scents he never could distinguish or name.

"Lady Winterburn. Been visiting my new estate, and I thought to offer you some news of Winterburn, but you've no doubt heard it from Mr. Hunt." He nodded to the latter, slouched in a damask armchair.

"About the scandal Winterburn has provoked in some village?" the countess asked.

"You see," said Barton, "nothing escapes your notice." He gestured to the wine decanter and glasses. "May I?"

"Yes. Mr. Hunt has been telling me that some poor country girl has accused Winterburn of seducing her."

Sydney pulled an armchair opposite the countess and settled himself. Polly Rees had let enough slip for him to know Lady Winterburn was playing games. "Only your own plans coming to fruition." He smiled and raised his glass to her.

Trevor Nash looked up abruptly, but the countess merely laughed. "Of course. I could not have Winterburn languishing forever in some country parsonage."

Sydney sipped his wine. Another of the riches of the lady's household, it had a fine bouquet. According to rumor the late earl had lost an enormous estate. Her third son must be penniless. "Hardly the place for the Earl of Winterburn, is it? Wonder why he stays?"

He studied his wine, not daring to look up. It had been a good stroke. He sensed the countess reevaluating Hunt's information.

"But what kept you there so long, Barton?" she asked.

"A sad affair. You didn't hear? Gerald Merrifield died, broke his neck." She was listening closely, sensing he had something to tell her, something Hunt hadn't revealed.

"You must have been grieved, Barton," said Hunt. "Your friend and partner, wasn't he?"

Sydney could not control a frown of irritation at the suggestion. "An unfortunate fellow, in the grip of gaming. Ruined his sister. She's quite penniless now."

"And soon to be homeless, is she not?" Hunt asked.

Sydney lifted his brows. "I don't know. I believe she's in London with her solicitor, trying to arrange to cover her brother's debts."

"The poor girl," said the countess without apparent sympathy. "She should be married off. With a proper sponsor, could she find someone appropriate?"

Sydney leaned forward. "Just what I suggested. I hoped to interest you, countess, in her plight, before she's hopelessly lost to good society. Sunk in service somewhere."

"It's too late for that, isn't it, Barton?" Hunt asked.

Barton turned to Winterburn's friend. He suspected Hunt of chivalry. He could not be sure, but he thought Hunt partly responsible for the girl's escape the night of Merrifield's party.

The countess had shifted her gaze to Hunt. "Do tell, Hunt. More scandal in this tiny village? What is England coming to if even the rustics are sinners?"

Hunt sipped his wine, making the countess wait. "Nothing so startling, my lady. The girl's brother tried to sell her to raise a stake for his gaming. There are several . . . gentlemen in town who could make the presentation of the girl to society most uncomfortable."

Sydney allowed himself a small smile. So Hunt thought to keep Winterburn out of it. "Where did she spend that night? At the parsonage?" He smiled at the countess. "Your son is kindness and solicitude itself in regard to this girl."

"Barton, you marry the girl, if you're so concerned about her," Trevor Nash suggested.

Sydney laughed. Nash had offered him a perfect opening. "I may yet." He looked at the countess. "Miss Merrifield is too unsettled to know her mind, but I could be the means of restoring her to her home and the house itself to its former glory." He took a sip of the fine wine, savoring its flavors on his palate.

The countess raised her glass to him. "Resourceful of you, Barton. A baronetcy in time, perhaps?" She lifted her glass.

Sydney rose, set his wineglass aside, and bowed. He thought it a good exit.

Trevor waited for the door to close behind his mother's guest before he heaved himself out of his chair and crossed to the wine. "I don't see why you put up with that fellow, Mother. Crows like a cock on a dung hill."

"He's useful to me," said the countess. "He tells me things." She handed her glass to Trevor for more wine. "Hunt," she said. "What is this girl to Winterburn?"

Trevor looked up. His mother was staring at Hunt.

Hunt toyed with his wine, making her wait, and Trevor felt his gut tighten. His mother did not like inferiors who tried to play games with her.

"To Winterburn? Nothing. As I understand it, Miss Merrifield's sole concern is preserving her hall. She's rather determined to see that it doesn't end up in Barton's hands. Means to auction herself off to the highest bidder to pay Barton off."

"Auction herself off?" Trevor sat down again.

"Come on, Hunt, where did you hear such a thing? Young girls, she is young, isn't she—"

"Twenty or so," said Hunt. He watched the countess closely.

"Young women of gentle birth don't sell themselves at auction," said the countess quietly.

Hunt smiled. "I believe they do, ma'am. At Almack's, every spring."

"But, Hunt," said Trevor, "this is a real auction? How'd you hear of it?"

"A fellow I fagged for at Eton. He was in India for years, and now he's come back a nabob. He's going to bid for her and wanted to know why a respectable girl was taking such a course."

"Wanted to know if she's a virgin, more like," Trevor said.

"Is she, Harry?" asked the countess. "A beautiful maiden in distress?"

Hunt shrugged. "Ma'am, you've been reading novels. She's a rustic, no polish, too much hair, too much color."

Trevor watched his mother. She did not like what she was hearing. Hunt was lying, he was sure of it. The countess rose from the couch abruptly and made a rapid turn of the room. She stopped at the large arched window overlooking her garden, her hand to her head. "Forgive me, Harry, Trevor," she said. "I fear the wine has given me a headache. Trevor, see Mr. Hunt out."

She was at her desk when Trevor returned. "How very unreliable Mr. Hunt has proved," she said.

"Mother, don't be put out with Hunt. He did

what you asked. Got a scandal. Uncle Ned's already in a wax about it."

She took up her pen, giving him the look he most disliked, the look that warned him not to tax her patience. "Hunt did nothing. That slut Polly has managed what the other three could not, but your brother has in fact remained chaste. Why?"

Trevor was not fool enough to offer the only explanations that occurred to him. He waited and helped himself to more wine.

"Trevor, dear." His mother beckoned him to her side. "Your lusty brother has plowed neither the voluptuous Polly nor the sultry Miss King. He has evidently been engaged in rescuing a virtuous maiden. It's not like him, and I fear it means he has foolish feelings for this girl."

Trevor nodded. She was probably right. She was inevitably right.

"So," she said, "you must discover all you can about the girl and her auction. I want you there. Make a bid for her if you must. I want you to make sure the girl is safely wed."

Trevor nodded. Then a thought occurred to him. "Mother, if she goes through with this auction, does that mean Barton won't get the house?"

She wasn't exactly listening to him. She was staring above his head, thinking moves ahead of him already. He had to admire that.

"I suppose," she said.

Chapter 16

The doors of Rowdene, which had slowly opened to him, were closed. His disgrace was known everywhere. He realized how accustomed he'd become to the shy smiles of children and brusque greetings of their parents. Now people openly turned their backs. Only the roads welcomed him, so he took to them. He met Braithe on the Merrifield rise where he'd stopped to look down at the hall.

"She's gone, you know."

Leigh turned to Braithe. Had he driven her out, or Barton? "Gone?"

Braithe's keen gaze pierced him. "To London."

"Because of me?"

The cold, blue eyes did not waver. "When she heard ye'd been showing yer scars to Polly Rees."

A short bitter laugh escaped Leigh. "I haven't, you know."

Braithe cast him a quick glance, then turned and began to walk on. "I know. I'd not be showing wounds to the likes of Polly Rees if I burned as ye do for the Rose."

Leigh fell into step beside the shepherd. Leigh did burn for her. There was no denying it to a man who knew the ailment well.

Braithe's staff touched the ground, marking their progress. " 'Better to marry than burn.' " He glanced up, a fresh challenge in his shrewd, blue eyes. "That's Scripture."

"Don't tempt me, Braithe," Leigh said. "I'd be a selfish beast to offer for her. The living will never be mine now. I've nothing of my own."

"Nothing?" Braithe snorted. "Beggin' yer pardon, *Lord* Winterburn, but ye don't know what nothing is."

They exchanged a measuring glance. "Not awed by the title, are you, Braithe?"

"Do ye want to be a great lord or a parson?"

"I'm not much of a parson at the moment. How did Vernon put it? 'A scandal to rock the church.' "

"Did ye hear yer cheese sold well? Could help a dozen families." Braithe shrugged. "Polly's lies will be discovered soon enough."

Leigh halted briefly. It was the first time anyone had believed him. The first time he'd heard how well they'd done at the fair. "It's not walking on water."

"It'll do."

"High praise, Braithe, but public opinion says my sins outweigh my good deeds." The lewd effigies were fixed in his mind. "I can't ask Rosalind Merrifield to take my name when I would bring disgrace and want upon her with it."

Braithe shook his head, his eyes solemn. "The Rose has left Rowdene. Yer likely the only man who can bring her back." He touched the brim of his hat and vaulted over a stile, disappearing across a meadow.

The Rose. Leigh stood at the edge of the green meadow. With sudden clear intensity his vision appeared, the rose opening sweetly, entwined about the hub of the wheel. To have her in his bed, a bed sanctified by the church. A painful longing gripped him.

He followed the road out of town, the idea of marrying Rosalind Merrifield pushing out all other thoughts. How could he conquer the temptation? Hours and miles later he had not shaken the hold of that idea. He returned to the parsonage weary in body and mind. Dowdeswell, who was now avoiding Leigh, had put his post and a cold supper on the table and disappeared.

Absently, Leigh opened a letter from Vernon.

Dear My Lord,

I must speak out. How may the flock be led in the paths of righteousness when the shepherd strays? I can hardly find words to describe my profound dismay at the prospect of leaving the people of Rowdene in your care. It is widely known that you have corrupted more than one young woman in your charge. Your deception about your rank and position in society and your carnal inclinations are a danger to the church in Rowdene, indeed to the church everywhere. Such sensuality is a natural extension of the papist leanings you betrayed from the first in your profligate use of candles. The cost of your sins can hardly be tallied. Lady Ellenby and Squire Haythorne may withdraw all support from the church.

I cannot condone your presence in the parsonage by meeting parishioners while you remain there. You pollute the parsonage of Rowdene with your presence, and should remove yourself at once from the premises.

Should you seek confession and counsel for your dark and troubled soul, I am, of course, available.

> *Your most humble servant,*
> *The Reverand Evert Vernon*

Leigh could not resist the mad impulse to reply.

My dear Vernon,

As much as my soul longs for consolation, I will seek it elsewhere. And I will continue to pollute this very snug parsonage until the false accusations made against my character are cleared up. You might best relieve your fears of pollution by urging the squire to make an investigation of Miss Rees.

> *Yrs,*
> *Winterburn*

He ripped opened a second letter with a flourish and found a few sobering words from Hunt.

Winterburn,

*Your resourceful love will auction herself as bride
to the highest bidder Sunday next. Barton will be
paid, the hall saved. Your turn to effect a rescue.*

                                     Hunt

He read the words again. Her intention was
unmistakable and beyond his grasp. He recalled
their conversation at the fair as they watched the
horse auction, recalled her determination to pay
Barton. She had spoken of auctioning the books,
but how had she come to this idea? He decided it
was not resourcefulness but despair. Or hope,
hope pursued too long and too far. That, she had
told him, had destroyed Mary Fletcher.

Anger curled his hands into fists, coiled in his
gut, maddened his brain. He crushed the letter in
his fist. It was necessary to move. He strode to
window and, looking out, saw the church. At
every turn heaven mocked him.

He acknowledged to himself that he was unfamiliar with the workings of divine will, and he
was undeserving of Rosalind Merrifield. He
tipped back his head and tried to say the words of
the familiar prayer. *Thy will be done.*

He could not. Human will, he understood—
selfish, stubborn, wayward, as his will had ever
been. He had no home to give her. If he interfered
in her plans, she would lose the home she loved.
She believed him false and carnal, and he knew
better than to call desire love. But the vision of the

rose twining sweetly about the center of his life haunted him. He could not let her go. She was the sweetness in his vision. The rest was unforgiving stone, cruel light, the burden of the wheel. Only the rose was sweet, soft, even as it pricked him. He would go to London to get her.

Leigh kept his left hand on his sword hilt, silencing the ring of the blade in the scabbard as he crossed his brother's bedroom. His plans were nearly complete. For a moment he stood in the dark, envying Trevor's sound sleep. He had slept little himself since he'd received Hunt's letter. Tomorrow, perhaps. He lit a candle on the bedside table.

"Trev, wake up."

Trevor rolled away from the light, and Leigh nudged his shoulder. He stiffened and lay back. His arm came up to shield his eyes. "What? Who?" He blinked. "Leigh?"

Leigh smiled tightly. "You're going to help me stop an auction today, Trev."

Trevor groaned and pulled the counterpane over his head. "Hunt told you?"

"What are friends for."

Another groan came from beneath the bedclothes, and Leigh lit a second candle.

Trevor pushed aside the covers and propped himself up against the pillows. "Hunt should know better than to cross Mother. She can ruin him."

"She won't know."

"She'll find out." Trevor rubbed a hand over his face, frowning. "She always does."

Leigh stepped back into the shadows, keeping his hand on the sword. "She won't know your part in this either."

"My part?" He cast Leigh a quick annoyed glance. "I don't cross Mother." He tossed the bedclothes aside, stepped into his slippers, and shuffled over to his wrapper hanging on a chair. "Leave it alone, Leigh. The girl doesn't need rescuing. Harwood's protected her interests very thoroughly. He's going to tie her husband's hands with more clauses than a damn peace treaty."

"Just how did you discover that detail, Trev?"

Trevor became absorbed in the tie of his wrapper. "Why don't you do what Mother wants for a change? Marry the Candover chit. She's clever, witty, and worth a fortune."

Leigh watched his brother steadily. "Trev, you're not going to bid for Miss Merrifield, are you?"

"I'm just to . . . be there, to . . . make sure she goes through with it."

"Good." Leigh stepped into the light. His sword jingled once. "I didn't want to slit your throat."

Trevor's head came up abruptly and his gaze froze on the weapon. "You're mad."

Leigh shook his head. "Find pen and paper. I want all the details you can give me. A floorplan of Harwood's—"

"No." Trevor lifted his hands, backing toward the door. "You can't go into Harwood's with a sword in broad daylight and . . ." He halted, a puzzled frown on his face. "What are you planning?"

Leigh shrugged. "You don't need to know."

"Damned if I don't." He strode back toward

Leigh. "Whatever you do, I'll be the one who has to face Mother."

"Then you'd be wise to help me come up with a foolproof plan . . ." He glanced at the clock on Trevor's wall. "This morning."

Trevor stalked into his sitting room, lit another branch of candles, and yanked a chair from the table. "Find some wine," he said.

Trevor relaxed. Leigh felt no serious religious call. There was nothing mysterious in his actions. Polly Rees's disturbing reports could be dismissed. Leigh might have been celibate for a few weeks, he might have taken an interest in the poor, but at heart he was as selfish as he'd ever been. He wanted his own way and would do anything to get it. And if Leigh got this girl, then Mother might finally turn from Leigh and put Trevor first in her heart.

There was light in the sky when Leigh was satisfied that he knew what he would face at Harwood's. The house was a familiar design, tall and narrow, with the rooms on each floor lined up one behind the other. The library where the auction would be was at the rear of the house behind the entry hall and the main stairway. There was one way in and out. He would have to conceal his intentions until he got to the library and Rosalind, then put obstacles in the path of potential pursuit as he escaped. His plan was far from perfect, and trusting Trevor was not the best insurance of success, but he would make it work.

"You've been helpful, Trev."

Trevor gave him a wry glance. "You may go too

far with Mother this time, Leigh. She'll not forgive you if you put yourself beyond the pale."

Leigh grinned. "Then she'll have to appreciate you, Trev."

"She should."

Trevor raised his glass in salute.

"There is one more thing."

"No, I'm in deep enough." Trevor drained the last of his wine.

"One more thing," Leigh repeated. "When I leave, confront Harwood. Complain. Play the outraged buyer."

Trevor tilted his chin at a haughty angle and gave a look to freeze any lesser mortal. "That I can do." He stretched. "Time for me to dress, Brother."

Leigh nodded. "I'll wait." He meant to keep Trevor in sight so that his brother could not slip a message to their mother.

When Trevor emerged from the ministrations of his man, Leigh had to admire his polished elegance. "You know, Trev, you should marry the Candover heiress. Surprise Mother. She likes a man who's one step ahead of her."

Rosalind waited with Mrs. Harwood in the back parlor, listening to the low rumble of male voices as the buyers gathered in the library. Mrs. Harwood adjusted the wreath of white roses on Rosalind's head, another concession she had made to her hosts' sentiments. They had found a gown of the whitest muslin, embroidered all over with white silk dots, so that it shimmered in the light. It tied under her breasts and fell to her ankles above white satin slippers. She had tiny puff sleeves and soft kid gloves to her elbows. She hardly recognized herself in the elegant attire.

She also hardly recognized herself in what she was doing, except that it was necessary to save Merrifield, to preserve what it was to her and others. Her limbs felt heavy and numb. She reminded herself that the man who bought her would have no power over Merrifield and that she would be free to return to it as she wished. She would manage her husband's household, serve as his hostess, and bear such children as he desired, but a part of her would be separate, inviolate. And he could not ruin her, could not beggar her children. She would have Merrifield. The idea did not ease the tightness in her body.

Mrs. Harwood gave her a pleased smile, and Rosalind thought of Jane. She should have Jane with her. "My dear," said Mrs. Harwood, "your beauty will slay your bridegroom."

Rosalind's stomach knotted. She was getting a husband, a comfortable gentleman who would look out for her interests, not a bridegroom. The word evoked Winterburn's ardent kisses. Rosalind shut her eyes as an unexpected wave of loss swept over her. She would not think of him on this day, not allow thoughts of him to weaken her resolve. She was seizing control of her future, holding onto her past.

Mr. Harwood appeared in the doorway. "It's time." He offered his arm, and Mrs. Harwood stepped back.

Rosalind started toward Mr. Harwood, caught

herself, and turned to give Mrs. Harwood's hand a quick squeeze. "Thank you."

She allowed herself to be led across the hall to the back door of the library, grateful for Mr. Harwood's stately pace, which concealed the stiffness of her limbs.

Mr. Harwood patted her hand on his arm and gave her a quiet smile. "I'm proud of you, my dear." He opened the library door and drew her inside.

"'The bride hath paced into the hall. Red as a rose is she.'" Mr. Harwood quoted Mr. Coleridge's poem.

There was a scrape of chairs and a rustle of movement. Six men rose as one, a wall of coats and cravats, a wave of sandalwood and musk. Rosalind halted, keeping her gaze steady, her chin up, meeting the scrutiny of her would-be buyers. It was nothing like the fevered gaze of the gamesters at her brother's party. Her brother's companions had been in the grip of a frenzy, their hot glances flickering over her. The faces turned to her now spoke of control and power. Cool eyes calculated her worth, reminding her of Mr. Harwood's words: "Commerce is king in London." These men were the dukes, the princes of commerce.

She slipped her arm from Mr. Harwood's, trying to take control of the situation, and gestured for the gentlemen to sit.

"Thank you, gentlemen, for honoring me with your interest." She picked out the nabob by his tanned skin, the young widower by the mourning band on his sleeve. "I'm sure Mr. Harwood explained the circumstances that have led me to this course." She thought the grain merchant must be the tall, broad-faced gentleman, and the banker, the man in gray. "However unconventional an arrangement, I do promise to be a faithful and dutiful wife." She recognized the white-haired lawyer, a friend of Mr. Harwood's. The last gentleman, the youngest, must be the gentleman of private fortune, who had entered the bidding late. "I will endeavor to promote my husband's concerns and learn his tastes and interests."

She thought she had amused the nabob somehow, for a faint ironic smile played about his lips. She hoped he would not outbid the others, then chided herself for the thought. She must have no favorites, no doubts.

"Gentlemen?" Mr. Harwood adjusted the spectacles on his nose. "You may begin."

"Ten thousand pounds," said the widower. His voice boomed in the small space. Something in Rosalind recoiled, but she held herself steady.

There was a moment of silence.

"Twelve," said the grain merchant more quietly.

"Thirteen." It was the banker.

She clasped her hands together. Her plan was working. Her debts would be paid. The buyers seemed intent on outbidding one another. An unexpected shiver started deep inside her.

The young man with the private fortune cleared his throat. "Fourteen." He seemed not to see her. His eyes shifted uneasily toward the front door, and she followed his gaze. There was no one there, of course.

"Fifteen," said the lawyer. The buyers were inching toward the sum she owed Barton. Merrifield would be hers. Strange that she felt herself shrinking inside the white shell of her bridal finery.

There were several bids in rapid succession, but Rosalind hardly heard them. The young man's nervous glances made her edgy, her muscles taut.

Silence fell, the ticking of the clock. They all seemed to hold their breath. Mr. Harwood looked from one to another. The nabob had made no bid.

He looked at the others then focused his gaze on Rosalind. "Twenty-five thousand."

From the shadows of a portico down the street, Leigh watched the bidders enter Harwood's, Trevor the last of them. They were solid, prosperous men, at home in the world of brick and stone around them. There was no madness in their manner or appearance. He did not think they had visions of roses twining about cart wheels or swords at their hips. But he knew they had their secrets. He'd investigated. He signaled the hackney he'd kept waiting at the corner.

When the driver reached him, he climbed in and gave Harwood's address. The cab rolled to a stop at the door, and he got down, hauling after him a tall urn filled with roses. He reminded the driver of the plan and turned toward the door. The urn weighed three or four stone and was awkward to carry, but he lugged it to the porch and stood behind its concealing bulk and knocked.

A maid answered, looking both interested and doubtful.

"Miss," he said. "Flowers Mr. Harwood ordered."

"He's busy." Her wide eyes were fixed on the roses.

"Can I bring them inside then, miss?"

"I don't know where." She darted a glance around the entry hall.

"Just point where Mr. Harwood and the other gentlemen are."

"Oh, you can't go in the library, sir."

"Then I'll put them in the hall."

"I'd best get missus." She hurried off.

The front hall led to the main stairway. Leigh set the urn at the foot of the stairs. The water rocked toward the lip of the urn, then settled, and Leigh slipped inside the closet Trevor had noted for him.

He heard two pairs of feminine footsteps arrive and halt.

"Oh," came a sweet matronly voice. "Mr. Harwood is a dear, dear man." There was a pause. "Did the florist's boy go?" Another pause. "I should have given him something."

The footsteps started to move away. "Go on now, Janet. Mr. Harwood will call us when they've finished."

Leigh waited, listening, until he was sure the stairwell was empty. When he left the closet, the door to the library was straight ahead on his right. He drew the sword from the scabbard at his hip, a slow, silent slide, and moved in on the door. The well-oiled handle made no more than a faint click as he turned it.

"Twenty-five thousand," said a smooth, cold male voice.

Leigh shifted his sword for a tighter grip. He let the door swing outward and stepped into the opening.

Rosalind Merrifield stood just a few feet beyond the tip of his sword, clothed in light, and the sight of her froze him, her beauty richer than he had ever seen it, her gown dazzling.

She turned. Her glance slid along the sword edge until her eyes met his. He saw the flash of mad joy in her gaze, felt it seize him, too. And knew she would fight it.

He forced himself to look away from her. She would cost him the advantage of surprise.

"Sir," protested Harwood, stepping in front of her. "I must ask what you mean, intruding in a private house?"

Leigh raised the tip of his sword level with the older man's breast. "The auction ends now."

The others were on the edge of his vision. The sun-darkened gentleman took a step toward him, and Leigh made a quick, thrusting cut, a slice that left the gentleman's buttons dangling from a loose flap of coat fabric.

Rosalind stepped from behind Harwood. "Stop!" Her eyes searched Leigh's. "You don't need to do this. I chose this auction."

He kept his gaze on Harwood and the others. He saw the cold, possessive drive in them. "It's customary before a wedding to ask whether there be any impediment to the joining of the man and woman."

The eyes of the buyers narrowed. "Now, sir," said Harwood, "there is no impediment here, only the urgency of Miss Merrifield's circumstances."

Leigh returned his gaze to her. "I think there is."

Her frozen figure came to life, and she took a couple of steps in his direction. "Why are you doing this?"

Silently he urged her onward. Just two more steps. He looked at the others. "Gentlemen." He held them with a pause. "The lady has given to me what by rights belongs only to her husband."

Her sharp intake of breath brought their eyes back to her, but they were wavering now, doubting. And she knew it as well as he did.

She strode forward, her eyes flashing. "It's a lie." Her anger carried her just within his reach. He shot out his left hand and caught her wrist, jerking her up against him, his arm pinning her waist and her right arm. She twisted, struggling against his hold, her free hand reaching up to hit him. "Liar."

The tanned gentleman grabbed a candlestick and hurled it. Leigh ducked and backed out of the room.

He heard Trevor shout, "Harwood!" Then he slammed the door. In two strides he was beyond the urn. He gave it a kick, sending it crashing to the floor, gallons of water gushing.

He clung to the bundle of writhing fury under his arm. Three more strides took him to the front door. He jerked it open as the first gentleman reached the flood. Then he was out the door, shouting at the hackney driver. He lifted Rosalind Merrifield, threw her into the cab, and flung himself in after her. The driver lashed the horse.

Chapter 17

R osalind's bottom thumped against the stiff seat; her head hit the side of the cab. Winterburn loomed over her but a moment, then dropped into the seat beside her. She righted herself and lunged for the door. His arm came up, pinning her against the squabs. The cab lurched forward, and she fell back.

For a moment there was only their harsh breathing and the rattle of wheels. She stared at him. Some fierce emotion possessed him and altered his face. She thought it the face he had shown his enemies in war. The blade in his hand made her think of the long, thin wounds in his flesh. He shifted his gaze to the sword, putting it away from him.

She straightened her skirts, freeing her feet from the damp hem that clung to her ankles. She needed to make him see reason. "You've lost your senses."

His head came up, his look a dark reproach. "No more than you."

"I did not come into a gentleman's house

waving a sword, knowing nothing of the situation."

He pulled a scarlet jacket from the seat between them and laid it across his knees. "I investigated your auction thoroughly."

"How could you? It was an entirely private affair."

"One of your would-be buyers is my brother."

"Your brother?" She felt a momentary weakness. He had been ahead of her somehow, had known her plans. She hadn't had time to think how he came to interrupt the auction. It had seemed as if her own doubts and longings had brought him, but it was his will, his doing. "Mr. Harwood will come after me."

His glance turned wry. He sat forward on the seat, his left hand flicking the buttons of his coat free. "I counted on that. First, however, he'll have to appease a few disgruntled gentlemen." He stripped off the blue coat. "When Mr. Harwood does follow, we'll be long gone."

There was nothing remarkable about a gentleman in his shirtsleeves and waistcoat, yet Rosalind felt her stomach take a sudden dip, as if the road had fallen away beneath them.

"Where?" She managed to ask. None of this made any sense.

He gave her an unpromising look, full of that hard-edged willfullness she had seen in him from the first. Reason seemed a puny weapon against him.

"The auction was a rational course, my only means of keeping Merrifield."

"Was it? Giving yourself to a man for money?" His dark brows lifted slightly. "It's a time-honored arrangement, I grant you, but I doubt you'd find yourself suited to it." He tossed the blue coat aside. "And for what? So you could keep a pile of bricks and mortar?"

She pressed her palms together. She wanted to slap him, but she sensed he wanted that, wanted a fight. "You don't understand what a home is, do you?" she asked quietly and saw that the words fell more heavily than a blow.

His movement was checked for a moment, but he didn't look at her. He shed his waistcoat.

She wanted to press the advantage, but he distracted her. "I would have been a good wife to whoever—"

"Whoever?" He gave her a savage look. "You were prepared to be flexible in your affections?" He thrust an arm into one sleeve of the scarlet jacket.

She gritted her teeth and took a deep breath. She would not allow him to humiliate her. "I have no cause for shame. If I gave myself without affection, it would not be without honor. Women have ever learned to care for husbands not of their choosing, and Mr. Harwood investigated the character of each gentleman."

He shoved his left arm into its sleeve. "Did you think the gentlemen were interchangeable? Did Mr. Harwood know your nabob's opium habits or the banker's relations with a certain brothel in Covent Garden?" He began to button the coat.

She stared at him. She was sure Mr. Harwood had not known such things.

"Did you think about going to bed tonight with 'whoever'?" He filled the word with contempt, as if he tasted bile.

She had tried to keep all thoughts of her marriage bed out of mind. What counted was keeping Merrifield. "It was a matter of indifference to me," she lied.

"Not to me," he said fiercely. He leaned over her, pressed against her from thigh to shoulder, his hand braced against the squabs. He was going to kiss her, his eyes heavy with the intention. "Tonight you're going to bed with me," he said.

"You can't mean it. You aren't so lost to decency."

"I am. We can be married first or not, as you please."

His faced dipped down to hers. She pressed her head back against the seat. She wanted to ask about Polly and Lucetta King. A whimper died in her throat. Resisting the promised touch was beyond her will. Their mouths met and clung and opened, and in the madness there was joy.

His hand fell away, and he turned to look out the grimy window, his ragged breath harsh in her ears. The cab slowed and came to a halt. He pushed open the door and leapt out, his sword in hand. She could not move. He had some words with the driver and planted himself below her on the paving stones, proud and implacable in his regimental jacket, wings of lace on the shoulders.

She thought he would do for one of the fiery cherubim barring the gates of Eden. If she went with him, she could not go home.

They had stopped in front of a brick church with plain white doors and a short, simple steeple. A crowd of mostly men stood on the steps, banging kettles and saucepan lids with tongs. A man with a fiddle plied it, his elbow pumping the air, but she could not hear the strings for the clang of metal. Then the crowd caught sight of Winterburn and cheered. He glanced at them over his shoulder and raised a hand in greeting, then he let his saber slide down into the scabbard. He reached up for her. He had planned this, too. She understood then that the regimental jacket was for this crowd, who saw him as a hero.

She wanted to refuse his hand, but that would be foolish. She had no idea where she was, but she was still in the city, still among ordinary people, and there might be someone who would be willing to listen to her, willing to help.

Only, the din was appalling. It smote her when she stepped down out of the carriage, her gloved hand in his. She held on just for steadiness. When she had her balance, she would let go. Another carriage drew up, and the banging intensified as the crowd waited for the door to open. Rosalind turned to see what stirred them. A young man jumped from the second carriage and offered his hand, and out came another bride. She smiled and clung to her groom's hand readily, her cheeks bright pink. Still another pair descended. Winterburn's threat was real. They were to be part of the usual Sunday weddings.

She pulled back. She needed time to think, to speak to someone over the banging of the pot lids.

Winterburn leaned down and spoke in her ear. "You once told me that to cling too long to a single hope can bring ruin. Let it go. Marry me."

Rosalind looked around wildly once, for what she hardly knew, as if she could alter or escape the moment. In some way she wanted this as much as Merrifield. To weigh them against each other in the awful scale of the moment was impossible. She might hate him when Merrifield was gone, but she could not summon the feeling now.

She looked up into his gray eyes. He touched her cheek with his lips, and she trembled slightly. *You don't know what there is to want*, he had said to her.

She yielded, and her acquiescence was met with a look of fierce elation which took her breath away. He drew her along in the wake of the other couples, tucking her arm in his. Behind them the carriages rumbled off. The crowd closed around them, pressing them forward into the little church.

Chapter 18

〜⌒◯◯⌒〜

Sydney Barton left Lady Winterburn at Melbourne House. His countess did not properly appreciate the change in his fortunes. She had allowed him to escort her this evening as if she were conferring one last favor. Her manner suggested he was insignificant, while elsewhere in London he enjoyed dozens of small acknowledgments of his new status. The change in his prospects, rumored about largely by Crawley, he suspected, had brought a gratifying increase in the cordiality of hostesses and acquaintances.

He could, he saw, put himself on the marriage mart. Though he was not in the bloom of youth, the Merrifield estate made him a catch. So why had his countess seemed indifferent? He had noted her coldness in small things. She had talked the better part of an hour with Eldon without so much as a glance in Sydney's direction. Most nights when he served as her escort, she played wonderful teasing games, allowing him to linger over the scent of her as he held her cape, his fingers brushing her shoulders. Tonight, as soon

as he leaned near with the cape, she stepped
forward. Unwilling to be humiliated a moment
longer, he had left Melbourne House. Now he
had the feeling that she had wanted that outcome,
had manipulated him into departing.

Deference from the proprietor of a gaming
establishment off Pall Mall restored a measure of
Sydney's humor. Then he spotted Trevor Nash in
a corner, raising a glass of claret with the abrupt,
deliberate jerks of a drunken man. Nash did not
see him; he could turn and try another establishment. Sydney weighed the distastefulness of an
encounter with another haughty Nash against the
possibility that a drunken Trevor would let something slip to explain the countess's indifference.
He crossed to the younger man's table, stopping
just where the wine fumes reached him. It was
not a bad claret.

Nash looked up and let his arm fall heavily,
sloshing wine. "Aren't you the lucky one,
Barton?"

"Am I?"

"Forgot. You don't know about the auction.
Drink?" Nash signaled a servant. "Join me. I
might be induced to tell you how lucky you are."

Nash refilled his own glass. Sydney watched
the dark stream of wine. Even this youngest Nash
made the careless assumption of power over
lesser men. But the word "auction" arrested his
thoughts. Had the girl put the property up for
sale? Was that the ploy behind her agent's delay-
ing tactics? He lowered himself into a chair across
from Nash. "What auction?"

Nash shook a finger in Sydney's face, and Sydney controlled himself to keep from slapping the insolent gesture aside. The sight of the wobbly finger offended him. His insides had had just that sort of unsteadiness tonight as the countess ignored him.

"You can't tell Mother, Barton. Got to tell her myself. Soon. Soon as I finish my wine."

The servant returned with another bottle and a glass for Sydney. He sipped slowly, his tongue savoring the excellent vintage even as he struggled to keep his features from betraying impatience.

Nash was halfway through a glass before he spoke again. "You nearly lost that Merrifield property today, Barton." He shook his head. "The girl was going to sell herself to the highest bidder. Nabob bid twenty-five thousand for her. Starting bid."

Sydney's stomach knotted. He made a conscious effort to relax his grip on the wineglass. "You are making little sense, Nash. Miss Merrifield raised twenty-five thousand, and I'm lucky?"

"No." Nash shook his head and paused, holding himself steady like a man trying to clear a clouded brain. "Harwood arranged an auction. Private sale, one gently bred girl, granddaughter of a duke, a beauty, a virgin." Nash made circles in the air with his free hand.

Sydney felt himself go cold. "How did you know about this auction?"

Nash blinked. "Heard about it from Hunt."

An instant memory of Lady Winterburn

flanked by Nash and Hunt came to Sydney's mind. Apparently the countess had known all along that he might lose his property. She had not warned him. No mention. Not a word. No offer of support. It was a matter of indifference to her. The wine soured in his mouth. He put down the glass. His child self, mocked by wealthy cousins for his poverty and dependence, took hold of him. He saw himself rising, hurling his wineglass against the wall, overturning the table, startling all those around him, as he had done in his mother's room whenever she told him to bear his sufferings with patience. He could not smash things here; he had to keep his head and find out whatever Nash was willing to tell him.

"What happened?"

Nash leaned forward conspiratorily. "Not a word to my mother, Barton."

Sydney raised a hand in a gesture of promise.

"Winterburn stopped it. Came right in waving a sword and stole her. He's mad about the girl."

"Where are they?" Sydney asked.

"Don't know." Nash shuddered. "Don't want to know. Hiding somewhere, I suppose." He lifted his glass in a toast. "To Winterburn. I hope you're enjoying her, Brother."

Sydney found he was sweating, actually sweating, from the relief of it. The girl had nearly cheated him out of his estate, but Winterburn's foolish chivalry had stopped her. The thought gave him only a moment's comfort. Of course, Winterburn would want the house, too. Sydney would call on the Merrifield man of business in the morning. He would make sure there were no more delays in the transfer of property. And he would make sure his countess knew he'd won.

Leigh, following his bride up the narrow stair, felt a rush of longing as if his soul were a trapped thing, struggling to be free, flapping broken wings against iron bars. He halted and leaned a shoulder against the rough wall while the strange feeling mastered him. The lamp in his hand lit the few steps above him. She limped on, her bridal finery wrinkled, the hem of her dress torn where someone at the wedding feast had trod on it.

He fixed his gaze on the torn lace. The tide of feeling in him swelled, his soul borne upward, a bit of foam on the surge. He struggled to contain that tide. Taking a steadying breath, he told himself she was a woman, with the lines and curves common to all females. It was blasphemous to think his vision had guided him to this moment. The feelings she roused in him were no more than the familiar desires of his carnal nature.

Three steps took her beyond the light cast by his lamp. She paused in the shadows on the landing and looked back uncertainly.

He came up a step, raising the lamp. The glow of it threw a nimbus around her, lighting her hair to fiery brilliance. The creamy roses of her bridal crown drooped. Again he felt his soul beat upward. He mastered himself. He would pull the roses from her crown one by one and let her hair down, fill his hands with it, bury his face in it. His gaze met hers and faltered. In her gilded face her eyes were deep wells of doubt.

Abruptly, he came up the last few steps, brushed past her to their room, and thrust his key in the lock. The door swung inward on a cold, dark space. Inside was the plain narrow bed to which he had brought her, his rose plucked from the green fields. When he made love to her there and wed his carnal nature to her spirit, he would take her forever from those fields. He was face-to-face with his selfish desire.

A glance showed Rosalind that the room was impossibly small. A sloping ceiling prohibited standing upright except in a few feet of space on the near side of the narrow bed. There was a rough dresser to her left and a faded screen to her right. She needed to distance herself from him. Since he had taken her from the Harwoods, she had allowed a hundred unguarded looks and touches to weaken her beyond resistance.

Behind her the door closed with a quiet click, and a sudden tremor shook her. She clasped her hands together and tried to still the treacherous quiver in her limbs.

"What now?" she asked.

"Bed."

He made no attempt to conceal it or disguise it with pretty words. He had told her in the hackney cab that their way led here, to a plain narrow bed with a worn counterpane. She glanced at him over her shoulder. He set the lamp on the dresser, and its light put half his face in darkness. It was the face she had seen at the fair, drawn in bleak lines.

She swung toward him. The sudden move made her head buzz mildly from the wedding toasts they'd drunk. She had not minded when they'd followed the others to a tavern. The crowd and the music had kept her mind from thinking of this moment. Now her ears, accustomed to the din of the marriage feast, felt strained in the silence. A backward step brought her up against the bed.

She pressed a hand to her spinning head. "Are we truly married?"

The question startled him. He looked at the bed, and the lines of his face settled in fixed purpose. "If we join our bodies in that bed."

"If we don't?"

The afternoon had passed in the swift rush of dreams. The flash of a sword blade, a clatter of carriage wheels, the din of the wedding guests, one quick, searing kiss at the altar. Somewhere she had lost herself, had signed her new name in a little book, and her world had contracted to this narrow room. Somehow, if she resisted him now, held him off, she might recover herself.

The moment hung in the balance. She tried to imagine walking past him, through the door, down the narrow stair to the crowded taproom, asking for a hackney cab, returning to the Harwoods. The images faded. Her will seemed paralyzed.

He drew back. "You're tired. That alone must make you eager for bed." He reached for the strap that held the sword at his side. His hands loosened the buckle, and her body answered with a quiver deep inside. He removed the sword and leaned it in a corner of the room beside the rough dresser.

"What are you doing?" Her voice sounded faint in her ears.

He turned back to her. "Seduction was what I had in mind."

He reached for the collar of his scarlet coat and unfastened the buttons with ruthless efficiency, his gaze on her, unwavering. With a single swift move he pulled his shirt over his head, baring himself to her: smooth, white flesh; dark, curling hair; and scars. She pressed so hard against the bed she sat down with a plop, her limbs shaking.

"You are eager after all," he said, taking a step forward.

She reached out a hand to hold him off, but he took it in both of his, twining their fingers briefly, then tugging at her glove, pulling it down, exposing her elbow and wrist, pulling it off, pressing their hands palm to palm. His fingers closed over the back of her hand, trapping it in his.

There was nowhere to look that was not him, his skin bathed in the lamp's golden hue. Her gaze settled on the long, curving ridge that scarred his ribs.

He bent his head, his gaze on their locked hands. "Rosalind," he said in a strained voice, "say my name." He raised their joined hands to his mouth and pressed his lips to the back of her hand.

Her hand tingled, and a lazy warmth stole up her arm, robbing her of strength. Her eyes fell closed, and her mind yielded for an instant. Just long enough for him to manage her other glove. He made her weak, like Gerrie. If she lost herself, she would lose Merrifield.

At the thought she snatched her hand away. "No."

He stepped back, his breathing uneven, the pulse in his throat visible. He turned to the door, pressing his crossed arms to the wood, resting his head against them. His body shook lightly, his ribs expanded and contracting with rough breaths.

"You said we would be married if we join in this bed," she told his back. "If we don't, then I might still have a chance to save Merrifield."

He spun around. His gaze stung her, the mockery in it unmistakable. "You find the prospect of the marriage bed daunting now? This morning you were prepared to sleep with a stranger to save your precious hall."

"Home," she corrected him quietly. He had called it a pile of bricks and mortar. He did not know what home meant. He might never know.

"Home then," he said. "We'll make another."

"I must not abandon Merrifield," she said.

He looked stricken, as if he'd lost some precious thing. "Then you must not lie with me tonight." His body shook, a fine tremor, like the inner shaking of deep cold.

She pressed her hands together in her lap.

"I'll leave you now." He gathered up his shirt

and coat and turned away. His hand on the doorknob, he stopped as if he'd remembered something and looked back over his shoulder.

"You have no maid," he said. "Let me help you . . . with your gown."

A long moment passed. She knew he had spoken the truth in Mr. Harwood's library. She had given something of herself to him that could not be reclaimed. As long as she remained near him, she would have to fight the enigmatic pull that drew them together. But he would stop when she said "no."

She came up off the bed and turned her back to him, bending her head, pressing her clasped hands to her mouth. His hands settled on her shoulders, and his thumbs began deep, soothing strokes, releasing the knotted tightness there.

He stepped nearer. She heard him take a slow, shaky breath, felt his touch at the buttons along her nape. He worked them one by one, swiftly at first, then fumblingly. The fabric parted; cool air touched her skin, sending a shiver through her. He faltered. Against her back she felt a little shake of his hands.

She tried to remember to breathe.

With his thumbs he brushed aside the edges of her dress, bunching the cloth, pushing the sleeves off her shoulders. She pressed her bodice firmly against her breasts. Behind her he seemed to freeze.

"The stays," he said.

Her heart pounded slowly, heavily, several times. She nodded. Then he found the ties and

began to pull at them. When he had loosened
several rows of tapes, his hands came to rest at
her waist. She waited for him to step away.

His right hand slid around her body and up the
bones of the loosened stays to cup one breast. She
watched the fine, strong fingers close over her.
His mouth descended to her shoulder, and he
pulled her tight against him.

He was afflicted as she was. She forced her eyes
open and twisted free, dislodging his hand from
her breast, turning her back to the bed, facing
him.

"Go," she said.

Leigh returned hours or minutes later; Rosalind
could not be sure. Pictures of the day flitted
restlessly through her mind so that she had no
sense of time.

She heard him move in the room, heard the
scrape of his boots, his minimal preparations for
sleep, felt the dip of the mattress under his
weight. She held her breath. He lay on top of the
blankets, his back to her.

She waited for some sign that he slept.

Instead he spoke. "Must you save Merrifield
alone?"

Her throat tightened. When she could speak,
she forced out a single syllable. "No."

There was no answer in the dark.

Chapter 19

~~~◦◯◯◦~~~

Deep bells woke Rosalind, ringing a change. She was alone in a pocket of warmth. She lay perfectly still. Her head ached, and she was conscious of her bare legs tangled in the sheets and the scent of Winterburn on the pillow beside her. A flash of heat warmed her from her toes to her cheeks. Her pulse beat in her throat. She glanced around the room. He was gone.

There was an odd mixture of disappointment and relief in the discovery. The danger of the night before had passed. She would remain strong, return to the Harwoods, and begin to untangle the complications an afternoon's madness had caused. She closed her eyes and pictured the green lawns of Merrifield with the sun rising over the hill, the sky pink with dawn.

She climbed out of bed, dragging a scratchy, brown blanket as a wrapper, and crossed to the door. Locked. He hadn't abandoned her; he'd made her a prisoner. She leaned her head against the wood, her hand on the knob. Her head throbbed. She had not slept well and would have to summon all her will to resist him.

She looked about the room. Her wedding dress was draped across the screen. Putting it on again seemed an admission of her helplessness, but she had no other clothes. The roses and the pins from her hair were on the dresser beside a basin and a pitcher. A thin towel hung on a rod to one side.

She ducked behind the screen and did what she could with her dress. Then she went to the dresser to work on her hair. The roses stopped her. She could not bear to see them fade. She pulled them from the garland, cut the ends with a razor she found lying there, and arranged them in a cup with some water from the pitcher. Her confidence returned as she worked at the little task.

She was pinning her hair up when there was a sharp rap on the door, a moment to pull the blanket up, then he was there, a large, black bundle under one arm.

She turned from the small cracked mirror, and he stopped dead, unmoving, his gaze fixed on her. All the danger she thought had passed crackled in his silence. "Good morning," he said.

Her skin flushed under his scrutiny. She straightened, bringing her gaze more level with his. "Do you mean to keep me a prisoner here?" she asked, as lightly as possible.

"Yes." A tight, dry syllable. He closed the door firmly and tossed his bundle onto the bed. Then he moved toward her, backing her into the corner beside the dresser. "I'm sorely tempted to do just that. To keep you here and woo you until you yield to me."

"We decided I mustn't yield."

"We?" He moved again, and she backed up against the wall. "I can be very persuasive." He flattened his palms against the wall on either side of her head, and concentrated all the intensity of his gray gaze on her.

"Don't," she said. She hoped he did not hear the effort she made to keep her voice steady.

"Don't what?" He leaned closer. "I haven't even touched you."

She clutched the blanket tighter. "Seduce me."

"You think I can?"

"You'll try."

"I haven't yet."

"Then be kind. Let me go."

He shook his head. "I can't," he said fiercely. He pressed his hips against hers, and she went perfectly still. The outline of his body at the juncture of her hip and thigh was unmistakable. She thought of Nan's words about a man's root.

The touch was wholly male, shocking in its frank admission of desire. But the look in his eyes made it something else, transformed the press of swollen flesh into an intolerable longing to leave the self's isolation. Inside her a taut emptiness answered with the need to be filled.

He tilted his hips up, a slow stroke, seeking to increase the contact, and brought his mouth to hers, taking possession in a fierce kiss, compelling her to open to him, and remain open, suspended, waiting, for something he was withholding, something that would release the tension inside her.

At last he broke away, turning his back, his shoulders stiff, his pent breath expelled in gusts, his hands buried in the folds of his arms. Rosalind pressed her lips closed and willed her heart to slow its beats. He straightened and moved to stand at the bed. "You want to get the hall back?"

"Yes," she said, though a moment earlier she had forgotten it, her will consumed in his.

"I think there's a way. I think Barton rigged those games to make your brother lose, and we may be able to prove it."

She studied his back, wondering where his thoughts were leading. He had mentioned Barton's cheating once before, but it made no difference. "The money my brother owed Barton was owed before the party began."

"If we can prove Barton lent Gerald the money in order to set him up, Barton can be prosecuted for fraud."

"Then he won't be able to collect on those debts?"

Winterburn still had his back to her. "Barton will have to flee or go to gaol."

"How can we prove Barton's intent was fraud?"

"We talk to the other guests." He picked up the black bundle and turned. She had no time to mask her surprise or misgivings. He must have read them in her face. "Can you do it?" His voice challenged her.

She met his gaze without faltering.

"I know what happened that night," he said quietly. "Hunt told me."

The humiliation of her brother's sale of her came back. "You knew and you married me?"

It was his turn to look away. "You don't want to hear my opinion of your departed brother."

"You must see then why Merrifield is important to me, why I must protect it from those who would lose it or ruin it."

"Even if you must sell yourself?"

"Yes."

"Is this some superstitious folly? The Rose of Rowdene must sacrifice herself for the village?"

Rosalind shook her head. "You don't understand. Merrifield doesn't belong to me. I belong to it."

A long moment passed. "Then you can face a few sots who happened to be at your brother's unfortunate card party."

She drew a deep breath. "Yes, but . . ." She held out the skirts of her ruined gown. "Like this?"

"Like this." He turned to the bundle on the bed, working the strings. "Your doublet and hose, Rosalind. You'll be a young clerk I've hired to take down our witnesses' statements."

She stepped forward, and he opened the paper.

"I borrowed this gear from a friend who's studying the law. You'll look a proper clerk in this." He held up black breeches and a judicial robe.

She took the unfamiliar clothes, conscious that he was offering much more than a disguise—a chance to free herself from Barton, from the consequences of Gerrie's folly. With Winterburn's help. She would not do it alone, nor would he do it for her. They would be partners, and she would not have to sell her possessions or herself.

"Thank you." She hugged the black robe to her.

"I'll give you a few minutes to transform yourself into my clerk." He stepped out, and she was left to don her disguise.

There was a strange ease in putting on a man's clothes. The fastenings and buttons were all in the front, the openings wide, requiring no wriggling, no assistance. There was nothing to tighten. She paused in the act of stepping into the pants, suddenly arrested by the thought that she was stepping into his life. She fumbled with the fall of the breeches, tucking in the shirt. She would have to ask for help in the matter of the neck cloth. She bent to check her appearance in the mirror and realized that the garments were no disguise unless she did something with her hair.

He knocked again, and when she called out that she was dressed, he entered. His gaze slid down her person to the plain hose and pumps, above them her calves and ankles exposed to his view.

"I need help with the cravat," she said, drawing his gaze up. "And my hair."

He had a kettle in one hand and set it on a towel on the old dresser. "Come here then," he said.

She took a cautious step his way. He took her

by the shoulders and turned her to face the mirror in front of him. Their eyes met in the glass for one moment of precarious balance between reason and madness. A fraction of an ounce more will on one side, and the scales would tip. His hands tightened on her shoulders, and he buried his face in her hair.

"The neckcloth," she reminded him. She raised a shaky hand, offering him the long piece of linen.

He lifted his head and took the cloth, draped it around her neck, and with a few deft moves produced a neat fold.

"My hair?" she reminded him.

"Smells like roses," he said.

"Needs to be disguised."

He smiled wickedly. "There was a wig in that bundle. Did you not see it?"

She stepped past him and looked at the remains of the bundle. On the floor was a short, gray wig with a pair of curls on each side and a queue. She bent, scooped it up, and settled it on her head, tucking in stray wisps of red. He looked a bit regretful as her hair disappeared under the gray, but she grinned at him. "Who am I now?"

"Mr. Ross Lind, clerk. And I expect you to know your place, Mr. Lind, and be a dutiful, discreet employee."

"I don't think so." She pulled the barrister's robe about her. "I think Mr. Lind is a fellow who knows the dignity of his position. He won't hesitate to advise his employer on even the most trifling matters."

She had caught him off guard. Suddenly he laughed. "I beg your pardon, Mr. Lind. Would you be so obliging as to occupy your keen legal mind for a few minutes while I shave?"

She kept her eyes on her robes, suddenly shy at this new intimacy, but her voice was steady. "Go right ahead, Lord Winterburn. I'll wait."

Images of Winterburn shaving came back to haunt her that night as soon as the bed dipped under his weight. It was near three, she guessed. The weariness that had made her eyes heavy as they ate a late supper had fled. She felt edgy and lay still with difficulty.

He lay with his back to her, his shoulder lifting the covers, creating a stir of air that brought her the scent of his shaving soap. She realized the smell of him was now as familiar as the smells of woodbine and meadowsweet at home, by which she could locate herself.

"Thank you for today," she said.

"You enjoyed your foray into male London, did you?"

"I had no idea of male independence before. I thought myself independent in Wiltshire, but now I see that a pair of breeches confers a great deal more freedom than I imagined."

It was an invitation to talk, but he didn't turn or speak. She tugged the covers closer about her body, and he shifted, releasing the blankets to her pull. It was so immediate a response that she caught her breath.

"I suppose you're tired," she said.

"Yes."

"And you are uncomfortable sharing a bed with me?"

He didn't answer at once, and she wondered if he meant to ignore her. "This is not sharing a bed."

"I didn't mean . . . we can talk, can't we?"

"Talk?" He rolled over, facing her.

They were just inches apart. The slope of the mattress inclined her body toward his. "I know I hadn't much to say earlier, but—"

"You want to review the evidence we gathered today?"

"Yes."

"When you speak, I can feel your breath on my face."

His words annihilated the distance between them. They were not so much separated then as joined by the air. She should turn away and remain silent, only she couldn't.

"There's only one act more intimate in a bed than talk," he said. There was a little rustle of the covers, and she felt his hand, warm and heavy, cup her jaw. He dragged the rough pad of his thumb across her lips. "Talk, then."

His thumb coaxed her mouth open, reminding her of that moment in the morning when he had kissed her and left her wanting. She struggled to recall what was important to say to him.

"Mr. Davies was helpful," she said. They had dined with Davies in a male preserve in Jermyn

Street, where Rosalind had spent the meal taking notes of Davies's observations on her brother's card party.

"Yes. Davies more than Maitland." Winterburn's thumb continued to stroke her lips.

He was touching only her lips, but the sensation seemed to awaken every nerve. She clutched his wrist, struggling to hold onto the thought she'd had earlier in the day. "You think Mr. Crawley was in on it with Barton? He always played at Gerrie's table."

"He probably signaled Barton, too, letting him know when to distract your brother. It's Crawley we have to get to tomorrow."

"Will that be difficult?"

"Less difficult than some things." His thumb stopped moving.

She held still. The friction of his thumb had made her helpless, clinging to him like a bit of leaf or blossom caught in her skirts. She wanted to lean toward him but knew that she must think of Merrifield and turn away.

"Tomorrow, then," she said. She released his arm and rolled over, a small move that required a great effort, tucking into herself, trying to compress the emptiness she felt into a tiny bearable knot, somewhere about her heart.

Chapter 20

 ⌒ ∽∽ ⌒

It was a fine June night. All London seemed to
be dancing, and Sydney needed a woman. His
countess's slights and his own impatience with
Rosalind Merrifield's man of business left him
restless and uneasy, and he needed to keep his
head. Of all the brothels in London, he had, over
the years, come to patronize only two or three
which met his exacting standards. He did not care
to be offended by a girl's accent or her odor. He
did not like places where the girls did not have
their own rooms, nor places where the patrons
could expect to be spied upon.

At a modest establishment not far from the
opera house, he greeted the madam, made his
discreet request, and was ushered into the salon.
There was Crawley, a woman on his lap, another
leaning over him from behind. His neck cloth was
missing, his shirt and waistcoat gaping wide.

Crawley looked up, his hands still fumbling the
woman's exposed breasts. "Ah, Barton. Thought
you'd show here sooner or later." He returned his
gaze to the mounds of flesh in his hands.

"You were looking for me, Crawley?"

"Winterburn is asking around about your card party." Crawley squeezed the tart's nipples between his thumbs and forefingers, and the girl arched toward him. He grinned and buried his face in her breasts.

"Crawley!" The sharpness in Sydney's voice brought the other man's head up. "Who is Winterburn talking to? What's he asking about?"

Crawley pulled the girl's wrapper closed over her breasts. "He talked to Maitland and Davies and . . ." He pushed the girl off his lap, and lifted away the arms of the girl behind him.

"You haven't done me, love," she complained, thrusting her chest into his hands.

"Patience, Sophie," he said. "Come sit here a minute."

The girl settled herself beside him with sulky dignity and a little wriggle of her bottom which brought her body flush against Crawley's. The girl on his other side responded with a similar tactic, and for a minute the three on the couch were lost in writhing giggles.

"Hush now," said Crawley. "I've got to speak with Mr. Barton, here."

"Who else did Winterburn talk to?" Sydney asked. He was aware of a vein in his temple throbbing just a tiny bit.

"Me, of course, this afternoon," said Crawley.

"You didn't tell him anything, did you?"

"I'm not an idiot, Barton." Crawley put an arm around each of the girls. "Winterburn seems to think there was cheating at Merrifield's card party. I told him that was crazy. It was Merrifield's party."

"Yes, but why is he asking?"

"Don't know. He's serious though. He's got some clerk tagging along, taking it all down."

"Clerk?"

"A fellow in robes and wig. A very earnest fellow, a bit delicate in the wrist, if you catch my meaning, writes down every word." Crawley slid his hands down, grasping a breast of each of the girls, who giggled and squirmed in response.

Sydney took a step back. He crossed the salon to a table where spirits were kept for the guests and helped himself to a generous dash of brandy. Winterburn must have some legal proceeding in mind if he hired a clerk. Sydney swallowed half the brandy in his glass. Lord, he needed to clear his head. He took another swallow of drink. Behind him the giggling had developed into panting and rustling of garments.

When the inner door opened, Sydney turned. The madam presented a demure-looking brunette, who dropped him a quick curtsy. Sydney put down his glass and signaled that the girl would do.

He sauntered toward the door, stopping in front of the couch, where Sophie had now wriggled onto Crawley's lap.

"I would have called Winterburn out, of course," said Crawley, "but he didn't actually suggest cheating, you know."

"Just stay away from him, Crawley." Sydney gave Sophie's breast a squeeze. "And let me know if you hear anything else."

Jeremy Braithe rose to his feet with the crowd in the common room. The bride and groom were about to withdraw to their chamber, and the last toasts were turning the bride's cheeks a rosy hue. He saw the happy couple exchange a glance of proprietorship and promise, and he burned to exchange that look with Catherine Cole.

Someone brushed his arm, and he leaned back.

"Beggin' yer pardon, Mr. Braithe."

He turned to the husky voice and found Polly Rees looking up at him. With the press of the crowd, she stumbled into him again and clung to his arm, lifting bright-blue eyes to his. He could have laughed at the invitation in those eyes, but he thought the better of it. The girl had her misfortunes, too.

"Ye'll not be interested in a poor shepherd, Miss Rees," he said.

"I can choose, can't I?"

"Ye've not chosen so well now, have ye?" he asked quietly, loosening her hold on him. "Ye've been forsaken."

She shook her head, and a sly smile raised the corners of her mouth. She swayed a little. He put out a hand to steady her, and she fell against him, her breasts flattened to his chest. He had a flash of Catherine Cole leaning into him and pushed Polly firmly upright.

"Now, Miss Rees, let me walk ye home."

"Too soon. No one's going yet. Another drink," she said.

He steered her to the end of a bench, and she sat down heavily, a little belch escaping her pretty mouth. She giggled. "I choose, ye know."

"Choose what?" he asked. He handed her his tankard, and she took a long draft.

"Men. Handsome men. Like you."

Jeremy glanced around. No one was looking at them, but he was sure the gossips would not miss their talk. "Ye like poor men, then?"

She shrugged. "Doesn't matter. Polly's rich now."

He was beginning to regret the charitable impulse to help the girl. "Don't look rich to me. Looks like ye've got no husband and a babe on the way."

Polly patted her slightly rounded belly. "Ye can't get another one in me, so we can do what we like." Again she gave him a sultry look. "I've been paid handsome to make this babe."

The girl's odd smugness triggered a suspicion in his mind. "Who would pay fer that, Polly?"

She laughed again. "The richest lady in London."

The girl was daft. Maybe the pregnancy had turned her brain. "Let's get ye home, Polly."

"No." She put her hand on his thigh and rubbed.

He jerked and pulled her hand away.

She leaned toward him, her breasts swelling

above the low-cut bodice. "It's too dull here, and I've been so good. I've waited ever so long."

"Waited for what?"

"For the bishop to come. Bloody bishop. Once he comes and I tell 'im my story, I'll get the rest of what I'm owed. And my 'old da,' too, though all he does fer it is lay about and grouse."

There was another toast for the new bride and groom, everyone shouting and banging the tables. He studied Polly as she downed a long swallow of his ale, the fragments of their conversation shifting about in his brain. Suddenly he understood with cold clarity that she'd set out to shame Winterburn for money and that she was willing to boast about it. Jeremy planted his elbows on the table and gave Polly his full attention. "Yer a clever lass, then, aren't ye?"

"You have no idea." She stretched.

"Tell me," he said. He ran a finger over the tops of Polly's breasts and prayed he would talk to Catherine before any gossip reached her.

Hours later, it seemed, he was free of the girl. He followed the moonlit road to Catherine's gate and stood, letting the night air blow away the ripe odor of Polly Rees. In the end she had boasted quite enough. Jeremy was sure the babe in her belly belonged to one of Winterburn's golden-haired friends or to Barton. And he knew Mrs. Cheek, sitting on the bench next to theirs, had heard enough to spread the truth abroad.

He took a deep breath of country air, of earth and cows and green, growing things. And whis-

pered "good night" to Catherine Cole, asleep in
her quiet house.

The hackney Sydney had hired pulled to the
curb a discreet distance from Revelstoke's town
house just before noon. After leaving the brothel,
he had recovered his wits sufficiently to consider
Winterburn's actions. If Winterburn had inter-
viewed Davies, Maitland, and Crawley, he no
doubt knew the names of the other guests at
Merrifield's card party. Winterburn would probably interview the lot of them. That train of
thought had led Sydney to visit Revelstoke.

He now had the advantage of watching Winterburn and his clerk as they left Revelstoke's and
made their way toward Piccadilly.

The young man's robes hung loosely about
him. He was, as Crawley had said, a delicate
fellow. He tapped Winterburn's arm, a feminine
gesture. He wanted Winterburn to look at a small
notebook, like a schoolboy's copy book. The clerk
jabbed the page and started reading to Winterburn, evidently excited. Sydney's stomach
twisted sourly as if he'd had a bit of bad meat.

The clerk's excitement raised annoying doubts,
undermining the certainty of Sydney's plans. He
reminded himself that whatever Davies and Revelstoke might suspect, only Crawley had been in
on it, and Crawley would be a fool to reveal his
part. Yet Sydney found himself staring at the little
book, as if it were a pistol pointing his way.

Too late, he realized Winterburn was approaching the cab. Sydney pulled his hat over his face

and slumped in the corner. He held his breath while Winterburn queried the driver.

"Sorry, sir, engaged," came the driver's response.

Sydney breathed again and waited for Winterburn to move on, but apparently the man was in no hurry.

"You don't mind walking, do you?" Winterburn asked his companion.

"Not at all."

Sydney stiffened.

"It's not Rowdene." Winterburn was plainly amused.

"I'll match you stride for stride, my lord."

Winterburn laughed. "I believe you will."

Sydney sat motionless. He dared not lift his hat to see the speakers. He didn't need to. He knew Rosalind Merrifield's voice. He waited until their footsteps faded, then he opened the cab door and glanced after them. The robes and wig concealed the girl's appearance, but Sydney had no doubt that she was masquerading as Winterburn's assistant. He gave the driver an order.

The driver turned the cab, and they followed behind the pair traveling on foot. Sydney's head pounded. He had been so careful to ensure that Gerald's debts to him were not the result of cards. All Gerald's vouchers had been properly witnessed and dated. Furthermore, Sydney had secured the support of Gerald's lessor creditors by promising them prompt payment once he assumed proprietorship of the hall. Only Rosalind Merrifield had stood in his way with the absurd delays contrived by her man of business. Now she was conspiring with Winterburn to cheat Sydney out of the hall.

The cab crossed a ditch of foul water. There the progress of a herd toward Smithfield held up traffic while the stench of dung and cattle rose around them. Sydney closed his eyes and saw the expanse of green acreage that would soon be his. He would not sit in hired cabs in the stink of London. He would be master of Merrifield, host to men of rank and fortune. The Countess of Winterburn would be pleased to lean upon his arm. In his own hall he would pump himself into her and erase the slights of the past.

He opened his eyes. His quarry eluded him, traveling on foot where he could not follow. His thoughts turned to the notebook Rosalind Merrifield held in her hands. He leapt from the cab and paid off the driver. If he could get his hands on it, the little book would explain what they were up to.

"You think we were followed?" Rosalind held the door while Winterburn brought in a tray from the inn kitchen. He had insisted they leave the common room where they usually took their meals.

"From Revelstoke's," he said.

She tossed the precious notebook on the bed and removed the basin and ewer from the dresser to the floor. He set the tray down.

"That cab!" She straightened, glancing at him for confirmation.

He nodded. He hooked a finger in the bow of his cravat and tugged. The knot gave, and he unwound the linen from his throat. She gripped the edge of the dresser with her fingertips, pressing firmly against the rough surface. After three days she should be inured to the little intimacies of sharing his room, but each day sharpened her awareness of him.

"You got a great deal out of Revelstoke today," she said, fixing her gaze on the white tips of her fingers. Their latest witness had been surprisingly forthcoming when Winterburn suggested that Gerrie's death would be investigated.

"The details about Crawley will help us." He shrugged out of his coat.

"Do you think we still need to talk to Jenny and Alice?" Her voice was faint.

He didn't answer at once. "Let me help you with your neckcloth." She turned automatically, then strained to stand straight and still under the light touch of his hands. Her heart thudded heavily, and her breasts ached with an immodest desire to arch upward toward his hands. She stared at his shoulder.

He turned to put away his coat and neckcloth. "Crawley is the kind who boasts to women. If he's seen Jenny and Alice since your brother's party, he's likely to have let something slip."

"Will they be our last witnesses?" she asked, watching the careless movement of his hands. He did not seem to feel the terrible pull of nearness.

"How many do we have?" he asked.

She sank on the edge of the bed and opened the book across her knees. The pages seemed heavy and difficult to turn, and her notes, incomprehensible. Each interview had yielded some clue to another witness, until they had spoken with servants and gambling hell proprietors and anyone to whom Gerrie owed money. She forced her sluggish brain to count the names.

"We have fifteen sure witnesses." She closed the book and laid it on the bed.

"Barton doesn't stand a chance."

She looked up. "I owe that to you."

He didn't return her glance. "It won't come to court, you know," he said quietly. "Barton will flee before he'll face a nasty scandal."

Rosalind stood. They had won and she should feel elated, but some alteration in his voice left her doubting she'd gained anything at all. She could summon no vision of Merrifield, only him.

He stood at the dresser, staring at the roses she had arranged in a cup the morning after their wedding. With a light brush of his knuckles, he disturbed the petals, releasing a faint, sweet fragrance in the air. The gesture stirred a deeper disturbance in Rosalind, a ripple of wakening sensation. She closed her hands to keep from reaching out to him. She wanted his touch.

It was a bad time for such a realization. The long, idle hours of late afternoon lay ahead of them before they would seek their next witnesses. The room offered no distance, no concealment. Deliberately, she crossed to the opposite corner and busied herself with removing her male disguise, first the heavy clerk's robe and stiff shoes.

"It wasn't Mr. Harwood following us?" she asked, keeping her voice even.

"No. I told Harwood I would return you to him by the end of the week."

She spun around. "You did? When?"

He picked up the ale cup from the tray as if it absorbed his entire attention. "By post. Monday."

She averted her gaze before he could see her surprise. He had accepted her choice. He would let her go. She should find no wonder in it. Even when she got her home back, she was merely a poor country girl. He was Winterburn. He had played at parson, but she had seen him in his world. In the night they had passed the glittering windows of the grand houses, watched the lines of crested carriages, entered the exclusive men's clubs and gambling hells. Winterburn knew them all and moved among them with careless indifference, his face, his very walk, altered from his familiar demeanor in Rowdene. His marriage should be a grand alliance of rank and fortune.

She shook off her clerk's robe, straightened its folds, and hung it on a wall hook. How pleased and hopeful she'd been to wear it not two days before. Now its black folds seemed a sad omen. She removed the cravat he'd undone, the waistcoat, and lastly the gray wig, shaking her hair free and twisting it into a knot at her nape.

"Your tea grows cold," he said.

She turned, and his gaze caught and held her

an instant; then he seemed to withdraw into himself. All her little keys, useless to open what was closed to her. A peculiar ache settled inside where she had not known she could feel anything. She went to the dresser. He stirred at her drawing close, a tightening of his frame she sensed rather than saw. Carefully she picked up the teapot, a plain glazed-clay pot, its surface an intricate maze of cracks, the spout chipped. She would never forget it.

He had told her she didn't know what there was to want. She knew only the wanting itself, which made her feel hollow and tight. She wished the teacup a deep well so that she could pour forever. The moment closed around them, holding her frozen.

When it ended, she set down the pot and took up her cup. He was strangely silent, and she realized how their talk had filled the space between them, which now seemed empty.

Winterburn lowered his ale cup to the dresser and moved unhurriedly to the door. "You'll likely be home next week."

It was what she wanted, what she'd fought for, but there was no triumph in the victory.

His hand was on the knob. If he left now, something would be lost, something she must have. She had to make him stay. She put aside her tea. "Wait."

He glanced over his shoulder. His hand slipped from the door.

A shaft of late-afternoon sunlight from the window made the dust motes sparkle in the air around him as he turned. The ordinary, insignificant substance of the world was made brilliant and set to dancing on invisible currents of air. Rosalind caught her breath.

Leigh felt a door inside him crack ajar and was powerless to close it. Her remarkable eyes hid nothing of what she wanted. What he wanted would mean her ruin. He had told her the first time he kissed her that she didn't know what there was to want. Now she wanted to know.

A small harsh laugh escaped him. "You touched me . . . five times today."

"Five?"

"Five." And every touch had made burning fuses of his nerves, igniting the desire in him. "Shall I catalog them?"

"Please." Her breath came out in a long sigh.

"A hand on my shoulder as we descended the stair, your elbow brushing mine at breakfast, your head against mine as we studied the book, a brief collision in Revelstoke's entry, and a tap on my arm outside his door."

She bowed her head, her hands clasped tightly. "I suppose in these circumstances knowing what one wants is worse than not knowing?"

He swore silently at her cursed perceptiveness.

"I just feel I want something, and the wanting consumes me," she said. "If it's worse for you, it is no wonder you were about to leave." She unclasped her hands, lifting them palms up in a gesture of appeal.

He swallowed. "I should have left." He should have retreated long before temptation reached this point, turned, passed through the door, locked it behind him. Instead he closed the distance between them, seizing her hands in a hard grip. "It's hard to stop once you've begun."

She lifted her head, her eyes bleak with comprehension. "You're saying we should do nothing."

He couldn't answer. Months of self-restraint counted for nothing, a candle's pale flicker in the darkness of his soul. A sharp gust of desire blasted that brief flame of resistance and left him shaking. He wanted her.

He lifted her hands and kissed one palm and then the other, placing them on his shoulders. He would not tie her to him. He would stop if it killed him. He cupped her face and brought her mouth to his, offering a taste of desire. Her kiss asked for more. He showed her how to open for him but held back his tongue and the plunge into mindlessness.

Again the sweet press of her mouth to his begged for more. He swept his hands down her back. A stumbling step brought her closer. Her breasts flattened against his chest; her hipbone brushed his taut male flesh. He froze and broke the kiss. The bed, he reasoned.

If they lay side by side, he could press his aching groin to the mattress. He nudged her up on the bed. The mattress sagged, and she tumbled onto her back with a surprised peal of laughter, a shining presence in the afternoon shadows. Her male garments hid nothing of the slim curve of hip and thigh, the juncture where he longed to be.

For a moment he could not breathe. Her wondering gaze passed over him, caught the rigid swelling of his sex, and returned to his face.

He joined her on the bed, braced himself on his elbows, and slid his fingers through her hair, freeing the knot at her nape, reveling in the silky softness, while her hands answered in kind, touching his face, tracing his brows.

His hand went to her waist and slid up along her ribs. She sucked in a breath, and he could feel a quiver deep inside her. He fit his hand to one small, firm breast, and a glad light shone in her eyes. He brushed lightly until the nipple tightened and her breaths grew shallow.

Her hands opened and closed against his chest, then flattened and stroked, mimicking his touch, asking for more. When she outlined his ribs, he grabbed her wrist, forcing it back to the bed, surging forward to cover her with his upper body and press his mouth to hers again.

He felt lifted out of himself. He allowed his hand to stroke down her side, over her hip, along her thigh to the bend of one knee. He pushed up on one arm, breaking their kiss and tugging her shirt free of the waistband. He freed her of shirt and shift, exposing her smooth, golden-hued skin. The trapped pulse beat in her throat as he traced the winged lines of her collarbone and lowered his head to her breast.

Then a tiny row of indentations caught his gaze, across her heart and ribs where the buttons of his waistcoat had pressed, his mark on that sweet flesh. He raised himself to his knees and stripped off the offending waistcoat, then his shirt.

Lowering himself again, he allowed the barest contact of skin to skin, a brush that woke the tips of her breasts. She clutched his arms and drew him down. *More, don't stop yet,* her touch said.

Braced on his elbows, he framed her ribs with his arms and buried his head in her breasts. Her hands covered his head, a flutter of touches.

He willed his body to stillness, but it would not obey. His knee nudged her limbs apart, that his hand might have access, and he stroked her thigh until she shifted restlessly and whimpered against his temple. Then he let his hand come to rest where her male garb hid the petals he must not touch. He lifted his head. She stilled, drawn taut with wanting, her eyes dark with it.

"I want to touch you," he said on a ragged breath.

"And I you."

He shook his head.

With a little cry she took his hand from her woman's place and pulled his mouth down to hers again. Her sweet self-denial pierced him, goaded him. A surge of desire bore him up, and he slipped between her thighs.

She smiled a welcome, and he rocked against her, tipping his body up in an accelerating cadence. She clutched his arms, and he felt the tension build in her until her slim form shuddered like a sapling quaking in the wind. Surprise blossomed in her gaze. A sigh of wonder floated up from her parted lips, and her grip on his arms slackened.

He felt oddly humbled and exalted. For once he had made of his body's urgings not a curse but a gift. He rolled onto his back and pulled her into the lee of his arm, kissing the damp curls at her forehead, brushing light feather touches across her breast.

She twisted toward him and with a sudden move cupped him gently in her palm. His breath hissed through his teeth, and his body flashed up to meet that touch before his startled will could take hold. He grabbed her wrist and pressed her hand to his heart.

"Don't you want me to touch you?" she whispered.

"You cannot imagine how much." He didn't release her hand. He coaxed her back into the circle of his arm and covered her with his discarded shirt. She nestled closer. His body shook, and he took a steadying breath.

She did not sleep as he had expected. Her breath made a warm halo above his heart. He could almost feel her thinking, a deep concentration he sensed through the stillness of her body.

Rosalind lay in his arms, thinking of what had passed between them. With his body he had coaxed some tiny hidden bud of pleasure to bloom and consume her senses. That was the first knowledge he gave her, a wicked grace.

In its light every meeting between them appeared altered. She saw that she must forgive him

for taking her from Mr. Harwood's. But she
needed his forgiveness, too, and could not beg his
pardon, for the second knowledge he gave was
terrible. In that stunned moment of her body's
awakening to its own sensuality, she had understood his self-denial. Schoolgirl whisperings and
intuition had fused into absolute knowledge, and
she had reached for him to offer something of
what he'd given her. His body had leapt in
answer to her touch, before his will had stopped
her.

With her wrist in his tight grasp, she understood that she had been right about his nature
when she believed in his goodness. And those
who thought him selfish and carnal were wrong.
He was, above all, generous.

Shadows had overtaken the room before she
spoke again. "I think you would make a good
curate for Rowdene."

"You think I should ascend the pulpit and
admonish the villagers to avoid sin?" The mockery was back in his voice, and she ached to hear it.

"I think you could preach to them about charity
and kindness, things at which you are good."

His hand drifted slowly down her arm.

"I did write a sermon once."

She held her breath. "Tell me," she said lightly.

"It was about the wickedness of lighting candles in church and playing ball on Sunday."

She sensed his smile and gave his hand on her
arm a sharp tug. "Tell me."

"I think there are only three sins I could truly
preach against." He paused. "I would say, don't

admire power; don't scorn the unfortunate; don't hate your enemy."

Rosalind felt the ache in her heart expand.

"No, I won't go back to Rowdene."

"Where will you go?" she asked.

"The army."

"But you'll return to Rowdene for your books and things?"

"Dowdeswell can see to packing up for me."

"You won't try for another living?"

"I think we've proved my lack of fitness for the clerical life."

"No. If not Rowdene, you must ask your uncle to see that you find a living elsewhere." She gripped his hand hard.

He gave hers an answering squeeze. "I have one last favor to ask of Uncle Ned, one he should be willing to grant."

Rosalind hugged the small notebook to her chest and slouched in the doorway. It was important to feign ease in her present surroundings. Gray light revealed the narrow street and carters and vendors going about their early business. A cab passed by, moving slowly, the horses' hooves a hollow clop against the paving stones.

At this last place she'd insisted on waiting outside. Winterburn didn't like their being separated, but he didn't want her inside where Alice and Jenny plied their trade. He would hurry the business. From women like them he had learned to know the mysteries of women's bodies that Rosalind was just beginning to learn. Their eyes would read every glance between Rosalind and Winterburn.

Much wiser to lurk in the doorway in this low neighborhood than to sit at Winterburn's side, conscious of all that had passed between them in the inn's narrow bed, though she could think of little else.

She tucked her chin over the top of the little notebook and stared at the pavement. Her life stretched out equally blank and hard. But to think that was to betray Merrifield. She took a deep breath and thought of home.

The hedges with their plumes of privet, the ditches lined with masses of creamy meadow-sweet, elder blossoms and purple foxglove mingling on the banks, the grass heavy with pollen—these would restore her to herself. The fields even now would be turning gold for the harvest ahead. The image of Winterburn striding the roads intruded. She suspected he had called on every house in the parish, a thing Vernon would never have considered. The thought that Winterburn belonged in Rowdene struck her with renewed force.

She was suddenly impatient for him to come down. There must be some way to restore him to the living. She raised her chin. Her feet were cold, and she wiggled her toes in the stiff shoes. Stepping down to the pavement, she paced back and forth in front of the doorway. The street was filling with people going about their morning business.

The slow hackney cab that had lingered at the

far end of the street came back her way. She made a few more turns in front of the house, restoring her numb feet to life. When she looked up again, the cab had stopped in front of her. The moment stretched as the door swung open, and the steps rattled into place, jarring her memory of the scene outside Revelstoke's. They had been followed again.

She spun and dashed for Jenny's apartment. She rapped the knocker, banging to wake the dead, and opened her mouth to shout. But she was slammed against the door. Her cheekbone and knuckles collided against wood with a dull crack. The gray wig slipped over one ear. A rough hand jerked her around.

For an instant she could only stare at Barton's face. Rage turned his sharp countenance feral. He clawed at the notebook, and she twisted away. Her foot missed the step, and she stumbled down to the pavement, fighting to keep her balance. Barton gave her a shove which sent her staggering against the hackney coach. She pushed off it and faced him. The house door burst open, and Winterburn leapt from the step with a shout.

Barton seized her arm and yanked her to him, making her body a shield. She felt the jab of cold, blunt steel under her chin, Barton's hot breath across her ear.

Winterburn froze, not three yards from them, his face altered in some fundamental way. Slowly his fists opened. He pulled himself back, assumed an air of indifference.

"You can't win," he said, his eyes on Barton.

"Oh, I think I can," Barton said. He sidled along the hackney to the carriage steps, dragging Rosalind.

"Here now, mate. What's this about?" the driver called from the box.

"Just drive," Barton ordered. "I'm returning the girl to respectable company."

The driver subsided, mumbling to his horse.

Winterburn's fists closed on air. Rosalind felt Barton behind her climb the cab step. She went limp, letting her weight slow him. Barton grunted, trying to drag her up the step. She forced herself to wait. He would have to lower the gun.

Barton panted, bending forward to pull her through the narrow cab door. She felt the strain in his arm as he bore more of her weight. The gun fell away from her chin. She tossed the notebook at Winterburn and grabbed the door frame with both hands. Winterburn kicked the notebook away.

She saw him spring toward her. Then a jarring blow to the back of her head knocked the wig over her eyes. She tilted her head to dislodge the wig, and the gun fired next to her ear with a deafening crack. For an instant her hold on the door frame slackened. Barton wrenched her into the cab. The startled horse shied, and the cab lurched forward.

Chapter 21

Rosalind tore off the wig and scrambled to her knees on the dirty floor of the cab, an unthinkable image driving her: Winterburn lying in the street, bleeding. She pushed aside the window curtain. The cab rocked with the horse's speed. A sick dizziness made her wobble on her knees. Houses slid by, but she could not see back along the street. She turned on Barton. "You shot him!"

His face was white. "No."

"Let me out. I've got to get to him." She grabbed the door handle.

Barton seized her arm, lifting her and flinging her against the seat. "I missed."

His voice sounded odd, distant. She clutched her ringing ear and willed her head to clear. The gun had been dangling in Barton's hand, pointing where? She could not picture the precise angle, nor the bullet's path to Winterburn. The crucial instant in which the wig had blocked her vision concealed everything. She could not be sure he had been hit.

Barton fumbled with the little pistol, reloading.

She lunged for the door. Barton's leg came up to block her, and with a shove he sent her sprawling.

"You'll hang," she told him.

He merely glanced at her, his gaze sliding to her legs, exposed in the man's breeches. She tugged at the robes tangled under her. He slipped the pistol into his coat pocket. "You should be grateful to me, Miss Merrifield. I've rescued you from the filthy embraces of the would-be parson."

Rosalind freed the robe from under her and started to tuck it around her legs, but Barton ripped the garment from her hand.

"Winterburn's not backward in the manly arts. He must have taught you a few tricks by now." Barton shoved a hand between her thighs, squeezing her flesh in a tight violating grip.

Rosalind gasped. Her legs closed against the intrusive hand, and she twisted, pressing back against the seat, tearing at the hand.

"Don't tell me Winterburn hasn't been here already." Barton's fingers probed. "I can smell him on you."

Rosalind raked her nails across his hand. He snatched it back, and she clamped her legs together, panting. Her head ached, her ear throbbed.

"You should have married me." Barton licked his wounded hand.

Rosalind gave him a look of loathing. "Never, not even to save the hall."

His nostrils flared, and he slapped her. "Bitch."

She thought her injured ear would burst. She tasted blood on her lip. Fighting him was not

working. She had to get back to Winterburn. She
lifted her chin and steadied her voice. "Let me go,
and you can have the house."

A flicker of doubt crossed Barton's face. "So
that you and Winterburn can take it from me in
court?" He shook his head. "What do you know?
What's in that notebook?"

It was a slip, a small one, but a slip. Barton *had*
cheated Gerrie. Rosalind composed her features.
She would give nothing away.

Barton seized her shoulders and shook her.
"You think you can scare me off, do you? Your
brother's vouchers were all signed and witnessed
long before that card party. He owed me." He let
her go.

Rosalind slumped back against the seat. "If that
were true," she said, "you would not have abducted me today." She had him there. His eyes
shifted right and left as if searching for a way out.
Then he seemed to come to himself again.

"You're very wrong, my dear." He leaned back
in his corner. "This is a rescue. Witnesses will
testify that Winterburn abducted you days ago
and held you for his filthy purposes. Until Sydney
Barton, dear friend of your late brother, restored
you to polite society."

She gaped at him. "Where are you taking me?"

"To Lady Winterburn. No one can object to
that."

Rosalind knew he read the disbelief in her eyes.

"Really. I have your best interests at heart." He
leered. "Even dowerless and deflowered, you can

make a suitable match with Lady Winterburn's help."

Rosalind started at the suggestion. He hadn't guessed the truth, and she musn't let him. She must keep him thinking about the hall. "I don't want a match. I want my house."

A nerve twitched in Barton's jaw. His hand jerked up as if he meant to hit her again. "*My* house."

Rosalind said nothing. His rage was unlike anything she'd ever seen. She must wait, but she had never despised patience so much. If Winterburn was bleeding . . . She tried not to think it. Jenny and Alice would come to his aid. If Barton was really taking her to Lady Winterburn's, there would be someone there who could help her.

They came into a larger street full of milling crowds. The cab slowed until Rosalind wanted to scream at the delay. Confused shouts reached her good ear. Barton cracked the window. "Victory," the voices cried. A man pressed the *Morning Chronicle* against the glass, the print plain: "Total Defeat of Bonaparte."

The cab spurted forward again, and Barton glanced at her. "Fitting. My day of victory, too."

They stopped at a brick mansion in a fine square Rosalind had never seen. Barton clamped a hand on her wrist and pulled her from the cab after him. Coachmen engrossed in talk stood along a row of elegant crested carriages. She shouted, but no one turned. Barton rapped sharply on the mansion door. A harried footman admitted them to an entry like a Greek temple with a dome of light far above them.

"Help me," Rosalind cried, but the man appeared not to see her.

The butler rushed forward, blocking their progress.

"The countess, Peck," Barton demanded.

"Is not at home, Mr. Barton," replied Peck. His correct gaze made no note of Rosalind.

She stepped forward. "Mr. Peck, please listen. I think Lord Winterburn's been shot."

Barton yanked her back and jabbed the small pistol into her ribs. "Lady Winterburn will receive me," he insisted to the butler.

The other man's eyes widened, but he repeated, "My lady is not at home."

"She is to me," Barton said, "or the scandal will ruin her sons."

Barton swung his gun arm wide, sending a tall porcelain vase crashing to the floor of the marble entry. The startled Peck retreated with an undignified hop. Two footmen edged back.

"I'll wait in the small salon," Barton announced. He dragged Rosalind past the three men, into a sumptuous apartment with blue brocade walls and a marble mantel flanked by fluted Ionic columns. He shut the door and shoved Rosalind onto one of a pair of red tapestry sofas facing each other in front of the fireplace. She pulled herself up. Footsteps hurried by outside the room, then the knob turned.

A tall, dark-haired woman entered, a sleek

gown of lavender silk rustling with her purposeful
stride. She stopped just inside the door.

"Barton?" The woman raised a brow, her blue
eyes contemptuous. Rosalind caught her breath.
The imperious manner was Winterburn's exactly.

"You've terrified my servants," the lady continued. "What is this intrusion about?"

Barton waved the pistol toward Rosalind. The
woman's glance registered the gun, but passed to
Rosalind and took in her male garments, her hair
tumbled down about her shoulders. The other
woman's brow went up again. "A doxy of yours,
Barton?"

Barton laughed. "May I present Miss Merrifield. I mentioned her plight to you a fortnight
ago."

The countess's glance, now sharp and assessing, came back to Rosalind. "I remember. And
you've brought her here today because . . ."

"He shot . . ." Rosalind began, but Barton
backhanded her, splitting her lip, numbing her
tongue. She clutched the sofa, black dots swirling
before her eyes. The countess gave her a contemptuous glance.

"Because she's become an obstacle to things we
want," he said.

"We?"

"Will you sit, Countess?"

"Barton, really, you've heard the news today.
Wellington's won, and there are many people
upstairs I must see." She glanced over her shoulder at the door.

"Sit, Elizabeth."

She gave him a frigid glare. "I beg your pardon, Barton. What you do with this girl is no concern of mine. Do excuse me." She turned to the door.

Barton spun away from Rosalind and sent a delicate figurine smashing from the mantel to the floor. The countess paused, her hand on the knob. Barton, panting, spoke again. "It must . . . be your concern, Elizabeth, unless you wish to ruin your sons."

The countess glanced over her shoulder. "Barton, come to your senses, or I will have you removed."

"Removed? Am I a piece of furniture?"

A short silence answered him before the countess spoke again. "I won't play games with you today, Barton."

"Thinking of Trevor's career? Think again, Elizabeth. Trevor made a scandalous bid for this woman not three days ago. Then Winterburn stole her to enjoy her favors in some love nest."

The countess turned with slow majesty and advanced toward Barton with a lazy stroll. "You've been listening to absurd fictions. Leave the girl and the gun, and come join everyone in the large salon."

She was coaxing now. Her voice drew Barton across the room. He halted before her, breathing deeply, as if he could drink her in. The hand with the gun dropped to his side. Then the countess made a miscalculation. A little clock on the mantel chimed, and she gave it a quick glance, full of her impatience with an unwanted caller. "We'll talk later," she said.

Barton shook his head. He raised the gun. "You must persuade Winterburn to abandon his action against me."

"I must? You will tell me what I must do?" Her voice was low, husky, and filled with soft scorn.

Barton ran the pistol along the neckline of her gown. "Yes."

She lifted her chin. "How can I persuade a grown son, Barton? You aren't thinking clearly."

He spun away from her, stalking to the mantel. Behind him the countess edged toward a small table. Rosalind scooted along the sofa toward the countess.

"He shot Winterburn," she whispered to the other woman.

"What?" The countess's head snapped up. Her hands left the table drawer hanging open. "You shot Winterburn?"

Barton whirled, pointing the gun at Rosalind. "Elizabeth, she's lying."

"Where is he?" The countess strode to the bellpull.

"Don't ring, Elizabeth. Look at me," Barton's voice implored. "I left Winterburn standing in front of a brothel not half an hour ago."

"You shot him," Rosalind said.

"I missed," Barton shouted.

The countess stared at him, her hand poised at the bellpull. The door opened, and a young man scurried forward. "Mother, the war secretary . . ."

He stopped mid-stride. "What's going on?" His gaze went immediately to the pistol. "Barton, are you mad? What are you doing?"

The newcomer was a sleek, ruddy version of the countess, and Rosalind recognized him as the last bidder among her would-be buyers.

Lady Winterburn crossed to him in a flurry of silk skirts, taking his arm, steering him toward the door. "He is mad," she said. "We've got to find Winterburn. Call Peck."

As she spoke, the door opened again, and there was Winterburn. Rosalind swallowed a cry of joy.

"Looking for me, Mother?" he asked. His appearance seemed to freeze them all. His eyes were on Rosalind. She licked her swollen lip, tasting blood, and reached up to brush it away.

Leigh could not move. There was a rushing in his ears like wind. The little door in his heart swung wide open, and two words escaped. *Thank you.* And he understood that he had been praying from the moment Barton stuck his pistol to Rosalind's throat. A dozen prayers, a litany of need and faith and thankfulness, rose easily from his heart.

He strolled forward. He had only to get the gun away from Barton.

Rosalind searched Winterburn for some sign of a wound. She could detect no hurt, yet she thought his face drawn, his skin ashen under the summer tan he'd gained in Rowdene. She measured the chances of crossing to his side against the danger from Barton's pistol.

Lady Winterburn's hands fell away from her other son's arm, and she tucked a loose tendril of hair back into place. "Winterburn." She looked him over. "You've not been shot then. Miss Merrifield alarmed us unnecessarily." With stately indifference she took a seat on the couch opposite Rosalind.

Barton's pistol followed her movement, and Rosalind held her breath. Barton had become a cornered snarling thing. Rosalind was sure he was more dangerous than the countess realized.

"Barton." Lady Winterburn's voice was coaxing again. "Be so good as to put away the gun. It's not the proper calling card in these circles."

"No, Elizabeth," said Barton. "The gun is just what we need. If it's all a game to you, we'll play one of your favorites, the exchange of favors."

The countess appeared bored. She smoothed her skirts.

Winterburn had come closer without seeming to move. He glanced over his shoulder. "Trev, bring Mother a fan from that drawer."

Trevor stiffened. His expression gave another meaning to the request. He hesitated as if torn between advancing and retreating, then moved to the little table, keeping his eye on Barton.

"What favors do you think we have to trade, Barton?" the countess asked.

As she spoke, Winterburn inched forward. He reached the edge of the rich carpet on which the two couches stood. If Rosalind stretched out a hand, she could almost touch him.

"Stop there," Barton commanded.

Winterburn halted stiffly, like a lead soldier at attention, his arms straight at his sides.

Barton's gaze returned to the countess. "Winterburn must agree to drop any action against me and see that I get Merrifield Hall without further delay."

"I can't do that, Barton." Winterburn glanced at Rosalind. "The hall isn't yours."

"But it is. I have Gerald Merrifield's vouchers. All signed before the card party. All witnessed." Barton's voice was high, strained.

"More evidence against you. You mentioned the scheme to Crawley as early as March, and Crawley talked."

"To whores. What court will take the word of a tart?" Barton looked around wildly as if he could find support somewhere.

Winterburn took a long stride closer to his adversary. "You slipped, Barton. You invited Maitland to visit the hall for the hunt. You talked to Revelstoke about new livery for your footmen."

"It's nothing. Idle talk. Only the vouchers matter. Merrifield owed me."

Winterburn lifted his left hand to the arm of Rosalind's sofa. He seemed to be lifting stone. His knuckles gleamed stark white against the red upholstery. Rosalind thought the brown sleeve of his coat was wrong.

With a petulant sweep of his arm Barton emptied the mantel of clock and vases and porcelains. Brittle figurines shattered on the hearth with a discordant clang of the clock chimes.

Winterburn took two more quick steps. He was in front of the sofa, fully on the carpet.

Trevor shouted, "For God's sake, Leigh! Have a care! The fellow's mad."

Rosalind's breath caught in her throat. She saw that Winterburn meant to interpose his body between hers and the madman's gun. She rocked forward with infinite caution, shifting her weight to her feet, ready to leap between them.

"You have one shot, Barton." Winterburn paused. "Fire, and you'll hang."

Barton raised the pistol higher, steadying his aim on Winterburn. "You can't have everything, damn you."

"You're not a murderer. Yet. You can flee." Winterburn's tone was careless. "The Continent will open again now that Bonaparte's lost. Paris will suit you, I'm sure."

"No." Barton swung the gun toward Rosalind again. "I'll have the girl. The girl or the hall. You choose."

Winterburn gave a single shake of his head.

"You've ruined her, and as her brother's friend, I will offer her the protection of my name."

"I'm afraid not." Winterburn smiled coldly. "She's my wife."

"What?" said the countess, jumping up from the sofa. "She's not!"

Winterburn held out his hand to Rosalind, a slow, stiff leverage of his arm, and she knew what was wrong. His coat should be blue, not brown.

"May I present the new Lady Winterburn?" he said.

"The marriage will be annulled," the countess said.

Winterburn raised his outstretched hand a fraction higher, lifting the edge of his coat, exposing white silk stained red.

Rosalind gasped. "He has shot you!" She seized his hand.

His mother's gaze flew to Winterburn. "Sit, Winterburn." She turned on Barton. "Murderer! What have you done?"

"It's a lie," Barton cried.

"You pathetic worm." She glanced at Trevor. "Call Peck."

"Don't, Elizabeth." Barton aimed the gun at her. "You owe me. You all owe me."

The countess snorted. Winterburn seized her arm, holding her back, his gaze on Barton. "Flee," he advised. "Now, while you can."

"Fool," the countess shouted, attempting to shake Winterburn's hold. "Did you think you could be one of us?"

The pistol wobbled in Barton's hand. His eyes went blank.

"Mother!" cried Trevor. "Don't goad him."

The countess wrenched free of Winterburn's hold and strode to Barton. She dealt him a ringing slap, rocking him back on his heels.

"You senseless, puffed-up nothing. A bladder of conceits. Get out. I despise you. Get out."

Winterburn lunged, and Barton fired. An unnatural silence followed. Rosalind's stopped ear opened.

The countess twisted toward Winterburn, groping for his hand. Her knees buckled, and she crumpled to the floor. Winterburn knelt at her head.

"Mother!" Trevor cried.

"Elizabeth!" Barton cried, a mewling whimper of sound.

"Barton," Trevor called. He stood at the little table, a dark pistol in his hand. "Go to hell, damn you!" He fired. Barton's face crumpled, and he pitched forward onto the carpet.

Chapter 22

Winterburn moved first, kneeling at his mother's side. Rosalind dropped down next to him. His fingers touched the countess's throat briefly, and he turned to Trevor, standing immobile, pistol still pointed where Barton had been.

"She's alive, Trev," Winterburn said. "Call Peck. Get a surgeon."

A blank look was Trevor's only response. Then he lowered the pistol and stumbled forward to where his mother lay. Blood rose in sluggish spurts from a wound below her right breast.

"Mother!" Trevor's stricken face twisted as his gaze shifted to the lifeless Barton, his fist closed around the hem of the countess's gown. With a savage thrust of his boot, Trevor rolled the dead man away.

"Trev!" Winterburn said sharply.

Trevor dropped the gun and fell to his knees, clutching his mother's feet.

Rosalind touched Winterburn's arm lightly,

and he looked her way. "I'll get Peck," she said, scrambling to her feet.

Peck was just outside the door, wringing his hands, his dignity forgotten, his proper face screwed up in alarm.

"Lady Winterburn needs a surgeon at once," Rosalind said. "Lord Winterburn, too."

Peck whirled and with a word sent two footmen running, the marble entry echoing with the sound of their footsteps.

"Good God," said a male voice from above them. "What's going on, Peck? We heard shots."

Rosalind looked up into the stunned faces of half a dozen or more gentlemen, peering down the great stairway.

Peck assumed his stoic mask as he turned to the gentlemen, and Rosalind slipped back into the small salon.

She found Trevor cradling his mother's feet in his lap while Winterburn pressed a small cushion to her wound with exquisite care.

Rosalind stripped off the clerk's robe and, kneeling, began to tuck it around the wounded woman. Winterburn lifted his head, and when their eyes met, she saw a new light in his. A dawn light, calm and clear, different from the careless certainty of his first days in Rowdene. She wanted him to mind his own wound, but she saw that he was beyond it for the moment, outside of himself, open to her as he had never been. It took her breath away.

Doctor Phillips arrived in minutes, his manner crisp and sharp as his shirt points. He examined the countess, ordered Peck to procure a table leaf to serve as a litter, and sent his own assistant with Trevor to ready the countess's chamber for surgery.

As he prepared to follow his patient, Rosalind touched his sleeve. She stood her ground when he flicked his impatient gaze to her.

"Lord Winterburn has also been shot," she said.

Phillips shifted his attention to Winterburn, who was trying to rise from one knee. As he came up, he swayed dangerously. His skin went whiter, then his knees gave way. Rosalind and the doctor reached him together and eased him down on one of the sofas. "A bit giddy," he said.

Phillips opened Winterburn's coat and discovered the stained silk. While his hands cut away Winterburn's garments and probed the wound, he ascertained the time and circumstances of the injury and what Winterburn had been doing since. Phillips was eloquent on the folly of a jarring carriage ride and an hour's standing confrontation with a madman.

With supreme indifference to the justice of the doctor's criticisms, Winterburn fainted.

Phillips rose and gave orders to Rosalind and the remaining footman. "He's in better shape than his mother," Phillips confided to Rosalind. "Keep him warm. If he comes to, get him to drink liquids, broth, water, anything." He headed for the door. "I'll remove the bullet after I see to her."

He bowed and was gone.

* * *

Rosalind did not leave Winterburn until a maid came to light the candles. She stood and stretched. The whole of a long summer day had slipped away while she sat at Winterburn's side.

Four footmen had moved him to his own chamber, where Dr. Phillips had removed the bullet from his shoulder. Phillips's hands had moved rapidly over Winterburn's wounds a few minutes, then he had given her clipped assurances of Winterburn's strength and health. She had indulged herself since in gazing unreservedly at Winterburn's still face.

His eyes had fluttered open briefly, once, after Phillips removed the bullet. He seemed to smile at her, then slipped back into a profound rest while she waited for him to awaken.

It was her one talent, really, waiting in hope. The great turning wheel of the seasons had provided her with practice in this endeavor. Waiting for the return of green in the spring, for the ripening of grain, for the fall of leaves, for the first snow. Winterburn belonged in this world that had lured Gerrie from home years before, a world of impatience and power, while she was rooted in Rowdene and must return there. The gulf that divided them had never been wider, but the wonder was that, even so, she felt full of hope. After the maid left, Rosalind leaned over him.

"I love you," she whispered. She kissed him lightly and went in search of Peck. She would request that a bed be made up for her near Winterburn.

She did not find Peck, who was apparently

busy on some errand associated with her ladyship's care, but a footman directed her to a grand
salon where a hundred candles blazed and Trevor
Nash sat at a large desk, a glass of spirits and a
decanter at his elbow. He had discarded his cravat
and coat and raked his hair into disorder. The
furious scratching of his pen was the only sound
in the room. Rosalind approached the desk and
spoke his name.

His head jerked up. "You here still?"

He threw down the pen and waved the paper
rapidly. A hasty fold and seal, and he sprang to
his feet, striding to the bellpull and handing a
stack of letters to the servant who answered his
ring.

The desperate insolence of his manner reminded Rosalind of Gerrie. "Your brother is resting now. Dr. Phillips removed the bullet from his
shoulder."

Trevor came back to the desk, sank into the
chair, and lifted his glass.

"How is your mother?" Rosalind asked.

Trevor took a long swallow of drink, emptying
the glass. "Phillips says she'll die."

"I'm sorry."

"Are you?" He toyed with his glass, slanting a
glance up at her. "You'll be Lady Winterburn
then." His blank gaze was suddenly calculating.

Rosalind sucked in a breath. Trevor was like
Barton. He saw others as having some imagined
advantage over him. He grasped at things around
him to make himself strong. She understood

Winterburn then, too. It was his cool self-sufficiency that made him different from other men. He was himself without a grand house or fortune or title. He could abandon them without a thought. He could lay down his life as carelessly. She straightened.

"I think you misunderstand. My marriage to your brother is a marriage in name only." It seemed the saddest truth she had ever spoken.

"Don't expect me to believe that!" Trevor filled his glass and drank again. "No matter. Whatever sort of marriage it was, it will be dissolved. It was my mother's last wish. I have written just now to my uncle."

"Then you have no worries on that score. Until our marriage is dissolved, however, I am your brother's wife and I would like a bed made up for me somewhere near him that I might . . ."

"No!" Trevor slammed the glass down.

Rosalind winced. His eyes gleamed with frenzied energy.

He pushed up from the chair, tumbling it backward. "I blame you for this disaster, and I won't have you in this house while my mother dies. Demurely waiting to take her place."

Rosalind gripped the edge of the desk. "You mistake me, Mr. Nash. I am not waiting for your mother's place. I will return to Rowdene as soon as your brother is out of danger."

"Hah!" He came around the desk, advancing on her. His gaze swept up her limbs. "I know what you are, willing to sell yourself for money."

Rosalind curled her hand around the base of a heavy candlestick on the corner of the desk. He stumbled to a halt in front of her.

"Did he have you on your knees under him? He likes it that way. He would see that flaming hair and not what you were after."

"I was not after your mother's place." Rosalind lifted her chin.

"Well, you won't have it. You have your house. You won't get this one." His breath, thick with spirits, washed over her.

"I never wanted more than my home."

He rocked back. "Go, then. Get out."

She didn't move. "Winterburn needs—"

Trevor gripped her arm, but she wrenched free, picking up the candlestick and brandishing it.

"Don't touch me, Mr. Nash." She backed to the door. "A carriage to convey me to Mr. Harwood's, please."

Leigh opened his eyes to morning light. Merely lifting his lids seemed to require the strength of Hercules. He stared at the ceiling until he felt ready to raise his head, a chore for Atlas. He pushed up against the pillows, ignoring the pain in his shoulder, then lay breathing shallowly, waiting for it to subside.

A footman, slumped in a chair by the door, roused at Leigh's stirring, came to attention, and disappeared through the door. In a minute quick footsteps sounded at the door.

Trevor came right to the bed. "How are you?"

"Among the living. Where's Rosalind?"

Trevor stiffened, and Leigh recognized that he'd blundered. "You mean, how is mother?"

Leigh nodded. He was in no position to antagonize his brother.

"Phillips says she won't last the day."

"Is she conscious?"

"No."

Leigh understood. Trevor had loved her and was on his own now for the first time. "What day is it?" Leigh asked.

"Saturday."

Leigh tried to take it in. He'd been asleep since late Thursday night. The last he'd seen Rosalind, that moment when she'd bent over him, lying here, when had that been?

"Where's Rosalind?" he asked again.

"Long gone." Trevor averted his gaze. "Left as soon as Phillips got the bullet out."

Leigh turned his head to catch Trevor's expression, sure he was lying. "Where did she go?"

"To Rowdene. That's her village, isn't it?"

Leigh stared at the ceiling. Had she really gone back to Rowdene without a word to him? "Did she leave a letter?"

Trevor shrugged. "Apparently your marriage was in name only. She told me as much right away. It eased her mind considerably to know I wrote to Uncle Ned. Of course, he'll take care of an annulment."

"Taking quite a bit on yourself, aren't you, Trev?" Now he could be sure Trevor was lying.

Again Trevor shrugged. He stood at the window, his back to Leigh. "You should be grateful to me. There were three cabinet members here when Miss Merrifield showed herself at the foot of the stairs. I had to act fast to avoid a scandal."

"You threw her out." With a surge of furious strength, he pushed himself up against the pillows.

"High drama is your forte, Brother." Trevor turned, but his face was still in shadow. "She was eager to leave and said as much. She had me call a cab immediately to take her to Harwood's. I could hardly refuse."

Trevor strolled back to the bed, his countenance composed, his voice easy. A minute earlier Leigh had been sure his brother was lying, but Trevor seemed to gain confidence as he spoke.

"She left me to your tender ministrations?"

Trevor laughed. "Your charm must have failed with the girl." He pulled a chair up to the side of the bed and sat. "She made sure Phillips and I would care for you, but she said she never wanted more than her home." He lifted a hand as if anticipating a protest from Leigh. "Her very words."

Leigh said nothing. Trevor seemed to have taken on their mother's character. He recognized the smooth, effortless manner of her manipulations.

"Worried that she'd settle in here and send you packing, Trev?"

"Not at all. Daresay, she was relieved to get away. A country girl, after all. That appalling auction, abducted twice. Between you and Barton, it'd be no surprise to me if she never wanted a man to touch her again."

"Laying it on thick, Trev," Leigh said.

Trevor stood. "Am I?" He smoothed the lines of his coat.

"I'm not going to stay." Leigh's lids closed against his will, and he forced himself to open them again. "I will help you settle the estate any way you like."

Trevor's head jerked up. A guarded look came into his eyes. "You don't mean it."

"But I do." He moved his shoulder, welcoming the sharp jab of pain that kept him from drifting off.

"Where will you go?"

"The army."

A wide grin broke across Trevor's face. He took a couple of quick steps toward the door, then stopped. "I don't understand you."

"I know."

Trevor's hand was on the knob.

"But, Trev, until my marriage is annulled, Rosalind is Lady Winterburn."

Trevor glanced over his shoulder, apparently willing to agree to anything now. "Of course."

Chapter 23

~~~⌒⌒⌒~~~

Leigh was back on his feet by the day they buried his mother, and following the lengthy rites, he received a summons for an evening interview with his uncle Ned. Shortly after eight the bishop's secretary admitted Leigh to His Grace's chamber where one of the tapestry settees had been invested with something of the dignity of an episcopal throne. A reclining nude on the wall had been covered with purple velvet.

The bishop was tall and lean with a lofty brow, an affable manner, shrewd blue eyes, and decided views. After insisting that his guest sit, he took his makeshift throne, sitting well forward, his hands planted on his knees. His voice, when he spoke, was like the last peal of a round, full bell.

"Time to settle this business of your profession, Winterburn. Tricky business, actually. Not the situation we had in March." The bishop pursed his lips. "Now that your mother's gone, your circumstances have changed. You have a bit more freedom, in any case."

Leigh knew exactly how much freedom he had:

all the freedom of an exile. The world was his if there was anyplace in it he wished to go.

The bishop regarded him with a slight frown, as if he were a puzzle to be solved.

"You've no doubt heard reports from Rowdene," Leigh said, wondering what his uncle thought remained to be settled.

"Yes. I was on my way there when the sad news of your mother reached me."

"You know then that I've been accused of a 'fatal error.' A village girl names me the father of her unborn child. And—"

"And you've been extravagant. Yes, I've had several reports." The bishop's expression was grave, his gaze searching.

"Then you will want me to—"

"Contradictory reports, actually. Some in Rowdene apparently find you humble and saintly."

"Who?"

The bishop waved away the question. "Frankly, Winterburn, I'm puzzled. Profligacy and extravagance were to be expected in a man of your stamp. Piety and good works are quite out of character. Apparently you may be faced here with a serious call to a religious life."

Leigh opened his mouth to deny it, to proclaim that he was selfish and had sought only to avoid a disagreeable dependence on his mother, but a stream of recollections stopped him. Ever since he met Rosalind Merrifield he had been acting less like himself until he had found himself on his knees in the street outside a brothel, bleeding and praying for Rosalind's life.

These mornings in London a certain slant of light entering his room whitened the walls briefly, reminding him of the vision that had started him on this unexpected path. The stone, the wheel, and the rose came to him, stirring an acute longing to return to Rowdene.

The bishop was watching him closely. "As I suspected. If you wish to keep Rowdene, much less advance in the church, we must contradict the existing impression of your unsuitability for the clergy. I have given considerable thought to the problem since this afternoon."

"Thank you, your grace," Leigh said, uncertain just where his uncle's considerable thought might lead him.

The bishop rose and, clasping his hands behind his back, began to pace with a measured stride. After a couple of turns, he paused. "You must marry." The bishop pronounced this with the air of a judge condemning a prisoner.

"But—"

"Hear me out. It's one thing to be a fine pulpit man or a good manager of money, but people expect their vicars to marry. Women resent an eligible male who has chosen celibacy over one of their number. Too Roman in any case. Men will think you a threat to their own wives if you aren't safely tied to someone."

"Your grace—"

The bishop shot Leigh a quelling glance. "The trick is to choose the right sort of girl—not too high nor too low. You want a girl with money, you understand. Even when you get a better situation, you'll want money, but not an heiress, not this Candover girl. Let your brother have her, if he can get her, much better for a diplomat."

"Of course." Leigh allowed himself a tight smile. Clearly, Trevor had taken pains to protect his interests.

"And you want a girl who wishes to marry into the clergy. Any other sort will soon be miserable in a parsonage house and make your life a misery. Now the best place to look for this sort of girl is in the neighborhood itself—"

"Uncle Ned, I am married."

The bishop halted abruptly, looking plainly astonished. "Trevor made no mention . . . When, who, how?" The bishop resumed his seat on the settee.

"Rosalind Merrifield."

There was a flare of recognition in the shrewd eyes. "I know the name. Don't tell me. Vernon wrote a lot of superstitious nonsense about the girl—Rose of Rowdene or some such legend."

"Whatever is said of her, she's of respectable birth and irreproachable character."

The bishop smiled, and Leigh saw that he'd given himself away with his hasty defense of Rosalind.

"Yes. The father was a scholar. Well, then, what difficulty are you concealing from me?"

"I want you to annul the marriage."

It was the bishop's turn to be surprised. "Dear God, why? On what grounds?"

"Nonconsummation."

"Not likely to be believed in your case." A faint

irritation crept into the smooth voice. "What are the girl's feelings toward you?"

"I don't know."

"Don't know?" The bishop's tone became decidedly tart. "Well, you'd best find out. Regularize this union of yours, and you may have Rowdene. Collins!" He called for his secretary.

Leigh rose. "And if Miss Merrifield refuses me, may we have your promise of an annulment?"

"Yes, and an end to your career in the church. Collins!"

"Thank you, Uncle. No need to trouble Collins, I'll find my way out."

Late on a clear, warm day, almost the last of June, Leigh returned to Rowdene. He left a bag at the inn and walked up through the village. Wild roses bloomed at the cottage doors, and as he passed, villagers startled him with nods and smiles of greeting. He halted below the parsonage where the road beckoned him on to Merrifield and turned in at the churchyard gate, taking the path to the rough old door. The cool darkness welcomed him, and he was startled to see the nave swept, the wall brackets unexpectedly filled with candles. In a daze he wandered up the aisle to the sanctuary rail and knelt.

Heaven still mocked his self-interested plan to buy his freedom by entering the church. The stones under his knees and the jewel-bright saints in the windows above him gave mute witness to the demands of the calling he had thought to take lightly. Months or lifetimes ago he meant to brush up on a few facts of church history, flatter his neighbors, and convince his uncle to ordain him. But from the start his vision had nagged him with the possibility of something more than a cynical escape from his mother's world. And then there had been Rosalind Merrifield, stirring him body and soul. Now he had to decide.

To deserve her he must be the sort of parson she could respect, but to have her no hypocrisy would be too great. The thought kept him on his knees a long time.

When he finally rose and stepped outside, the brightness of a golden sunset stopped him, and when his eyes adjusted to the light, he found Braithe leaning against the gate.

"Staying this time?" Braithe asked, his blue gaze sharp.

Leigh worked the rusty latch. "Perhaps."

Braithe, his feet planted wide, blocked the path. "Or have you come to take her away w' you?"

"Not that. She belongs here."

A thrush in the hedge began to sing, and Braithe shifted aside. "She's done wonders since her return. Ye saw the church. And she's got folk milking their sheep."

Leigh turned and began walking toward Merrifield. "I met with some smiles in the village earlier. Is she responsible for those, too?"

Braithe shrugged and matched his stride to Leigh's. "Polly's lies were found out."

Leigh halted. "How?"

Braithe looked out over the golden fields. "Polly got to boasting in the inn about the pretty penny yer brother gave her to seduce you. Said she was promised another sum for telling her tale to the bishop, but she tired of the waiting."

"So my reputation's been restored in Row-dene?"

" 'Tis white as fleece."

"And Miss Merrifield's?"

"Unstained as ever."

They reached the brow of the hill looking down to Merrifield. The hall stood surrounded by the green and gold of summer, its bricks mellow in the rosy light of the sunset. A flock of birds rose in a great wheeling pattern above the house, then settled again, peace descending.

"So why have ye come back, Lord Winter-burn?"

Leigh raised a brow at the title. "To see if she'll have me."

"Ah," said Braithe. He looked very grave and backed a few steps away. "Then ye'd best return to the parsonage."

Leigh swung to face his companion. "Why?"

Braithe doffed his hat and turned the brim uneasily in his hands until Leigh thought he might crush the thing. Then the shepherd looked up. "She's in yer garden, tending the roses." Braithe laughed and vaulted over the nearest stile, and from the safety of the other side, he called back, "Try putting some butter under yer hat, Lord Winterburn."

Braithe's whistle faded, carried away by a whisper of breeze, before Leigh could rally his stunned senses. He turned back, his step light, impatient.

At the parsonage a smiling Dowdeswell opened the door.

"Miss is in the garden," he said.

"So Braithe told me. Is there anyone in Rowdene who doesn't know my intentions?"

Dowdeswell's expression sobered briefly, then a grin nearly split his face.

In the garden Leigh's stride faltered. A stab of joy left him unable to advance when he caught sight of her, his rose among roses.

The canes she had tied to the arches of the arbor in April had become a canopy of flowers, from which the light and air took their taste and hue. He could be content to stand and let the joy pierce him forever, but she saw him, and he went to her.

An old straw bonnet, a tan apron, and gloves concealed her person from his hungry eyes. The curve of one cheek, golden in the fading light, held his gaze.

"I've come from London," he said.

She stopped then, just out of reach. "I didn't expect . . . You said Dowdeswell would collect your things."

"I changed my mind."

She considered it, taking a minute to remove her gloves, then seemed to remember the proprieties. "Your mother?"

"Died Sunday last."

Her gaze dropped. "I am sorry." And lifted again. "And you?"

"Healing." He raised his arm to show her.

Her eyes met his and looked away. The silence

hummed with bees, and their buzzing seemed to fill his body, a furious trapped longing.

"I think we should talk about our situation."

She nodded. "Here?"

He wanted to say "in bed" but couldn't. "Fine."

She put her gloves and basket of roses on a bench and, turning her back, asked for help with her apron.

He untied the strings, careful not to touch her waist. He felt himself walking on a steep edge and struggled to keep his balance. "You are learning to ask for help."

"A good lesson, you must agree, as you were the one who taught me."

His throat was too thick for speech, so he merely offered his arm, and they began to stroll the grassy path under the roses.

When he had grown somewhat accustomed to her light touch, he spoke again. "You left London without a word."

Her gaze came up to him, full of regret. "Your brother made certain things very clear to me."

A little hopelessness intruded then as he thought of what Trevor might have said. "My brother had his own interests to protect."

"But his selfishness does not permit mine."

"So you think we should part?"

She studied the path. "We can easily do so. Your brother said the bishop would annul our marriage. That's what you meant in the inn when you told me you had a favor to ask of him, isn't it?"

He could not deny it.

"Then you would be free." Her voice gave nothing away, and he couldn't see her eyes.

"And you would be safe at home."

They reached the end of the arch of roses. The acknowledgment of their contrary ends stilled his tongue. A desperate sense of loss gripped him, and he seized her shoulders, turning her to face him. He stared into eyes as dark and bleak as wintry fields and, in the face of them, felt a blade of hope spring up. "It is plain you don't know the first thing about selfishness."

She shook her head. "But I do. I know what I want."

"What do you want?"

"To be your wife."

"Here in Rowdene?" His voice dropped to a whisper.

"Or anywhere," she whispered back.

He broke away. "Don't be so generous. I cannot match you in that. I want you, and I will make you mine, not the Rose of Rowdene, but Winterburn's rose. Though I burn in hell for it."

"How could you?"

"My uncle has offered me the living after all, if we regularize our marriage."

"Then you will be ordained."

He could not mistake the gladness in her voice, but he didn't turn. He made himself ask what he had vowed to ask an hour earlier in the little church. "Do you think I will ever be fit for the clerical life?"

Again the silence hummed, the air between them a taut string, vibrating with a single note low and sweet, and then her voice came. "You don't know half of what you are or what you can be." Her hand tugged his good shoulder, compelling him to turn. "You pretend to be selfish, hide behind your indifference, your lifted brow." She reached up and with a finger lightly traced that brow. "But what you are is strong and kind and generous. You will make a fine parson for Rowdene."

He grabbed her hand, stilling her touch. "When I look into my heart, I don't see goodness, only that I want you."

She smiled a small, sad smile. "I am not your equal in the eyes of the world. I cannot bring you even a modest dowry, only duties and cares."

With a careless gesture he abandoned the world and undid the strings of her bonnet. The old straw hat slipped down her back and fell unheeded to the grass, while he threaded his fingers through her hair, scattering pins. "A dowry of lights and fires," he said, bringing his mouth down on hers.

His kiss was an invitation to union and change. His heart beat wildly against hers, as if to break down the barriers of flesh. With the press of her whole self, Rosalind answered, *Yes*. When he raised his lips from hers, he whispered, "Come, love."

Taking her hand, he led her into the house, pausing only long enough to summon Dowdeswell and make a quick announcement of their marriage. The old man offered to take their message to Merrifield, and Winterburn swept her up the stairs to the bedroom.

In the fading light he came to stand before her and drew her into his arms. He kissed her again slowly, letting desire build in them both.

He knelt and removed her shoes and stockings, causing her to hold his shoulder for balance. He shed his own boots clumsily because he would not look away from her as she stood barefoot and waiting for him. When he came back to her, he unwrapped the cord at her waist that held all her keys. A jingle and she was free of them.

"From that first day," he said, "I have wanted the key to unlock your secrets, wife."

The light of joy was back in his eyes, as she remembered it from the fair, and it made her bold. She pulled at the knot of his cravat and unwound the linen cloth. She eased the coat from his shoulders and tended each of the tiny buttons of his waistcoat. When it fell open, she paused, her hands at the band of his breeches, wanting to touch him there, too. But he distracted her, offering his wrists, and when she'd freed them from the cuffs, he pulled his shirt over his head. She smoothed her hands over his shoulders and kissed the angry red pucker of his recent wound.

He turned her, working swiftly to free her from her gown, his fingers a flutter of touches along her back, sending rills of sensation through her, weakening her knees. He paused at her stays and kissed her shoulder, a reminder of their wedding night. Then she was in her shift, watching the rise and fall of his chest, feeling the burn of his gaze even in the cool of evening. He swung her up and laid her on the bed, stretching out beside her on his stomach, one hand brushing lightly across her breasts until she arched to him. Then he covered her body with his own, and all thought was drowned in touch.

The empty wanting consumed her, but she felt him holding back, doubting himself. She wrestled with his doubts, pushing him off of her and onto his back and bringing her hand down his chest, learning his contours as he had learned hers, lower until he guessed her intention and gripped her wrist. She coaxed him with kisses and patience until he yielded and let her touch his swelling male flesh.

With a groan he lifted himself away to shed the last of his garments.

When he returned, she whispered, "Teach me." She reached for him again, but he pushed her onto her back and positioned himself between her legs, his breath a harsh rasp in his throat.

He held himself above her, his head down, letting her feel the press of his body against hers. When he lifted his head, his eyes questioned hers. "The last key, the last lock," he said. "When I fit my body to yours, I am home."

"Then come home," she said.

He did, sliding into her, filling the emptiness that consumed her. The barrier of her untried flesh yielded to a quick thrust of his body, and he kissed her, sweetly soothing the sudden pain, whispering his regret.

She stopped his words and made him see her joy. And he began to move inside her. She met him, catching the rhythm, making her own coun-

terpoint to it, persuading him that she could love
him wholly. She saw in his eyes that doors he had
long kept closed were open to her.

They lingered in their joining, descending
slowly from the height they had reached together.
Then he nestled her under his arm.

"I was wrong about home, you know," she
said.

"You were?"

"Yes. I thought a woman made the house a
home, but I see now that it is the bond of man and
wife that makes the home."

"You're sure, or are you merely making the best
of a bad bargain? You're stuck with me as perpetual Curate of Rowdene now," he said.

"I have only one regret," she said.

"You do?"

She could feel him looking at the top of her
head.

"Yes. What if you give up your fine coats? I
don't know if I will like you so well in black."

He tickled her waist, and she squirmed, catching his hand. "How soon can you be ordained?"

"Are you in a hurry to hear me preach?"

"No, but Jeremy Braithe is."

"You joke, but the whole thing is heaven's joke,
I think, making a clergyman of a worldly, carnal
soul."

"I knew you belonged here when you brought
light into the church, only I didn't wish to give in
so easily."

"It was all I could think of to do. In Portugal . . ."

Rosalind waited, sensing he was about to reveal something he had not told anyone else.

"The fields caught fire after our last battle, and the army thought me lost in the blaze. But one of the guerrillas had dragged me into the road, and a farmer left me at a convent where the sisters tended me, though they had little hope at first that I would live.

"When I began to come to myself, their cure was to put me to work, and eventually I regained my strength and sense of who I was. By then I thought I owed them a good bit for all they'd done, and I stayed to work, restoring fields and gardens and buildings damaged by the war.

"One afternoon I was hoeing a row in the kitchen garden when I saw a bright light against the outer wall. It seemed to come from nowhere, and I felt drawn to it. As I approached, I saw a dusty road leading me. Ahead in the light lay the hub of an old wheel, just the hub, lying against the stone wall, a rose twining sweetly around it.

"When I reached the wall, of course there was nothing there. Sister Luzia, a particular friend of mine from the kitchens, said I'd had . . . a vision. She made me tell the head of the convent, and the mother superior wrote to the bishop. The bishop told the army where I was, and I received word I'd inherited. I thought the vision would fade when I left Portugal, but ever since then I've had flashes of it."

"So you never discovered its meaning?" Rosalind asked.

His fingers drifted through her hair. "I've been fighting it, but I think I understand the rose."

Rosalind turned in his hold, resting her folded arms across his chest and looking at him where he lay propped against the pillows. "Your vision makes perfect sense of everything," she declared.

"How?" One black brow rose a fraction.

"The stone is the church, the people, your own heart." She went on, feeling the certainty of her understanding. "The hub is the dailiness of life, the ordinary small cycles, even and constant, not the exhilarating rise and plunge of the rim. The hub is the life of work and caring you have chosen."

"And the light?" he asked, his expression less doubting, more wondering.

"Is mercy, love, grace, seeming to come from nowhere, but in your heart all the same." She placed her hand there.

With a sudden swift move, he rolled her on her back, pinning her under him.

"That's it? You've explained it all?"

"Yes, perfectly." She smoothed his hair back from his brow. "I have always felt, even when I didn't like you, that I was seeing things through your eyes. It angered me sometimes, the feeling was so strong."

"You forgot the most important part of the vision. The rose."

She smiled, and his arms tightened around her. "You are the rose in my vision," he said.

"You don't believe the superstition, do you?"

"That you're the Rose of Rowdene? No. You don't have to save the village from every disaster."

She pressed closer to him. "I love you," she said.

"I love you, Rosalind, my rose. Winterburn's rose."